WHISKEY FOR BREAKFAST

AN ADDISON HOLMES MYSTERY (BOOK 2)

LILIANA HART

Published by 7Th Press

DEDICATION

For Scott,

Because you're my hero and my heart.

OTHER BOOKS

The MacKenzies of Montana

Dane: Volume 1
Dane: Volume 2
Thomas: Volume 1
Thomas: Volume 2
Riley: Volume 1
Riley: Volume 2
Cooper: Volume 1
Cooper: Volume 2
A MacKenzie Christmas

MacKenzie Security Series

Cade
Shadows and Silk
Secrets and Satin
Sins and Scarlet Lace
Sizzle
Crave
Trouble Maker
Scorch

Lawmen of Surrender (MacKenzies-1001 Dark Nights)

1001 Dark Nights: Captured in Surrender
1001 Dark Nights: The Promise of Surrender
Sweet Surrender
Dawn of Surrender

The MacKenzie World (read in any order)

Trouble Maker
Bullet Proof
Deep Trouble
Delta Rescue
Desire and Ice
Rush
Spies and Stilettos
Wicked Hot
Hot Witness
Avenged
Never Surrender

JJ Graves Mystery Series

Dirty Little Secrets
A Dirty Shame
Dirty Rotten Scoundrel
Down and Dirty
Dirty Deeds
Dirty Laundry
Dirty Money

Addison Holmes Mystery Series

Whiskey Rebellion
Whiskey Sour

Whiskey For Breakfast
Whiskey, You're The Devil
Whiskey on the Rocks
Whiskey Tango Foxtrot
Whiskey and Gunpowder

The Gravediggers
The Darkest Corner
Gone to Dust
Say No More

Stand Alone Titles
Breath of Fire
Kill Shot
Catch Me If You Can
All About Eve
Paradise Disguised
Island Home
The Witching Hour

Books by Liliana Hart and Scott Silverii
The Harley and Davidson Mystery Series
The Farmer's Slaughter
A Tisket a Casket
I Saw Mommy Killing Santa Claus
Get Your Murder Running
Deceased and Desist

AN ADDISON HOLMES MYSTERY

WHISKEY FOR BREAKFAST

NEW YORK TIMES BESTSELLING AUTHOR

LILIANA HART

PROLOGUE

T*uesday*

I'M NOT the kind of person to dwell overmuch on the details, but even I knew I couldn't talk my way out of my current predicament if I got caught.

I looked both ways down the deserted alleyway to make sure I was alone. A dumpster and crumpled trash that rolled across the cracked pavement like tumbleweeds were my only company. I'd gotten lucky—the moon was only a sliver in the sky and not enough to make me visible to any passersby. I was still new at this whole breaking and entering thing.

I opened my brand new Kate Spade clutch and pulled out the black cloth packet of lock picking tools I'd bought online. I'd had to practice my new hobby incognito because my best friend and boss, Kate McClean, sometimes got an eye twitch when she knew the lengths I'd go to research my job.

My name is Addison Holmes, and I'm a private investigator in training for the McClean Detective Agency. That basically means I spend most of my time spying on adulterers, making coffee, and being babysat by my trainer since I have a tendency to get into trouble whenever I'm out on my own. But in my defense, I usually managed to get the job done. I had the scars to prove it.

I'd been practicing my B&E skills by watching YouTube videos and using the back door of my house as a test dummy. It had only taken me three tries before I'd managed to click the tumblers into place, which was terrifying considering I was a woman living alone and there were more talented lock pickers than I out there. I couldn't really afford better locks, so I kept a chair pushed under the door and my gun under my pillow.

It was fortunate the back door of the clinic I was trying to break into couldn't afford better locks either, but it still took a good fifteen minutes before the lock gave. The night air was cool, but I was sweaty as a stripper's G-string due to nerves. I had to rub my hands on my shorts twice before I could turn the knob. I cursed as I thought about fingerprints, so I quickly wiped off every surface I'd touched with the hem of my Bon Jovi T-shirt, pulled a pair of rubber medical gloves out of my purse and snapped them on.

I slipped into the clinic, closed the door at my back and then swallowed a yelp when the air conditioning unit came on with a rumble.

"Shit," I breathed out. I relaxed and decided I should've gone to the bathroom before I'd left the house. My bladder couldn't take the stress of illegal activity.

The clinic smelled of Lysol and antiseptic and it was long and rectangular in shape. Ugly gray brick on the outside, metal roof. White industrial blinds were on all the windows so those who frequented the clinic had ultimate privacy.

The reception desk divided the rectangle into two parts—offices on the left and the patient rooms toward the right. Even the thought of what happened in those rooms made me throw up in my mouth a little. There wasn't enough Lysol in the world to cleanse away what happened in there.

The door I'd entered was on the side with the offices, and I passed through a long narrow hallway with white floors and wood paneled walls. The lights were off and the only reason I could see at all was because of the red nightlights spaced every twenty feet or so in the ceiling.

I stifled a nervous giggle at the thought that I'd once seen a horror movie that reminded me an awful lot of my current situation. I reached into my purse and pulled out my gun just in case there were zombies. At least I'd worn tennis shoes instead of high heels in case I had to make a run for it.

I'd wasted enough time building up my courage so I set forward with determination. I snuck past two bathrooms and a water fountain and wondered if it was against the criminal's code to sneak into the bathroom and relieve myself. But with my luck, that's when the SWAT team would break down the doors and the Enquirer would be standing there to take pictures.

I pulled the strap of my purse over my body and held the gun in a two handed grip. In my mind I was just like Laura Holt from Remington Steele, only curvier and without eighties hair. I made my way to where the hallway met the main area, squatting low and peeping around the corner to make sure I was alone.

The place was silent as a tomb and I crossed in front of the reception desk without even a squeak from my sneakers. My stealth abilities had improved by about a hundred and fifty percent since my first day on the job. Which wasn't saying much. It was the same thing as saying a kindergartener could finally use the paste without eating it.

My heart was thudding a hundred miles a minute and the red glow from the lights was creepy as shit. My goal was fairly simple: I needed to get into the locked room I'd noticed on my first visit to the clinic and search the files. The room was at the end of the opposite hall past the patient rooms, made to look more like a janitor's closet than anything else, but I'd glimpsed the rows of file cabinets during my tour a couple of days before.

I was halfway down the hallway when I heard a horrible moan. My heart stopped and I turned around to run back from the way I'd come when I heard it again. And though it *was* horrible, it wasn't a death moan. I'd heard a few of those sounds over the past months. Back when I was having regular sex I'd even moaned like that myself. From the increasing volume I was guessing she was enjoying herself, whoever she was. Either that or she was declawing a cat without anesthesia.

To say my curiosity was piqued was an understatement. I'd never been very good at listening to the part of my mind that told me I shouldn't stick my nose where it didn't belong. I made my way closer to the sounds, hurrying my steps because it sounded like she was winding up for the finale, and I noticed the door was open a crack and light flickered from beneath.

I meant to be quiet. I really did. But the sight that greeted me was enough to draw a gasp from my lips. A pair of familiar blue eyes met mine and widened in surprise. My own eyes narrowed and I felt sick to my stomach as I took in the scene. It was worse than I could've imagined.

The woman reached a climax shrill enough to break glass and the tension ratcheted up the temperature several degrees. A pregnant silence followed her cataclysmic orgasm, and I realized if I didn't breathe a little slower I was likely to end up hyperventilating.

"I should've known you'd show up here," Nick Dempsey said, closing his eyes and shaking his head in disbelief. "I don't suppose I could talk you into turning around and going back home so I can get this straightened out."

I raised a brow and cut my eyes to the loaded weapon in his hand. "No, I don't think so."

He sighed and put his gun away, reaching over to turn the TV off and the X-rated flick that had been playing. The smells of old sex and new death assaulted my senses, and I swallowed back the bile that rose at the sight of the body at Nick's feet.

"At least you put on gloves when you came in," he said, nodding at my hands. "I'd hate to think you smudged the prints of whoever broke in."

"Someone broke in?" I asked, guilt sending a rush of heat to my cheeks.

"You didn't see the front door shot to shit and standing open when you came inside?"

"Umm...sure I did. How could I have missed that?"

CHAPTER ONE

T*hursday...Six days earlier*

"FIF—TY..."

I flopped back onto my yoga mat with a thud and a *whoompf* of expelled breath, and I stared longingly at the cup of coffee I'd placed at the edge of the kitchen counter for inspiration. I didn't have the energy to get up and get it, not to mention it probably wasn't all that hot anymore.

"Go-go-gadget arm." I flung my limp hand out toward the coffee cup, but much to my continual disappointment, saying those words never worked. It wouldn't stop me from trying in the future though.

I mostly lived in a realm of my own imagination and fantasies because the things that happened there were way more interesting than what happened in real life. I figure as long as I recognize the issue instead of living in denial it makes it an acceptable practice.

My abs burned like fire, and it felt like someone had

rearranged my intestines. I stared at the clock for a few seconds, waiting for my vision to come into focus, and I groaned at the time.

"Fifty sit-ups in eight-minutes and fifty-two seconds. A personal best. But still pathetic, Addison."

It was never the first thirty sit-ups that gave me any problems. I could do thirty in about two minutes. It was the last twenty that had me using every creative curse word I'd ever heard as the daughter of a cop. I couldn't seem to get over the hurdle. And my time was running short.

A couple of months ago I'd lost my job as a teacher in the small town of Whiskey Bayou where I'd been raised. It hadn't come as that big of a surprise since I'd gotten caught stripping at a gentleman's club in an act of desperation to bring in some extra cash. It hadn't mattered that I'd been the worst stripper ever born or that I'd only managed to hold the job for the minute and a half I'd been on stage. It had been long enough for my principal to see me and snap off a couple of photos.

I'd like to think I could've bribed or blackmailed him into keeping my secret safe, but by the time I'd made it to the parking lot he was already dead. I fell over him quite literally, and the rest, they say, is history. Once the police became involved there was no way my secret wouldn't get back to Whiskey Bayou and the residents there who thrived on gossip as if it were mother's milk.

Needless to say, my financial situation hadn't improved since the loss of my job. My unemployment benefits were only good for another couple of months, and I had regular rent payments I had to make and all the bills that went along with living in a house. Not to mention credit cards I was still paying off from a wedding that never took place.

I'd been engaged once upon a time, but my fiancé had decided he'd rather play sink my battleship with my arch-enemy, Veronica Wade, rather than walking down the aisle with me. I didn't think so at the time, but it turned out being stranded at the altar was the best thing that ever happened to me because it led me to my current job opportunity.

I'd been moonlighting at the McClean Detective Agency to bring in a little extra cash before my unfortunate dismissal from James Madison High, otherwise I never would've had the opportunity to talk Kate into hiring me full time. I wasn't exactly a full time employee yet. I did contract work and a lot of background checks—spying on adulterous spouses and the occasional case of fraud. Savannah was a hotbed of lust and debauchery if the cases that crossed my desk everyday were anything to go by.

I'd basically caught Kate at a low moment when I'd convinced her to hire me on as a full time private investigator. The only stipulation for my employment was I had to pass all the tests at the top of my class.

I'd spent the last couple of months taking the Citizens' Police Academy classes once a week, studying manuals thick enough to use for kindling, practicing my shooting at the range, and...exercising. I'd passed my conceal to carry test with flying colors, mostly because my dad had taught me how to shoot when I was still in diapers. A cute little H&K my mom and her new husband had bought me as a congratulations gift sat in my purse on the counter. Though if anyone had tried to break in at the moment I would've been too tired to grab it.

The written exam I had to take the week after Christmas would be a piece of cake as well. I was an expert researcher and test taker thanks to my degree in history. I could recite rules and regulations out the wazoo. The problem was, my mind didn't always want to follow those rules and regulations. Sometimes a situation called for thinking on your feet instead of going by procedure. I just made sure to leave the thinking on your feet parts out of any reports I had to write for Kate. Bless her heart, she was a rule follower through and through. She always had been, even when we were in grade school.

The only section of the test I couldn't quite seem to master was the physical fitness portion. At the rate I was going, I wouldn't pass at all, much less be in the top of the class. The requirements were a two-mile run in under thirty minutes, followed immediately by fifty sit-ups in five minutes, followed by 10 pushups in however long it took you to do them. And those were just the minimums.

I rolled over onto my hands and knees, thinking I probably needed to run my yoga mat through a car wash since it was soaked with sweat and smelled of things that no Southern lady should ever smell of.

A whimper escaped my mouth, and I crawled from the living room to the kitchen where my cold coffee waited for me. I managed to use the drawer handles as a way to lever myself to a standing position and the drawer pulled out and conked me on the head.

"Ouch." I rubbed my forehead and managed to make it upright. My hands shook like a wino in a dry spell, but I managed to wrap them around the coffee cup and bring it to my lips, only spilling a little down the front of my black sports bra.

The cobwebs started to clear little by little and I

groaned as I realized I still had to fit in a run. I'd finally made it to the mile mark without having to stop and throw up in someone's yard, so I was at least making progress on that front.

I grabbed the binoculars from my kitchen drawer and went to stand at my front window, just like I did every morning. I cracked the blinds just the slightest bit and then put the binoculars to my face. They were already adjusted exactly how I needed them to be.

When I'd rented this house a couple of months ago, it was at the suggestion of a very sexy FBI agent I'd been working with at the time. His name was Matt Savage and I'd never met anyone whose name fit more perfectly. He looked like the love child of The Rock and Pocahontas—dusky gold skin stretched over sharp features and muscles that would make any woman sit up and take notice. I'd taken notice all right. But as much as I liked Savage and as much as I was curious to find out what he looked like under those black suits he always wore, I'd decided to keep my distance.

Savage was a nice guy, but he wasn't someone who'd be great for the long term. He liked to play fast and reckless, and there was an element of danger about him that not even I was comfortable with. And that was saying something.

When he'd made the suggestion about the house I was currently residing in, I'd had no idea he lived just across the street. This caused me a lot of anxiety. Mostly because I was currently single and every time he got within a five-mile radius my hormones started to sing. So I'd gone out of my way to make sure I had as little contact as possible. That didn't stop him from coming over with takeout or mowing my lawn like clockwork every Saturday morning, but I was still trying to make an effort.

Men like Savage were no good for small town girls like me. And as odd as it seemed as a woman in twenty-first century America, I still had hang ups about casual sex. I couldn't do it without there being some kind of emotional attachment or hope that something long term could come from it. I was pretty much a big fat failure according to the feminist movement.

I held the binoculars up to my face and watched Savage's house for a few minutes. He liked to run first thing in the morning before he went to work, and I tried to coordinate my schedule so he was already gone before I took my turn through the neighborhood—mostly because I didn't want him to witness my resemblance to an arrhythmic heffalump.

There wasn't a car parked in the driveway, but that wasn't unusual since he normally parked in the garage. The blinds were all closed and I couldn't see any lights on in the house. I let out a relieved breath and scanned the street in both directions just in case he was still out running, but I was pretty sure the coast was clear.

It was on my second scan down the street that I got a weird tingly feeling at the back of my neck. Usually that was my internal warning that something bad was about to happen, but considering the results of my morning work-out, it could've been nerve damage as well.

I don't know what made me glance at my neighbor's house—the one directly to my right. It was a little square of a house almost identical to mine, only it was painted canary yellow with white shutters. I'd never even met who lived there, or seen them for that matter since my work hours were on the odd side.

The binoculars stopped of their own volition and peered into a large square window with slatted blinds that were all the way open. Another pair of binoculars stared straight back at me, wide blinking eyes magnified through the opposite end of the lenses.

"Jesus," I screeched, stumbling back a step and tripping over a rug so I landed on my ass. My lungs heaved as I tried to suck in oxygen and figure out what had just happened.

Obviously my neighbor was a peeping Tom. The only problem was technically so was I, and I couldn't exactly make accusations. I crawled on hands and knees back to the windows and closed all the blinds.

A knock at the door had me biting back a scream, but I realized I needed to get a grip. I was supposed to be a professional for Christ's sake. Adrenaline gave me an added rush of strength and I vaulted myself toward the kitchen and pulled my gun out of my purse before skulking to the door and looking through the peephole.

I didn't recognize him, but I had a sinking feeling I was about to meet my new neighbor. He was probably an inch shorter than me and had a face soft with baby fat. His eyes were very round in his pudgy face and I couldn't tell if he had eyelids because he didn't blink. At all.

Black hair stood in wild tufts around his head and a pencil thin mustache I was pretty sure he'd drawn on sat just above his lip. He wore khakis that were at least a size too big and a Star Trek T-shirt that was a size too small. His binoculars hung around his neck.

I stood as still as possible, wondering what I should do, and praying he'd get tired of waiting and go back to his own house. He kept staring at me through the peephole, never blinking, and when my fingers cramped I realized I was squeezing my gun too tight.

"I can hear you breathing," he finally said through the door.

I let out a sigh as I unlocked the deadbolt and undid the chain, but I didn't bother to hide my weapon.

He looked me up and down with those wide, unblinking eyes, and I was suddenly very aware that the only thing I had on was a pair of spandex bike shorts and a sports bra. I could mostly be pretty attractive when I gave half an effort—my hair was dark and shiny and never frizzed in the humidity, and my eyes were a nice chocolate brown. My skin was good and my features put together an attractive package.

But after a morning workout, my face was probably flushed red and blotchy and patches of sweat darkened my clothes. My hair was up in a crooked ponytail, I had on no makeup, and I probably smelled like a locker room. Chances were pretty good he probably didn't come over to attack me.

"You're Addison Holmes," he said, and I was slightly taken aback by the fact that he not only had been spying on me but also knew my name. "Agent Savage speaks highly of you, but I had to see that you would fit in for myself. We don't just take anyone off the street, you know."

"I have no idea what you're talking about."

"Neighborhood watch." It was then I noticed he had a folded T-shirt in his hand and a dayglow orange vest and he shoved them both at me. "I've been watching you since you moved in, and I could tell this morning that you have a good eye for what's happening in the neighborhood. We try to keep crime to a minimum here. I'm Leonard

Winkle, but everyone calls me Spock. I'm the president of the NAD Squad. It's your turn to host Saturday since you're the newest member. We'll be here at 9am sharp. Wear your shirt. Mrs. Rodriguez likes cranberry muffins."

With that he turned on his heel and headed back across the small expanse of lawn that separated our houses.

"What the fuck?"

I closed the door and locked it up tight. I put my gun back in my purse and tossed the ugly vest on the counter before holding the shirt up in front of me so I could see what it said. NAD was spelled in giant block letters in the same dayglow orange as the vest across the front of the shirt. And underneath it was the word SQUAD in much smaller letters.

"NAD Squad," I murmured. I turned the shirt around so I could read the back. "Neighbors Against Delinquency. Of course that's what it means."

I tossed the shirt on the counter and poured another cup of coffee, deciding to take it into the shower with me. Running wasn't going to happen this morning. In fact, I was contemplating just crawling back under the covers and starting the whole day over again. Unfortunately, Kate was expecting me at the agency for a meeting.

She'd called me the night before driving back from the airport and reception had been spotty, but I'd caught the words sperm and billionaire, so it was enough information to have me sufficiently intrigued. Though a part of me was wondering if Kate was trying to set me up on a blind date.

CHAPTER TWO

Since my move to Savannah, I'd somehow managed to add ten extra minutes to my commute. Instead of taking the highway all the way around the outskirts of downtown Savannah like I had when I was living in Whiskey Bayou, I now had to maneuver my way through the congestion of historical Savannah, where drivers felt the need to sightsee from the middle of the road instead of going straight to their destination, and the one-way streets made it impossible to get anywhere without a lot of creative cursing and a half tank of gas.

The McClean Detective Agency was just across the street from Telfair Square in a two-story brick corner building. Riotous green ivy covered the walls and black shutters framed the windows to give it the same charming appearance that all of the businesses had around the area. The front door was black as well and a gold plated plaque with tasteful lettering was the only advertisement as to what went on within.

Six months ago I'd been driving a sweet little cherry red Z that had been worth every penny of the price I couldn't afford. Unfortunately, when hard times had come it had been the first thing to go. I'd found a Volvo that had seen better days at a salvage yard for five hundred dollars. Sure, it had some exterior paint issues, but I kept telling myself that I wasn't so shallow that appearances made a difference to me one way or the other.

The interior smelled like Mexican food farts and mountain pines because of the little scented tree I had hanging from the rearview mirror, and there was a hole in the floor of the passenger side big enough to drop a toddler through. But for the most part, the car got me where I was going, and beggars couldn't be choosers.

I floored the gas pedal so I could pass a car that was trying to figure out how to parallel park, but as soon as the pedal touched the floor the car shuddered hard enough to snap my teeth together and a high-pitched wheeze came from somewhere under the hood. I barely caught my purse before it bounced off the passenger seat and fell through the hole in the floorboard.

"Come on, come on. Don't do this to me now."

The car was making enough noise that people had stopped to stare—probably to see if it was going to blow up with me inside—and all of a sudden the car shot forward and the awful noises stopped only to be replaced by a growling engine and the sound of my wheels whooshing against the pavement.

"Oh, shit."

Horns blared as I sped through a red light and I dodged pedestrians and other cars with wild-eyed panic as the car seemed to take on a mind of its own.

"Oh, shit. Oh, shit."

My heart stopped in my chest and my bowels turned

to liquid as I weighed my options. It turns out I didn't really have any options other than crashing in a fiery heap of metal and rust and that wasn't really something I was looking forward to. Though if I died today I'd no longer have to be a member of the NAD Squad, so there was an upside to everything, it seemed.

I took a hard right onto York Street on two wheels, my foot pressing the brake over and over again with no success. The smell of rubber made my eyes water. Or it could have been the black smoke rising from the hole in the floorboard. Whatever it was, I was in big trouble.

Kate's building came into view and I gave one last ditch attempt to stop the car, pressing the pedal all the way to the ground, my ass coming up from the seat and my grip on the steering wheel so hard I was afraid it might pop right off. All I could do was close my eyes and pray.

The car stopped so suddenly I screamed into the silence, and when I found the courage to open my eyes I found I was about an inch away from the bumper of a black Mercedes. God and I'd had a pretty tenuous relationship over the last couple of years—ever since the whole wedding fiasco. But occasionally He came through for me and saved me from sudden disaster, and I figured I probably needed to start paying Him back a bit by going to church so my prayer points weren't all used up in the event of a real emergency.

The good news was I was mostly close enough to the curb to be considered parked, so I pulled the keys out of the ignition and grabbed my purse, looking around to make sure no one had witnessed my grand entrance. Unfortunately, it was peak hours for professionals going to work and joggers making use of the park across the street, so I ducked out of the car as fast as possible and ran through the front door of the agency to the sound of catcalls and slow applause.

I slammed the door at my back and stood in the lobby of the McClean Detective Agency, reveling in just being alive. That had been too close to call, and already I was mentally rearranging my checking account and wondering what I could sell so I could get another car, but there was nothing in my checking account to rearrange. I had rent due in another week, and I didn't even have enough to cover the whole amount.

The only thing I had left of value to sell was internal organs and thick brown hair that came just past my shoulder blades. I figured if shearing hair to the scalp and selling it for cash was good enough for Jo March, then it was probably good enough for me. I wasn't quite as enthusiastic about getting rid of the internal organs yet.

Lucy Kim stared at me from behind the ornate cherry wood reception desk with soulless black eyes and an impassive face. She was so still I wondered if she was real or one of those blowup dolls that were sold in naughty novelty stores. I was ninety-eight percent sure that Lucy was one of those day-walker vampires, but I hadn't been able to prove it yet.

The front lobby of the McClean Detective Agency was tasteful Southern elegance. The furniture was leather and placed in front of a massive fireplace that never got used because this was the South. Rugs were scattered across the floor and expensive paintings hung on the walls. It was made to look like a home instead of an office from the front to make people more comfortable.

"Hey there," I said, just to fill the uncomfortable silence.

Lucy was a mystery. She was several inches shorter

than my own five-foot-eight, and her skin was golden and flawless. Straight black hair rained down her back to her waist and shone like silk, and I was thinking her locks would probably sell for a hell of a lot more than mine. She wore black from head to toe, as she always did, and five inch heels that would be good for stabbing someone in the eye in an emergency. Her nails were long and blood red to match her lips.

I had no idea how old she was or anything remotely personal about her other than she'd worked for Kate since the agency opened a decade ago. She never took a sick day or a personal day and I'd never seen her eating in the break room or from the snack trays that were brought out for clients. Like I said, *vampire.*

Lucy held out a couple of file folders to me without saying anything, and when I took them from her she immediately went back to whatever she'd been doing on the computer.

"I'm a little early for the meeting," I said. "Is Kate already in her office?"

I'd been on a personal quest lately to get Lucy to speak to me in the hopes that I'd be able ferret out some personal information about her. It just wasn't natural for a woman to live in the South this long and not want to talk about herself, her family, and her ancestors from a hundred years past.

Lucy jerked her thumb towards Kate's office, never looking away from her computer screen. I rolled my eyes and sighed and headed down the long expanse of hallway where all of the agents in Kate's employ had their offices.

Kate's door was closed, which meant she was probably in the middle of something important. Our meeting wasn't for another twenty minutes so I had time to look over the two new files Lucy had handed me.

I'd been using Carl Jansen's office while he'd been on medical leave for a herniated disk, but Carl was back and I'd been ousted to a refurbished janitor's closet. The gray metal desk filled up almost the whole space and the computer was probably a dozen years old, but it still did the same invasive searches on people's lives that the newer models did—only a lot slower. I mostly used my personal laptop at home.

The walls were oyster gray and new industrial carpet with maroon flecks had been laid for my benefit, only the smell of the glue was so strong my eyes started watering if I stayed inside for more than ten minutes at a time. I'd put a few personal touches around to make myself feel more at home—candles, family photographs, and a dartboard that hung on the back of the door—but in my experience there was never much point in polishing a turd.

The most important thing on my desk was the Keurig coffeemaker, and I dropped in a pod and pushed the button as I opened the first file. I raised my brows at the note Kate had stuck to the first page. It was a request for an assist from the Savannah PD. Requests came through the agency a couple of times a week, but they never came to me, or at least hardly ever. I'd assisted the FBI and the local police in a call girl murder case not too long ago, but I'd ended up mostly naked and with a broken heart by the time the case was solved, so I'd been steering clear of the boys in blue lately.

The department kept Kate's agency on retainer because it was easier to hire her agents out by the hour rather than pay overtime for a cop's salary, and a lot of cops worked for Kate in their off time just to make extra money. Budget cuts had hit the city hard over the last couple of years.

"Johhny Sakko," I read aloud, my brow furrowing as I tried to remember where I'd heard the name before.

It looked like Johnny owned a couple of parking garages right in the middle of the city. He also owned several restaurants, including a place called Mambo that was all the rage right now. I remembered where I'd seen the name now. There'd been a write-up about it in the papers and he'd been featured on the national news.

According to the police, the valet service at Mambo used one of Johnny's parking garages close by, and while people sat and had what was surely an overpriced dinner with mediocre food, Johnny's employees were suspected of using the cars to make drug drops all over the city. They had a tendency to use the flashier cars for their dirty work. Different cars on different nights and different times, and the police were running in circles. They knew Johnny Sakko was guilty. They only had trouble proving it.

My job was pretty cut and dried. I had a reservation for two for Saturday night at nine o'clock and the use of a brand new Porsche that had been loaned from the dealer. All I had to do was slip the camera inside the car and go in and enjoy a free meal. Easy enough. Except I had no date to bring with me, and I'd be caught dead before eating in a restaurant alone.

I'd seen women eating by themselves from time to time, usually looking forlorn and trying not to make eye contact with the other diners so they wouldn't see the pity in their gazes. I'd heard women ate by themselves all the time in the north. But in the South eating alone was like proclaiming to the world that no one wanted you.

I made a couple of notes in the Johnny Sakko file and opened up the second file.

"Good grief."

I didn't have anything against old people, but there was nothing I hated more than spending time in a nursing home, even an upscale assisted living center like the one in the file. It was filled with nothing but randy geriatrics who thought it was okay to pat you on the ass because they were over the age of seventy-five.

I knew this to be fact because my Uncle Milton spent the last twenty years of his life in Sunnydale Assisted Living, where he met the last two of his four wives and finally keeled over from a heart attack during the throes of passion. Uncle Milton had been a firm believer in male enhancement and erectile dysfunction medication. Not that it had done him a lot of good in the end. They'd had a hell of a time getting Milton's coffin closed, and I shudder to think how scarred the poor intern was who was relegated to massaging out the rigor.

I was looking for a woman named Virginia Peterson, according to Kate's notes. Apparently Virginia had decided she didn't like how her children hovered over her, and she was paranoid they were going to take all of her stuff and stick her in a nursing home. According to Virginia's doctors and her children she had the early stages of dementia, but she also suffered from delusions and extreme paranoia.

So Virginia bought fake IDs on the Internet and cashed out her entire life savings, and she slipped out of her home in the middle of the night.

"Damn," I muttered. For someone close to eighty years old she was pretty spry.

I snorted my coffee when I read Kate's handwriting at

the bottom of the page. Apparently she thought I should take notes on how to sneak around without being seen or heard from Virginia Peterson. It would serve Kate right if I took her up on it.

Virginia took her new identity and all her money and rented an apartment at the Summer's Eve Retirement and Assisted Living Home.

"That's an unfortunate choice of names." The images in my head of what went on at Summer's Eve was enough to make me want to run screaming.

The case was simple enough. Virginia's children were frantic with worry and Kate had tracked her down this far. All I needed to do was go in and give a visual affirmation that it really was Virginia and then I could leave and let the family take over.

I made a call to Summer's Eve and made an appointment to tour the facilities later in the evening, with the small lie that I had an ailing grandmother. With that done, I stuffed the files in my bag and looked at the time. My eyes had started to water a few minutes before so I knew I'd already spent too long in the space that was called my office. I grabbed my coffee cup and my purse and closed the door behind me, breathing in the fresh air from the hallway.

My keen sense of smell noticed something that hadn't been there on my first walk down the hallway.

"Chocolate." I stopped and inhaled again. The smell was coming from beneath Kate's door and I didn't even stop to think as I knocked on the door. I had the knob turned and was halfway in before I heard her say "Come in."

"I wondered how long it would take you to sniff them out," Kate McClean said from behind her desk. I looked at the chocolate scones on the sofa table next to the Keurig and my mouth started to water a little. "You're losing your touch."

"The carpet glue threw me off. I think it's done permanent damage. All my nose hairs are singed."

Kate and I had been best friends for our whole lives. There wasn't anything we didn't know about each other, and when we did try to keep secrets we could usually tell and ferret out the information anyhow.

Her office was a replica of an old noir film, from the lettering on her office door to the slatted blinds at her back that looked out onto York Street. Her desk was dark wood and masculine, and so was the leather couch and chairs off in the sitting area. An antique hat stand stood against the wall and it held a variety of umbrellas and a raincoat. Kate was always prepared for any situation.

Kate's appearance had never been very important to her. That was probably our biggest difference. Kate was one of those women who was perpetually cute. She looked exactly the same as she had in high school—chin-length blond hair, a cute button nose, clear gray eyes and dimples she didn't like others to see because she thought they wouldn't take her seriously. She never wore makeup unless forced to at gunpoint, and she wore a different boxy suit every day and her shoulder holster. Today's suit was a brown pinstripe and her shirt was white oxford.

I looked down at my own clothes—bright red ankle pants, a black and white polka dotted silk shirt and a strappy pair of Jessica Simpson heels that would have my feet screaming by the end of the day. And yes, I was well aware that I'd be better off financially if I could manage to stop maxing out my credit cards, but sometimes ice cream wasn't enough to chase away the blues. Sometimes a girl needed shoes.

I wondered briefly if I'd be taken more seriously if I wore ugly brown suits too, but quickly discarded the idea. I looked horrible in brown.

I grabbed a scone and took a seat in one of the leather club chairs where we'd be meeting the client. "You want to fill me in on what's going on? I caught enough of your phone call last night that I'm assuming we're meeting a billionaire with a sperm problem."

Kate's mouth quirked in a smile. "Something like that. Or maybe I'm just setting you up on a blind date."

"Then I'll pass. I don't want anyone with sperm problems, no matter how much money he has. My ovaries would kick his ass. These suckers are primed and ready to go. They seem to want children whether I'm ready for them or not. Weird, isn't it?"

"Not really. We're past thirty. I can say children have been an occasional topic of conversation in our house too. But then that changes in a heartbeat whenever I go to the Piggly Wiggly."

"Maybe that's what I should do."

"It's the best birth control ever."

A knock sounded at the door and Lucy stuck her head in before opening it wide. She stood aside as an older gentleman stepped in. Kate and I both rose to greet him as Lucy quietly shut the door at his back.

"Mr. Tannenbaum?" Kate asked, holding out her hand.

"Yes, ma'am. And you're Ms. MacLean." He had the true Southern drawl of a Savannah native, so his words extended over several extra syllables. He took Kate's hand in a limp grasp and leaned over it as he kissed it softly.

Mr. Tannenbaum looked to be somewhere between eighty and a hundred and forty—his hair was a solid shock of silver and his eyes were a rheumy blue. His hands had liver spots and his skin was too big for his bones. I could tell he'd been a charmer in his day, but behind the charm he looked ill. His complexion was pasty and I noticed his hand trembled slightly as he let go of Kate. He wore creased linen slacks and a blue button-down shirt with a white handkerchief sticking from the pocket. An ornate cane topped with a gold horse's head was held loosely in his hand. I was willing to bet he'd hung a fedora on the hat rack in the lobby. He seemed like the type to wear a fedora.

"It's a pleasure to meet you," Kate said smoothly, showing him to the sitting area. "This is Addison Holmes. She's going to be assisting me in some of the research for your case. From what you've told me so far, I hope you understand this case isn't going to be easy. It could take time."

"Time, Ms. McClean, is precisely what I don't have. I'll do whatever it takes to get this resolved quickly."

"Then let's get started. Can I get you some coffee?"

"Please. Two sugars. And one of those scones I've been smelling since I walked in the door if you don't mind."

Kate made his coffee and brought him a plate back to the table with his cup. "Why don't you start at the beginning?" she suggested. "We need as many names and dates as possible. Accuracy is going to be key with this case."

I was completely in the dark as to what Kate and Mr. Tannenbaum were talking about, so I just took my seat and grabbed the legal size pad from my bag to take notes.

"I was seventeen years old when the war started," he began.

I assumed he was talking about World War II and not the War Between the States, but considering how old he looked I couldn't be a hundred percent sure.

"I didn't have any money then. We were about as dirt poor as you could get. The Depression had hit my parents hard, and my daddy died in thirty-nine working on the railroad. That left me as head of the family to take care of my mama and my little brother. I wasn't Tannenbaum then. That came later. I was Frank Hannigan in those days. They called me Little Frankie because my daddy had been Frank too."

He paused and took a sip, his hand shaking so bad I was afraid he might spill hot coffee on himself.

"I'll admit I got into a bit of trouble back in those days. I started hanging with some unsavory young men a little older than me. I played a lot of cards, gambling with money I didn't have. When I needed to steal I did so. I worked a job along the same railroad that had killed my daddy, but the money wasn't much. Not enough to keep food on the table on a regular basis."

"Then the war started and my mama went to work at the defense plant here in Savannah. I didn't want to enlist. I had no plans to do so, and some of the crowd I ran with had ways to access and alter medical records so we were all listed as not fit for duty. It seemed like a good plan to me." He looked up and stared directly at me, the blue of his eyes piercing. "I'm not proud to say that I wasn't always a good man."

I nodded, encouraging him to continue on. I hadn't written one single word on my paper. I think I was waiting for the other shoe to drop. I had a feeling things were going to get interesting with this case.

"It's those same medical contacts that opened a clinic right here in Savannah. About two blocks over from where we're sitting right now. Doctor Horace Neeley ran a legitimate practice in the front half of the building he owned. But even doctors then weren't making a lot of money. They were paid in food and goods more often than money, and Doc Neeley had a young wife half his age and a mansion over in Forsyth Park to maintain."

"So out of the back of his shop in his off hours, Doc performed the treatments that paid only in hard cold cash. I know women nowadays think you invented the feminist movement and fighting for your rights, but the same problems existed back then as they do today. Unwanted pregnancies were common, especially when birth control was so frowned upon here in the South. No one wanted to acknowledge such things existed. On the other end of the spectrum were the women who had trouble conceiving. Most times when a woman couldn't conceive she was the one considered inferior—barren—not her husband. But that wasn't always the case, and Doc started doing experiments."

Mr. Tannenbaum flushed bright red with embarrassment, and I raised my brows at the thought of what kind of experiments would embarrass a man of Mr. Tannenbaum's experience.

"Doc Neeley was a shrewd businessman. The first "unofficial" sperm bank in Georgia was opened right there in Doc's clinic. Turns out Doc was a sick bastard. Pardon my language, ladies, but that's what he was. His experiments went further than inseminating the women with the samples he'd managed to collect, most of them his at the beginning."

My nose scrunched and I might have whispered *Eww* because Tannenbaum turned his gaze to me and nodded.

"Indeed," he agreed. "But infertility was a money making business, even back in those days. It was still highly illegal, but word spread about his services all over the state. Before long he was looking for more donors, and he came to us first. He thought it was funny to impregnate these highbrow ladies with the criminals and lowlifes of every kind. He offered us twenty-five dollars apiece to donate to his experiments. That was a lot of money in those days. Enough to feed my family for a couple of months at least."

I looked at the wizened man in front of me and my nose scrunched higher. I had one of those minds that put images to every situation. The images in my head now were bad enough to make me want to bleach my corneas.

He laughed when he saw my expression, and I tried to blank my face of all emotion. I'd never been very good at that. Mostly what I think is always plastered all over my face.

"How long did Doc Neeley keep his clinic open?" Kate asked. "Surely the authorities were aware?"

"Oh, sure," he said nodding. "But the Savannah police had a reputation of being corrupt back in those days. I'm sad to say it was true, though friends in the right places kept me out of a few scrapes a time or two. But Doc Neeley wasn't able to keep things running more than a couple of years. It turns out he'd decided to inseminate one of his patients the old fashioned way, if you know what I mean." Tannenbaum waggled his eyebrows and my lips twitched.

"What happened?" I asked.

"The wife confessed everything. And then one night Doc Neeley's clinic caught fire and burned to the ground, along with half a dozen other businesses around it."

"Arson?" Kate asked.

"Oh, yes. Without a doubt. Doc Neeley's house over in Forsyth Park received the same treatment, only Doc and his wife and children were all inside. It wasn't a good time around these parts. Tensions were high and the police were trying to cover that they had any knowledge, but they were between a rock and a hard place because the man who set the fire had a lot of power, though they knew they had to make an arrest because the people were demanding it."

"Let me tell you, seeing that fire that killed the Neeleys opened my eyes. I was well on my way to becoming much worse than he ever was. It was almost '42 by then, so I gave my mama every penny I had and went and enlisted in the army. Best thing I ever did."

"I think I'm confused," I said. This didn't sound like the type of case Kate would take on. "I'm not sure what we're supposed to investigate. The man who killed the Neeleys was known."

"True enough, and he was finally arrested, though he hung himself before he could get to trial. I've hired this agency because of another matter entirely. I'm a wealthy man, Ms. Holmes. My time in the army taught me how to work hard. When the war was over, that's exactly what I did, and I'm fortunate I had a knack for buying and selling real estate. It's like gambling, you see," his eyes bright with excitement. "And I was always a very good gambler."

"What I haven't been very good at is family. I regret

that now that I'm at the end of my life. My first wife was a good woman. I loved her until she died more than twenty years ago, but business always came first."

The sadness and regret in his voice had tears pricking at my eyes. I was a sap. I cried at commercials for Pete's sake. Kate rolled her eyes at me and I looked down at the hardly eaten scone on my plate and picked at a few of the crumbs to get myself under control again.

"Darla and I weren't blessed with any children, though we tried. And then about ten years ago I married my second wife," he said, rolling his eyes. "I was seventy-six years old and I was tired of being alone. That's my only excuse. But Lord, that woman was annoying. And it's not like she married me for my body anyway, so at least I had peace and quiet while I was sleeping. I divorced her after about six months and she got a nice settlement to make her happy."

"And then three years ago I married my third wife." He frowned and paused while he tried to catch his breath. I gave Kate a worried look, but she shook her head at me to not make a fuss. Something was very wrong with Mr. Tannenbaum.

"She was an older woman—I'd learned from my first mistake—but she was still a good thirty years younger than me. She had two sons and a daughter from her first marriage, but they were all grown so they were never around much. She wasn't the love of my life, but we had a fondness and respect for each other. She was killed in a car accident last month."

"I'm sorry to hear that, Mr. Tannenbaum," Kate said softly.

"Yes, well, none of us can live forever. Not even me." His mouth quirked at the corners and I couldn't tell if it was a smile or a grimace. "Three weeks ago I was diagnosed with a rare form of cancer. My body is riddled with the disease, it seems, and there's nothing they can do for me. So you understand what I mean when I say I don't have time to wait."

"What, exactly, is it you want us to do for you?" I asked. I was ready to get out of the room and take a deep breath of fresh air. Mr. Tannenbaum's story had depressed the hell out of me. He'd had so much loss over his life, and then for him to know he only had weeks of his own life left made me think about my own mortality.

"As I looked death in the face, I realized I had wealth, but no one to give it to. I had no family left. I have my company, but it's run by a board of directors filled with much younger men. I've got my staff, but they're not the same as family."

"What about your step-children?" Kate asked.

He waved a hand in dismissal. "Wastrels, each and every one of them. They live off their trust funds and never do anything more to replenish the coffers. My late wife was quite worried about their habits, but there wasn't much she could do. I'll not be leaving them anything if they're just going to squander it."

"So who are you going to leave it to? I'm sure there are plenty of local charities who would be glad for the money," I said.

"I'm sure they would be. But that's not what I'm going to do." He took another shaky breath and the handkerchief from his shirt pocket to blot his brow. "I'm going to leave it to my child. I just need you to find him first."

It took me a second to process, but then I remembered what he'd said about donating to Doc Neeley's back alley infertility clinic and the light bulb went off. "Holy cow," I said, my eyes wide. "That's going to be a heck of a surprise for someone."

"I hope so." He smiled and leaned over to pat my hand. "I do know for certain that my sample was used and that the process was successful. Doc always told us if it was with glee. He frequently hobnobbed with society, and he found great entertainment in knowing people so high and mighty were bringing bastard children into the world without their knowledge."

"Do you know the mother's name or anything about her?" Kate asked.

"Not much, I'm afraid. Her name was Rose and she wasn't a Savannah native. Her husband was a banker."

Kate wrote diligently in her notes, but she looked up when he stopped talking, eyebrows raised. "Is that all?"

"I'm afraid so," he said sadly. "I only glimpsed her once you see. She was a pretty thing with red hair. And I was told she had a son."

"What year was his birth?"

"I donated in June of '41 and I believe she was inseminated in the same month, or at least the beginning of the next. That would put the birth sometime around March of '42 I believe."

"That's at least somewhere we can start then," Kate said. "What happens if you pass on before your son is found, Mr. Tannenbaum?"

"While my wife was still alive, I had my will set up so all my assets and the majority share of my company would go to her. I also had it set up that her children would receive a substantial amount to add to their trust funds. But as of today that's going to change. I'm headed to see my attorney and sign the final papers for my new will. Even if I die before you find my son, I have it stipulated in the will that the money will stay in an account for him, or in the case that he is also deceased, for any of my biological grandchildren. And you will keep getting your retainer every month until he is found. I want everything I've built to go to my own blood, even if they don't know who I am."

CHAPTER THREE

Twenty minutes later, I was standing outside of Kate's office feeling a little sad and a lot contemplative. Some of the things Mr. Tannenbaum said had really hit home.

I didn't have a husband or children to leave a legacy of memories to. Sure, I had my mother, but she was newly remarried and I wasn't about to encroach there. A couple of months ago when I'd been living at home I'd had the misfortune of hearing more than I'd wanted to about my mom's sex life—quite literally. My bedroom walls were thin, and Vince, my new stepdad, was apparently a thoroughbred in the bedroom department if the sounds I'd heard were anything to go by.

I'd quickly moved out and left them to their privacy. I was happy for my mom. Really, I was. She'd been hit hard by my father's death a few years ago, and some of the spunk had been knocked right out of her. Now that she was married to Vince she had that vibrancy of life that had been missing. I just always thought I'd be the next one to get married.

I stepped outside and breathed in the damp air. Savannah was beautiful in October. The temperatures stayed in the seventies, but the humidity was thick like syrup. Heavy rain clouds had gathered while I'd been meeting with Kate and Mr. Tannenbaum, but the rain was holding off for now.

I hitched my bag up on my shoulder and started toward the curb where I'd left my car. The black Mercedes was exactly where it had been a couple of hours before. But all that was left of my Volvo was the rusted bumper. I just stared down at the empty space, sure that if I waited long enough it would materialize exactly where I'd left it. But it was no use. The car was gone.

I looked up and saw a homeless man sitting on the bench in the park across the street, a brown paper bag stuffed with clothes sitting next to him. A gray ski cap was pulled down over his ears and his beard was long and wiry.

"Hey, what happened here?" I asked, pointing to the bumper.

He cackled once, showing a gap-toothed grin, and he rubbed two fingers and his thumb together so I'd know he could be bought for information.

I sighed and dug around in my purse for any cash. I didn't have much. I'd raided my change jar earlier, so all I had was a roll of quarters and a couple of crumpled bills I'd found in the dryer.

I crossed the street and handed him the crumpled bills. "What happened to the white car that was parked there?" I repeated.

He took the money and it disappeared into his pocket. "It was the aliens. Straight from the sky."

I narrowed my eyes and put a fist on my hip. "That was my ice cream money you just swindled."

"Ice cream sounds pretty good," he said, licking his lips. He picked up his paper bag and shuffled off down the street.

"Dammit." I walked back to the space where my car had been and evaluated my options. I could call a cab, but I didn't have money for the fare. I could call my mom, but then I'd have to listen to her "the world is going to hell in a handbasket" speech. I could probably borrow the agency car Kate sometimes used for stakeouts, but last time I did I'd gotten something sticky on the seat of my pants I'd been afraid to evaluate.

I pulled my phone out of my purse, figuring I had no choice but to call my mother, when I realized a shiny black pickup truck was stopped in front of me with the window rolled down.

"Looks like you've got a problem," Nick Dempsey said, his mouth quirking in a smile. I didn't smile back. My insides had just turned to jelly at the very sight of him.

We'd been lovers only a couple of months ago, and for the first time in any relationship I'd ever had, I finally felt like I'd found the person I was supposed to be with. Unfortunately, he hadn't felt the same way. My predilection for getting into trouble and the new career I'd decided to pursue had been a deal breaker for Nick. He was a cop through and through, and he'd broken my heart when he'd walked out of my life.

We'd only seen each other a handful of times over the last couple of months. He worked for Kate on occasion, and I did my best to avoid him whenever possible, even when he'd tried to speak to me. I still wasn't quite over him yet, and if I was honest with myself, I was pretty damned angry at him as well.

"It's no big deal. I've got it covered," I fibbed.

He looked good. I mean *really* good. He'd recently had a haircut so the slight curl that had a tendency to get out of control was ruthlessly tamed. He was dressed for work—pressed slacks and a blue button-down shirt that matched his eyes to perfection. His shoulder holster and weapon were visible and his sport coat lay folded over the back of the seat.

Cops in Savannah had a strict dress code and a lot of them were young and attractive, but Nick was movie star handsome, which was why he was often the media liaison for the department even though he was a homicide detective. There was more than one woman I knew who tried to get pulled over on occasion just in case she got lucky enough to meet her future husband.

"You're such a liar," he said. I could hear his sigh from where I stood on the street. "Get in the truck, Addison."

"Nope, I don't think so." I'd decided to stand firm, even though I wanted nothing more than to do what he said. I wanted to breathe him in—the scent of his cologne and the detergent he used on his shirts. It was all so familiar it made my chest hurt just thinking about it. "Really, I'll call a cab and it'll all be good. You're working."

"Please." His gaze was direct and there was something else I didn't recognize in his eyes. It might have been panic. "I need your help."

Against my better judgment I got in the truck.

~

I REALLY STARTED to worry when Nick got in line for the drive-thru at Dairy Queen. We hadn't said a word to each other and the air was tense with anticipation. I accepted the hot fudge sundae with raised brows and stared Nick down.

"Things must be pretty bad for you to stoop to this," I said.

"You looked like you could use a hit. You'd been standing there staring at the empty parking place for five minutes before you noticed I was in front of you."

I rolled my eyes and dug in, moaning as the sugar hit my system.

"Thanks for the ride, but you just missed the turn to get to my house."

"I'm taking the long way."

Oh, boy. I was pretty sure I wasn't cut out for the long way. I was about two minutes away from stripping down and doing something bound to get us arrested. Whenever I was within a few feet of Nick my hormones took over and my brain stopped working.

"You can just do a U-turn up here," I said. "People miss that last turn all the time. Really, there's no need to take the long way."

"You're pretty jumpy. Is something wrong?"

I turned in my seat and narrowed my eyes. "Really? Why would something be wrong? Just because you left me in the hospital with a gunshot wound and walked out of my life forever, that's no reason for you to think something might be wrong. I'm fine. You're obviously fine. We're all just *fine*."

Nick's knuckles tightened on the steering wheel. "Maybe if you hadn't been in the hospital for a gunshot wound then I would have stuck around."

"Maybe you should tell me why the hell I'm sitting in this car instead of reaching for my gun."

"Jesus, you're armed?" The horrified look on his face made me feel a little better and I smiled.

"I'm a single girl in the city. Of course I'm armed. I was the top shooter in my conceal to carry class too. I'm sure you remember better than anyone that I know how to handle a loaded weapon."

The sexual tension skyrocketed as Nick raised a brow at me. "Oh, I remember. I have fond memories of how well you hold a loaded weapon."

My body temperature went molten and I was pretty sure I might have had a small orgasm. "I think I'll get out here. Just drop me at the corner. I'm close enough to walk."

"Are you dating Savage?" he asked out of the blue.

"What?" I asked, surprised. "Why do you even care? It's none of your business who I date."

His jaw tightened and his eyes narrowed as he took yet another turn in the complete opposite direction of my house.

"Maybe I'm dating a different guy every night," I pressed on. "Maybe the reason I'm so good at holding loaded weapons is because I've been practicing. What's it to you? You're the one who walked away. I'm about two seconds from opening the door and jumping out into the street, so you should probably tell me what you want."

I was starting to think I was angrier than I'd originally thought. Smoke was coming out of my ears and my hand gestures were getting more aggressive.

"You're right. You're right. I'm sorry. It's none of my business." He deliberately relaxed his grip on the steering wheel and the tension seemed to drain from him. "I'm asking for a favor and I know you have no reason to help me out, but I'm going to ask anyway."

"I'm not dressing up in a hot dog suit."

His gaze jerked toward me in surprise and then he swore as he looked back at the road in the nick of time to swerve around a car. A blare of the horn followed us.

"Sorry," I said. "I have bad memories from a summer job."

"No hot dog suits, though I'm intrigued. My brother is getting married Saturday night and I need a date for the wedding."

I laughed out loud before I could control it. "You're kidding me. Surely you could find someone other than me to take with you. I can't imagine you haven't met someone else in the last couple of months. You don't seem like the type to let your bed get too cold."

His jaw tightened again and I saw a vein throb at his temple. "I've been busy with work. I haven't had the time to date anyone. Besides, after dating you everyone else seems a little boring. They're certainly less reckless."

"And you were doing so well..."

"Listen, I'll pay you."

My eyes widened at that and my first thought was that I should be angry. I wasn't a hooker for crying out loud. But then the practical side took over. I needed the money.

"How much?"

"A hundred bucks."

"A hundred bucks? You're kidding me? Five hundred and you've got a deal."

"Five hundred dollars?" he choked. "Are you fucking serious? I could hire an escort for that and at least get sex out of it."

"Stop the car. I'll just get out here."

"Fine, fine." He raised his hands in surrender. "Five hundred dollars."

"Believe me, you're getting out with a bargain. Mostly I still want to do bodily harm to you whenever I see you."

He slammed on the brakes and before I knew it my seatbelt was unbuckled and I was sitting on his lap, my empty ice cream container tumbling to the floor. His lips touched mine and every protest I had leaked right out of my brain.

Nick was a damned good kisser. Legendary even. And I'd missed it. Missed *him* more than I wanted to admit. His lips were soft and his tongue pressed forward so I had no choice but to open my mouth and let him in. I moaned and my fingers pressed against his shoulders as the world spun around me. Places on my body were getting very warm—warm enough that I was close to combusting. Definitely warm enough that as soon as I got home I was going to help myself self-combust with the memory of this kiss.

We broke apart, both gasping for breath, and he had that soft, unfocused look in his eyes like he got when we were making love. I knew if I didn't put a stop to this then things would get out of control.

And then he did something completely out of character. He rested his forehead against mine and just held me as our pulses slowed and the urge to stake a claim passed.

"I've missed you." His breath whispered against my lips and I held on to him for a few seconds longer, soaking in his warmth and just the feel of his touch again. "I didn't want to."

"I can't do this, Nick." I pushed away and shakily

moved back to my seat, fastening my seatbelt. "It hurts too bad."

He sighed and put the truck back in gear. "I know, babe. Believe me, I know."

Tears pricked my eyes and I blinked rapidly so they wouldn't fall. I looked out the window for the rest of the drive to my house. By the time Nick pulled into my driveway I'd gotten myself under control and was trying to think about anything besides the sorry shambles that was my personal life.

"Thanks for the ride," I said, opening the door before he'd even stopped all the way.

"Any time. And I mean that, Addison. Call me if you find yourself in trouble."

I'd just closed the door when he rolled down the window and stopped me. "Oh, and Addison? I'll be by to pick you up at six-thirty Saturday night. It's black-tie."

My mouth was still hanging open when he put the truck in reverse and sped away.

CHAPTER FOUR

The sky opened up about two seconds after I bolted the front door. I kicked off my heels and padded barefoot into the bedroom and then fell face first onto the bed. I tried to make myself fall asleep but all I could think about was that damned kiss, so I tossed and turned for twenty minutes before finally giving up and reaching for the Mr. Incredible I kept in my bedside table. I'd bought it a few months ago at one of those home sex toy parties. It had been worth every penny, though I hadn't had to use it once while I'd been dating Nick. His Mr. Incredible was more than enough to keep me satisfied.

An hour later I'd showered and changed into jeans, a blue silk shirt, and a pair of low-heeled black boots. My hair was styled and my makeup finished. I felt refreshed, relaxed, and ready to take on Virginia Peterson at Summer's Eve Assisted Living. The only problem was I didn't have a way to get there. I only had one choice really.

Rosemarie Valentine teaches choir at James Madison High where I used to be gainfully employed. My classroom had been right next to her for years, and I'd heard show tunes sung in Rosemarie's Southern vibrato in some of my worst nightmares. Her hair was blonde and curled around her round head Farrah Fawcett style, and she always wore two perfect dots of rouge on the apples of her cheeks. Her eyes were cornflower blue and guileless and she was round. Everywhere.

I'm not sure quite how it happened, but Rosemarie and I were friends. She liked to tag around whenever I was doing easy surveillance, and I enjoyed her company because I never quite knew what was going to come out of her mouth.

I called her up and asked her to pick me up at my house at five, and it just so happened she was free and completely excited about visiting an assisted living facility. Rosemarie didn't get out much. She lived with two Great Danes the size of bulldozers. I'd once seen Rosemarie kiss one of the dogs full on the mouth with tongue and everything, so I could see why it might be hard for her to find a man that appreciated all her qualities.

I made another call to the police station and reported my car stolen. I described the car as best I could and the cop I talked to said it sounded like someone did me a favor, but they'd put a BOLO out for it just the same.

By the time five o'clock rolled around, all the tension that had been released with the help of Mr. Incredible was back. Mostly because I'd just watched Savage pull into his driveway. I looked at my watch and bit my lip as I saw it was exactly two minutes until five. If I was lucky Savage would disappear inside his house before Rosemarie showed up.

The rain had stopped, but the ground was soggy and the sky still gray and dreary. I stood as still as possible because Savage had superpowers and always seemed to know when I was trying to avoid him. Or maybe it was X-ray vision because he turned and looked directly at me, like he could see straight through the blinds.

I dialed Rosemarie and waited for her to pick up.

"Where are you?" I hissed.

"Turning onto your street as we speak. Am I late?"

"No, but I've got a problem. Savage is standing in his yard and I'm avoiding him. Pull in front of the house and push the car door open. I'm going to run out and jump in before he can talk to me, and then you can drive away."

"Oh, boy." I could hear her breathing grow heavier over the line. "My palms are getting sweaty. I don't do well under pressure."

"You'll be fine. It's no big deal. I'm at the door and ready to run."

I grabbed my purse and heard the squeal of tires from down the street and I had a sudden thought that maybe I was asking too much of Rosemarie. I opened the door and caught a glimpse of Savage with his mouth hanging open as Rosemarie's bright yellow Beetle jumped the curb in front of my house, taking out my trashcan. The passenger door swung open and I was out the door like a shot, avoiding the puddles as best I could.

I looked up in time to see Savage start my way and I squeaked and ran faster. I could see Rosemarie through the car door, her head turning back and forth between me and Savage, the panic obvious on her face. I was almost home free when Rosemarie pressed on the gas pedal and the car shot forward. The door was still hanging open as the wheels left the curb and bounced back onto the street.

"Rosemarie, stop!" I yelled.

"I'm sorry! I got nervous!" she yelled back. But she didn't stop.

I was running alongside the Beetle as fast as I could, trying to figure out how to jump in without killing myself. If I hadn't been jogging every day for the last month I never would've made it. We were halfway up the street when Rosemarie slammed on the brakes and I thunked my head against the door as it swung back at me. I hopped in the passenger seat and slammed the door closed while Rosemarie laid rubber.

I turned in my seat to look back, but all I could see was Savage bent over at the waist shaking with laughter.

Rosemarie and I were both out of breath and my hair and makeup were probably no longer as perfect as they'd been before I'd left the house.

"I don't think I'm meant to be the getaway driver," she finally said. "I sometimes get a little excitable."

"That's okay. If I ever rob a bank I'll make sure to call someone else."

SUMMER'S EVE Assisted Living sat on top of a hill in Chatham County. Black iron gates surrounded the estate on all sides and the grounds were lush and green. Rosemarie pulled up to the closed gate and rolled down her window to press the intercom. I expected there to be a crash of thunder at any moment because it would've been perfect for the atmosphere. Summer's Eve looked more like a prison than a place to spend your final days.

The gates opened after Rosemarie gave my name and she drove up the long driveway and pulled into a little parking area to the side of a large gothic mansion of gray stone complete with gargoyles. We both got out and looked around. It was completely silent. No birds, no animals, no car motors, no airplanes, and no leaves rustling—nothing.

"This place is creepy as shit," Rosemarie said. "I think I'd rather eat a bullet than ever have to live in a place like this."

I hmmmed in agreement and we made our way to the front door. It opened before I could press the buzzer.

"Ms. Holmes?" The woman was somewhere between twenty-two and seventy-two. There was too much plastic surgery getting in the way to make an accurate guess, and I was thinking we'd probably have to chop her in half and count her rings if we wanted to know her real age. She had honey blonde hair and the whitest teeth I'd ever seen. She wore an expensive black suit and red heels that made my mouth water with envy.

"Yes, I'm Addison Holmes." I stuck out my hand when she offered hers. Her grasp was firm and businesslike and I found myself continuing to stare. I'd never seen anyone put together quite like she was. She was pretty at first glance, but the closer I looked at her features, it was like she'd been dealt her nose, eyes, and mouth from a Mr. Potato Head grab-bag.

"I'm Vicki Dawson. I'm glad you're here with us," she said, closing the door behind us. "I'm sure your grandmother is going to love it here at SEAL. Our residents enjoy an active social life, have spacious living facilities, and round the clock care if they have any health concerns or an emergency."

I was still trying to figure out what SEAL meant when it hit me. It was probably smarter on their part to use the acronym. Much better to think of sea mammals than feminine care products.

"If you'll follow me, I'll introduce you to your tour guide." She smiled and I was blinded again by all those teeth. "We let our seniors volunteer in our community, and the tours and customer service are just a couple of the opportunities they have. Every apartment has maid service three days a week. Breakfast, lunch, and dinner is provided daily, plus an afternoon snack. On Thursdays we do a high tea and social hour and everyone dresses in their best. We offer a church service on Sunday, and on Mondays the bus takes anyone who wants to go into town for shopping and lunch. On Wednesday the bus takes them to whatever activity we have scheduled. We have a movie theater in house as well as an indoor swimming pool and an exercise area."

"Wow, your grandmother is going to love this place," Rosemarie whispered.

I was tempted to move myself into Summer's Eve. It had everything. Except for young people, but I was willing to overlook that.

I had yet to see any of the residents, but a man who had a startling resemblance to Vicki came out of an area that looked like private offices. He was probably a foot taller and had the same honey blonde hair and blue eyes as his sister.

"This is my brother, Victor," Vicki said.

I shook hands with Victor as Vicki introduced us and immediately felt sorry for the two of them. It must have been hell growing up with those names.

"I'm sorry to interrupt, but we have an important conference call coming up," he said apologetically.

"Oh, yes," Vicki said. "I'd forgotten. Just let me introduce Ms. Holmes to Deloris and she can take over the tour from there."

Victor nodded goodbye and Vickie opened a pair of heavy oak doors to reveal a giant ballroom. Music played from the speakers—big band era I recognized from my mom's collection—and several couples danced in the open space on the far side of the room. A long bar with stools sat against the back wall and was made up to look like a soda fountain complete with a soda jerk behind the counter with a paper hat. A ping-pong table was set up in one corner and a pool table in another. There were tables for dominoes and cards as well. It was a senior citizen's paradise.

"Holy cow," I whispered.

"Isn't it fabulous?" Vicki asked. "Let me introduce you to Deloris."

I remembered I was there to work and wasn't actually scoping the place out for my grandmother who'd passed away several years ago. I did a quick scan of the room for Virginia Peterson, but I didn't see her. Of course, I'm not sure I would've seen her if she'd been standing right in front of me. People after a certain age had a tendency to look an awful lot alike.

It was obvious they all used the same stylist. The women all had short hair that varied in color from steel gray to white to peach, and they all had perfect sausage curls lined straight as soldiers.

Vicki led us over to the ping-pong table and I watched in rapt fascination while a woman in a bright red dress that showed entirely too much loose skin talked trash to her male opponent.

"Is that the best you got, Wilbur? I got hangnails that can swat balls better than that."

Wilbur didn't look so good. He was sweating profusely and his face grew redder with every taunt. And then Deloris spiked the ball for the winning point and threw down her paddle like a rapper throws down his microphone.

"Booyah! Take that, you old coot. No one knocks me off the throne."

"Maybe someone will knock you off the balcony instead," I heard someone say from the crowd.

"I heard that, Janice Walker. Maybe you oughta mind your own beeswax. It seems to me you should be more worried about George making time with Netta out in the garden."

The woman I assumed was Janice Walker narrowed her eyes and turned around in a huff, making a beeline for the double doors that led out into the back gardens. And then Deloris turned her eyes on me.

"Are these the newbies?" she asked Vicki, and then her blue eyes narrowed on me. "You play ping-pong?"

"No, ma'am," I answered, taking a step back. Deloris scared the crap out of me, though she barely came up to my shoulders. Now that I saw her from the front, I really appreciated my view of the back of her a lot more. Her red dress was cut in a deep V to the middle of her chest, but there was no cleavage there to support it. From the lumps around her middle I was pretty sure there was no bra in the world available to give that dress the support it needed.

"I've been known to slap balls around the table," Rosemarie piped in.

I closed my eyes in horror at the image of Rosemarie and Deloris doing a ping-pong fight to the death.

"It's a shame we don't have time for you to play

today," I broke in before Deloris could extend the challenge. "We'll be able to spend more time here if this is where my grandmother ends up."

"Right, the tour," Deloris said. "Come on then. I've got this, Vicki."

I saw Vicki's lips twitch as she waved us goodbye. At least she had a sense of humor.

Rosemarie and I followed Deloris out of the activity room and back into the lobby area. "You know the one good thing about getting old?" she asked.

"Nope." I couldn't think of one thing that I was looking forward to in my old age. Looks went to hell and the memory function of the brain seemed haphazard at best. Forty-two medications had to be taken daily to keep you alive and you had to wear diapers.

"I don't sweat anymore. It's like all my body fluids dried up. Check out this dress. It's red satin and dry as a bone."

"I've been admiring that dress," Rosemarie said. "I'm thinking it's a good cut for a woman with my attributes."

Deloris nodded sagely. "I used to have attributes like that. I don't know what happened to them. Woke up one morning and I just all of a sudden had three stomachs and a flat chest."

I was hoping there'd be wine somewhere on this tour because I could use a bottle or two.

"What's your granny's name?"

I realized she was talking to me when no one else answered and I figured it was best to stay as close to the truth as possible.

"Madeline," I answered.

"Does she like ping-pong?"

"Not to my knowledge. She likes soap operas and

bourbon." That was pretty much all I could remember about my grandmother.

"Sounds like good Southern stock to me. Let's go up this way so you can see the rooms."

We followed Deloris up three flights of stairs and Rosemarie and I were huffing like steam engines by the time we got to the top. I guess I wasn't at the age where all my body fluids dried up because I could feel the sweat running down my back.

"Are there no elevators?" I asked. "I'm not sure my grandmother could take these stairs every day."

"Oh, sure. But I don't like to take the elevator. Elevators are for sissies. No offense to your granny."

"None taken."

She showed me several apartments bigger than the size of my whole house, as well as a parlor, a library, and a music room. I didn't see Virginia Peterson in any of the social rooms, and I was starting to feel that maybe Virginia was holed up in her room.

We were on the second level and I was pooped and ready to call it a day.

"What's that noise?" Rosemarie asked.

I stopped to listen and I could barely hear a slight humming sound. I hadn't even noticed it until Rosemarie said something.

"Huh," Deloris said. "I've been hearing that for two days. I just thought my eardrums were about to burst or something."

"It sounds like it's coming from here," Rosemarie said. Apparently Rosemarie had ears like a bat and the determination of a pit bull.

"That's Martha Martin's room." Deloris went to the door and put her ear against it. "She was having chest pains and shortness of breath yesterday so the ambulance came and picked her up. I guess they left the TV on or something."

The door next to Martha's room opened and bingo, just like that, Virginia Peterson stuck her head out the door. I'd found since I'd been working for Kate that I didn't really have a lot of skills at finding people. I was mostly lucky, and luck was exactly what had just happened.

"Why are y'all makin' so much racket out here? I'm watching a Buffy marathon."

"There's humming coming from Martha's room. I think they left the TV on."

"Huh," Virginia said. "I wondered what that was. Thought I was about to go deaf." She came out of her room and closed the door behind her. It was definitely Virginia Peterson. And thank God for that because I was stick a fork in me done.

"I've got a key," Virginia said. "We'll just shut it off for her. I heard she was supposed to be back from the hospital tomorrow."

Virginia unlocked the door and we all trooped into Martha Martin's apartment. It looked like every other apartment. Martha liked Queen Anne furniture, lace doilies, and teapots. There were teapots everywhere.

But the TV wasn't on. We all looked around, listening at the vents and other electronic devices, but the humming wasn't coming from there. It was coming from the bed. The four of us stood on one side, and I watched with horror as Deloris picked the mattress up like it weighed nothing more than a pillow.

"Well I'll be," Virginia muttered.

Rosemarie was squeezing my hand so hard I was

surprised I didn't hear the bones crunch. Martha Martin's giant purple vibrator sat on the box springs, bouncing slightly, since it was turned to the highest setting.

"I guess we know why she was having those heart palpitations," Deloris said. "It's a nice size too, but mine's bigger."

"Mine is too," Virginia piped in. "I've got one of those Dr. Thunderhorse models and you've gotta be careful or it'll knock your fillings loose."

Deloris matter of factly reached over and switched off the vibrator and then dropped the mattress. "I don't know about you ladies, but I could use some wine."

CHAPTER FIVE

F*riday*

MY TONGUE FELT like sandpaper when I woke up the next morning, but I forced myself to get out of bed. There was no way I was going to exercise before a cup of coffee this morning, so I downed a quick cup and didn't even care that my taste buds were mostly singed off.

I changed into neon pink spandex shorts and a sports bra and stretched before I tortured myself with sit-ups. My mind was still in a wine fog from the night before, so I barely winced as I saw it took me twice as long as normal to complete the routine. If my brain hadn't still been in a wine fog, I would have remembered to check the neighborhood for Savage before I started my run.

I was just past Spock's house when I saw Savage coming from the opposite direction. It looked like he was finishing up his run. He was shirtless, his muscled chest slicked with sweat, and his athletic shorts hung low on his hips. I watched with amusement as screen doors opened and women from the neighborhood stuck their heads out to watch him go by. His body was a beautiful sight to see.

He cut across the street headed right toward me and I realized I had nowhere to hide. Not that I could in hot pink spandex. I kept running and hoped he would get the hint, but he fell into step right beside me.

"How's your head?" he finally asked when I didn't say anything. Mostly because I was concentrating on breathing, not because I was being rude.

"It feels like I drank too much wine with old ladies last night."

I saw his lips twitch from the corner of my eye. "I meant from where you bumped it on the car door."

"Oh, that." I already had a stitch in my side and we weren't even halfway around the block. "My head is pretty hard. I hardly notice the bumps anymore. Aren't you done running for the day?"

"I can always get another couple of miles in. It's no big deal."

"Must be nice," I wheezed. The spandex was already soaked through with sweat and I knew my face was probably the color of a tomato.

"I can help you with your workouts and get you in shape before you have to take the physical fitness part of the test, you know. You're doing better than you were, and people in the neighborhood are no longer complaining about you throwing up in their yards."

"Aren't you supposed to be getting ready for work?"

"Nah, I took a long weekend. I just had a case close yesterday so it was good timing. Why don't you want me to help you? Do I make you nervous?"

"Like a prisoner who just dropped the soap. I'm thinking having you as a personal trainer is not in my best interests at the moment."

We were coming up on the home stretch and my house was in sight, but I didn't know if I was going to make it. I was thinking it would probably be okay to just lie down in Mr. Sandusky's yard and crawl into the fetal position.

Talking was no longer an option as I was trying to focus on breathing and the horrible stitch in my side. I noticed briefly that Savage wasn't even breathing hard, and the competitive part of me wanted to see if I could make him bend just a little. So I kicked it into high gear and sprinted the rest of the way down the street to my house.

As soon as I hit my driveway a charley horse gripped the muscles in my calf like a vice and I went down with a scream.

"I hate this," I said through gritted teeth as I rubbed at the knotted muscle. "I hate running and exercise and sweating and yoga, and most of all I hate fucking sit-ups."

Savage kneeled down beside me and took over massaging the charley horse, and I scowled as I realized the sprint was for naught. He still wasn't breathing hard.

"Why are women expected to put our bodies through this? Doesn't society know that we're supposed to be soft and round and bake pies all day?"

"I'm guessing you don't get a lot of calls from feminist organizations."

"I need a donut."

"I don't mean to change the subject during your time of need or anything, but your driveway is strangely vacant. I'm surprised your car lasted as long as it did though. It was a deathtrap on wheels."

"Someone stole it from in front of the agency yesterday."

"I hate to break it to you, babe, but there's no way someone stole that car. Are you sure it wasn't mistaken for trash?"

"It was a perfectly good car. It ran. Mostly. And now that it's not so hot outside the smell isn't as bad."

The muscle was beginning to unknot and my brain functions were starting to return. Savage's hands were hot against my skin and I realized he was no longer rubbing my leg, but gliding his fingers up and down my calf in a way that had heat gathering in places best left unmentioned and my eyes rolling back in my head.

"What's all the racket out here?" Mr. Walner was my neighbor on my other side. He lived on his pension and drove a 1952 boat of a Cadillac that never fit completely in his driveway.

"No worries, Mr. Walner," Savage answered. "Just a muscle spasm."

"Why is everyone screamin' out here? I'm trying to watch my soaps." I groaned as I recognized Jemimah Blaze's voice. She didn't really fit in with the rest of the neighborhood. Mostly my street was filled with newly married couples just starting out and old people who lived on fixed incomes. Savage and I were kind of the anomaly. Jemimah Blaze was just a freak show waiting to happen.

She'd been a carnie before she'd retired to the suburbs, guessing people's ages and weights. She had tiny hands like a raccoon, a lot of body hair, and a mouth like a sailor. She scared the hell out of me.

"It's all good," I told her. "I just fell."

"Next time you fall like that you gotta make sure you trip him a little so he falls on top of you. That's how I lost my virginity. Of course, we were in a circus tent and he only had one leg, so it was hard for him to get up once I hooked on."

"Sweet Jesus," I said, meeting Savage's laughing gaze.

"I got some horse liniment in the house," Mr. Walner said. "Smells like bear piss and graveyard dirt, but I'm told it gets the job done."

"No, thank you," I called out before Savage could answer. "I'm fine now." I rolled over to my hands and knees and took the hand Savage held out to so I could stand. I sucked in a breath as I put weight on my leg and I walked around in a circle for a couple of seconds with a limp.

"Nothing good ever happens in this neighborhood," Jemimah said. "I was hoping for some full frontal."

"Not today," Savage said.

"Hmph." She slammed her screen door and went back to her soaps.

"The neighborhood was a lot quieter before you moved in," Mr. Walner said before going back inside his own home.

I sighed and headed toward my front door and I didn't realize Savage had followed me until I tried to close the door behind me and heard a thump.

"Thanks for your help," I said, heading to the shower. "You can go home now so I can die in peace."

"You'll feel better after a good breakfast."

"And yet no donuts have magically appeared on my counter."

"Go get in the shower, Grumpy, and I'll handle breakfast. We're going to get you in top shape for that test. You don't have a lot of time left."

I'd stopped listening by this point and barely noticed as I heard the front door close. I stripped out of sweaty spandex and stared at myself in the bathroom mirror.

"Good, God." My hair had grass and leaves stuck in it and my skin was flushed with big red blotches from head to toe. The good news was that my body itself looked pretty damned good. I could button all my pants every day and my stomach was mostly flat. My breasts had always been pretty good, but I was past thirty now so I didn't know how much longer they'd be upright and perky. I expected them to collapse under my armpits at any time.

I took a good twenty minutes in the shower, using all the hot water, but when I got out my muscles felt relaxed and I no longer wanted to vomit. I'd decided to work at home this morning, so I pulled on a pair of soft cotton pajama pants in gray and an old Metallica concert T-shirt I'd gotten in high school. It had a giant rip in the armpit, but I couldn't bear to get rid of it.

I pulled my hair up in a ponytail and slathered cream on my face and then I headed into the kitchen. Only to stop short at the sight of Savage making himself at home.

"What are you doing?" He'd managed to shower and was dressed in cutoff khaki shorts and another tight T-shirt—this one in blue. His feet were bare and he was slicing bananas and feeding them into the blender.

"Breakfast protein smoothie. It'll give you a boost for the day."

"Are there donuts in there?"

"If it'll make you drink it, then yes."

I sighed and then pulled up a bar stool, watching how natural Savage looked in the kitchen. "Do you do a lot of cooking?"

"You bet. I'm a single guy with a crazy schedule. It's cook or starve." He set the smoothie in front of me, and I couldn't bear to ask why it was green. Anything green made me a little nervous.

"So this is going to help me pass the physical portion of the test?" I was highly doubtful.

"This and a solid regimen of cardio and muscle training. One feeds the other. And it'll help if you'll lay off the donuts."

I took a giant sip of the smoothie and tried not to gag. It tasted like grass and bananas. Savage sucked his whole drink down in a couple of gulps and looked entirely too pleased with himself.

"There are no donuts in here."

"So I lied."

"You wouldn't be the first. Now if you're done trying to kill me I've got some work to do."

"What are you working on?"

I pushed the file for Johnny Sakko across the bar. I wasn't ready to share any info on the Tannenbaum case yet. Savage had a way of horning in and taking over. He and Nick had that in common.

Savage let out a low whistle. "Johnny Sakko is bad business. Every law enforcement agency in the country has been looking at him a long time. He's slick. Who's taking you to the restaurant? You need good backup."

"I can take care of myself. I don't need any backup." I told the lie with a straight face. On even my best day I needed backup.

"You can't go eat dinner alone at a place like Mambo.

You'd look like a loser eating there by yourself on a Saturday night. Good thing I'm free tonight. Besides, you don't have a car."

Damn. I'd forgotten about that. "It's not a date."

When I'd first met Savage a couple of months ago he'd blackmailed me into going on a date with him. We'd actually been on a few outings over the last couple of months, but I never called them dates because Savage had mentioned something about taking things to a whole new level by the time we made it to number five. The whole new level had a lot to do with being naked and sliding together horizontally so I was staying far away from the date label.

"Just business," he said, mouth twitching. "Mambo is a place to see and be seen. Make sure you look hot."

Savage left and I locked the door behind him. I was a little worried about going out on a non-date with Savage. He was the Devil in disguise, a temptation I knew I shouldn't have, but wanted anyway. And the longer I spent in his company the harder it was to resist him. It would be a mistake all around.

I washed out the blender and put on a new pot of coffee. I figured it would take at least two cups to get rid of the grass taste in my mouth. Once the coffee finished brewing I took my laptop, coffee cup, and the Tannenbaum file to the kitchen table.

It was disturbing how easy it was to dig up information on people, especially with some of the programs that were available to the agency. I did a full background check on Mr. Tannenbaum for my own records and then started the search for a woman named Rose in the state of Georgia who was married to a banker in the 1940s.

I let the computer work for a while and went to make

myself a sandwich. I felt a little guilty for using the white bread instead of wheat and mayo instead of mustard, but I figured the grass smoothie probably evened it all out. I added a fruit roll-up for dessert so the meal was more balanced.

By the time I was finished with lunch the computer had completed its search for Roses. There were more than three hundred of them to go through. I was actually expecting it to be worse since Georgia's population was somewhere over 3 million during the 1940s.

I needed to weed out the ones who didn't have sons and then I could narrow my search from there. The problem was this was all extremely time consuming. I had to do it name by name since there wasn't a program that was accurate enough to do it for me.

I looked up at the clock and saw it was past 7:30 and went into an immediate panic. I didn't have very long to look hot. And I was finding the older I got the longer it took. I closed down the computer and dashed into the bedroom to my closet. I pulled out a red tube dress that fit like a second skin. Red looked excellent against my olive complexion.

I didn't have time for hot rollers and big hair so I settled on straightening it so it ran sleek down my back. It would last all of two minutes after I walked out into the humidity. I put on my makeup and shadowed my eyes dramatically. And then I slicked on red lip stain that would make my lips feel like sandpaper as it dried if I didn't put on a coat of clear lip gloss immediately after.

All in all, I didn't look bad for half an hour's work. I also couldn't breathe in the dress, but oxygen was apparently overrated next to looking hot. I decided on nude skyscraper heels to make my legs look longer and when I went to get them from the floor of the closet I found I could only bend halfway, so I kicked them out of the closet and across the floor until I came to the little covered bench at the end of my bed. I put a hand behind me and sat down slowly, hoping the dress didn't roll down from the top or up from the bottom. I slipped my feet into the shoes and somehow managed to hike my leg up so I could buckle the straps.

The dress rose up to my hips and I felt a twinge in the calf that had knotted earlier that morning. If anyone had walked in at that exact moment I never would've gotten past the embarrassment of them seeing more of my lady bits than my gynecologist. Fortunately I had everything pulled down and back in place by the time Savage knocked on the door.

I made sure I had the file and tucked it into my purse, and then I went to answer the door. I was ready to get the job over with so I could get back home and let my internal organs breathe, so I didn't stop to let Savage in. I was almost positive it was his grass smoothie that was making my dress so tight. Everyone knew all that healthy stuff caused bloating.

"Nice dress you're almost wearing," Savage said. "You think it'll hold? I don't want to have to kill anyone tonight."

"It's a precarious situation, but I'm afraid to take it off and put on something else at this point. I don't want to rupture anything."

I walked over to Savage's black Expedition and I could feel his gaze like a laser beam against my backside. I turned back to look at him—his mouth was slightly open and his eyes were almost black, the lids hooded. I arched a brow and he shook his head a couple of times as if he were coming out of a trance.

"Do you need help getting into the truck?"

I sighed and looked at the side step on the Expedition. "Just watch where you put your hands."

"Oh, I'm watching." He opened the door and then picked me up around the waist like I was a bag of flour and then tossed me into the seat. I kind of teetered back and forth like a Weeble since I couldn't bend all that well, and managed to prop myself up in a slanted position against the bench seat.

"We're supposed to pick the Porsche up from Kate's office. She said it'll be parked right in front and you'll just need to run in and grab the keys from Lucy. The camera and everything will already be set up inside and the company credit card will be in the center console to pay for dinner."

"10-4, Kemo Sabe."

The ride was short and silent, mostly because I wanted to conserve my breath, and Savage was able to park directly behind the silver Porsche. It was a beautiful car, but I had no idea how I was going to squat that low to get inside.

Savage, gentleman that he was, came around and helped me out, and then I propped myself up against the Expedition while he went in for the keys. Kate and Lucy often worked late hours, well into the night, and when Savage came back out with the keys they followed behind him and got ready to lock up. Only I wasn't expecting Nick to come out with them.

I was a mess. I didn't officially have a man in my life, so it was completely unfair that I had the kind of reaction I did to a man I couldn't even lay claim to. Nick's gaze raked me over from head to toe, and his eyes turned to blue chips of ice.

"Busy weekend," he said.

"A girl's got to pay the rent."

Kate burst into laughter and the tension eased a little, but I wanted to remind Nick he had no say in my life anymore, and the only reason I was going with him to his brother's wedding was because he was paying me. But I wasn't going to lie, maybe it was a little nice to see the jealousy.

"Jesus, Addison," Kate said. "How are you supposed to sit in that dress?"

"I'll let you know when I figure it out."

"It's like paint. How in the hell did you get underwear on under that?"

I heard Nick and Savage both suck in a breath and I felt heat rush to my face. "Let's just say it's a good thing I have police connections if the seams happen to unravel. I can probably get out of a public indecency charge. And please don't tell my mother I'm not wearing underwear. She'll kill me."

"If you walked out of your house like that then she probably already knows. Mother's intuition."

Kate was right. My mother had radar when it came to me doing inappropriate things.

"The camera is already in place in the car and it's live. Hopefully they take the bait. Vice is waiting to step in once the car leaves the garage and any deals are made. Hopefully they'll be able to get someone to roll on Johnny."

Savage opened the passenger door of the Porsche and raised his brows at me to get in.

"No time like the present."

A collective breath was held as I lowered myself into the seat, and I managed to do it without displaying the results of my last bikini wax. Savage slammed the door closed and went to the other side, and I caught one last glimpse of Nick staring back at me, the thoughts unreadable on his face.

CHAPTER SIX

"You're awfully quiet," Savage said as he weaved in and out of traffic.

Savannah nightlife had picked up over the past several years, especially in the riverfront area. Bars and clubs popped up overnight within walking distance from hotels and apartment buildings, and the cops mostly did a good job of keeping the drunks from drowning in the Savannah River.

My cell phone rang and I saw it was my mother calling. Someone in my neighborhood was a snitch, but I had no idea who it was. The first time Nick had spent the night and his truck had been parked in my driveway all night I'd had so many calls from her I was surprised the phone didn't go up in smoke.

"Are you going to get that?"

"I'm thinking about it." And then I sighed and answered the phone. "Hi, Mom."

"Addison, I wanted to invite you and your man friend to lunch Sunday after church. You could even bring him to services if you'd like. He can sit in the family pew."

I turned to look at Savage and saw he was biting the inside of his cheek to keep from smiling. My mother had a voice like a freight train.

"I wish I could, but I've got work."

"On the Lord's Day? This is why the world is going down the toilet. No one takes time to rest anymore."

I'd heard this speech before so I was mostly on autopilot. We were getting close to the restaurant and I could tell she had at least another half hour of conversation in her.

"I'm going to have to call you back, Mom. I'm working tonight."

"Who is the man you're working with? Do you think he's good husband material?"

"I'm working with Agent Savage. And no. He most certainly is not."

"Is he gay?"

Savage cracked out a laugh and I slunk lower in my seat. "I have no idea. Maybe." Savage stopped laughing at that and I knew I was probably going to regret saying it.

"Just because he's gay doesn't mean you shouldn't wear underwear. It's not nice to tease a man. You remember what happened with your Uncle George. He was as gay as the day was long and then all of a sudden he fell in love with that nice Anastasia Dupris from Jersey, and now they're living happily ever after."

"That's because Anastasia Dupris is a drag queen."

There was a pause for several seconds on the other end of the line and I knew my mom was processing that information. "I never would have guessed. How do you think she gets her skin so smooth?"

"I have no idea. Maybe you should ask her."

"You're getting me off topic, dear. What I'm saying is

that you don't want men to think you're too easy by advertising your goods everywhere. Men like a little suspense when they're wooing a lady. Maybe this is why you're not married yet."

"I'm sure that's what it is," I said dryly. "I've got to let you go. We're just pulling up to the restaurant."

"Have a good time, dear."

I disconnected and immediately felt the pressure headache right behind my eyes. It was a miracle I managed to live eighteen years under the same roof with my mother without my head exploding. I loved her dearly, but a little Phyllis Holmes went a long way.

"Your mother reminds me a lot of my own," Savage said, stopping the car in front of the valet stand.

"Oh, good. I thought it was just me."

Savage got out and passed off the keys to a white male in his early twenties. He was blonde and blue-eyed. Frat boy was my first thought, and I was probably right. Those were the kinds of people Johnny Sakko would be looking to hire. Someone who looked respectable and probably came from a good family. But I'd taught kids like the one taking our keys, and they were always the ones I kept an extra eye on during test time.

Savage came around and opened the door for me before the frat boy could reach it, and he blocked the door so I could get out with a modicum of respectability. Savage was a good guy all in all. It was too bad I didn't love him.

By law, the restaurants and businesses had to fit in architecturally with the rest of downtown Savannah, so Mambo was in a two-story crumbling brick building facing the waterfront. It had black wrought iron railing around porches on both floors for outdoor seating, but that was pretty much where Johnny had stopped with the authentic Savannah architecture.

The inside was pure Miami. Including the pulsing salsa music that was already changing the beat of my heart so it thumped in time with the bass. Red lights flashed from the ceiling and bodies were crushed together on the dance floor. The entire lower floor was a giant bar and club.

Savage managed to give our names to the hostess without yelling, and we followed her tight leather skirt up a spiral staircase to the top floor where the restaurant was located. All of the waitresses were in leather mini skirts and bustier tops and the waiters were in leather pants without shirts. Clearly Johnny Sakko was as crazy as everyone said. No one wore leather in Savannah.

Physical fitness seemed a requirement to work at Mambo. There were no spare tires hanging around anyone's middles. Of course, it was a lot easier not to have a spare tire when you were eighteen and all your body parts were still in the correct location.

Once we reached the top floor the music lessened so we could only hear the dull thud of the bass through the floorboards. Savage's hand was warm on my back as he led me to a round corner booth that looked out over the waterfront.

"Too bad this isn't a date," Savage said. "This would be a pretty nice table."

"I'll have some wine, please." I smiled brightly at the sommelier. "A bottle will be fine."

Savage's lips twitched but he nodded that he'd have wine as well. Now that we were here and I wasn't thinking about what was happening with the car, it kind of did seem like a date. And then I saw my saving grace bouncing toward us in a tight blue sweater that showed an enormous amount of cleavage and a black wrap skirt that showed way more thigh than I was comfortable with with every step.

I heard Savage's groan, but my smile kept getting bigger. I didn't know what I'd done to have such luck, but if I had the money I'd send Rosemarie Valentine an edible fruit basket in thanks.

"What a surprise," Rosemarie said, her face pink like a cherub.

I could tell Rosemarie had already had a glass or two of wine. Her eyes were glazed over and her lipstick was smeared at the corner of her mouth.

"I had no idea you had a date here tonight," she went on. "I had to make reservations six months ago."

"Agent Savage has connections," I lied smoothly.

Rosemarie's eyes got big and round in her face just like they always did when she stared at Savage for too long. "I bet he does," she whispered, nodding her head.

"This is my date, Leroy." Leroy was about five-foot-three and looked a lot like Danny DeVito. So much like him that I had to stare for a good thirty seconds before I saw the large mole with the little hairs sticking out of it just below his ear. He wore brown slacks and a cream colored Hawaiian shirt with hula girls on the pocket. A wiry bush of chest hair stuck out just above the top button. His gaze hadn't strayed very far from Rosemarie's cleavage since he'd been standing there.

"Leroy, this is my friend Addison Holmes and her date Agent Savage. I don't think I've ever caught your first name," Rosemarie said to Savage.

"It's Matt, but no one ever calls me anything but

Savage." Savage shook Leroy's hand and Rosemarie fanned her face.

"I bet they don't," she said, licking her lips. "A woman likes a man who is a little unrefined. Isn't that right, Addison?"

"Absolutely. Shouldn't the wine be here by now?"

"They seem a little slow with the service," Leroy said.

"We were just headed to our table when we saw you sitting here." Rosemarie's hint was obvious, and I had two choices. I could invite them to join us and keep ordering more wine. Or I could send them to their own table and have what would most certainly feel like a date with Savage, where we'd talk about our personal lives and I'd surely end up saying something embarrassing and end up drinking more wine then I should. Then his thigh would touch mine and he'd lean close and, and then I might end up doing something I'd regret. Like seeing how high quality his sheets were.

Savage was dangerous, and I knew my resolve would weaken with him unless I was in a committed relationship with someone else. I had strong feelings about fidelity since I'd been on the receiving end of unfaithfulness before. And the thing was, I was perfectly in my right to have a fling with Savage and ease my curiosity. But my gut was telling me it'd be nothing but trouble. My gut was usually pretty accurate. It was my brain that wasn't always willing to listen to it.

"Why don't you join us?" I said. "We haven't ordered yet either."

I felt Savage's sigh more than heard it and I scooted toward him so Rosemarie and Leroy could fit in the booth. Once we were pressed thigh to thigh I realized I'd made a mistake of epic proportions.

"Didn't think that one through, did you?" Savage said against my ear. He put his arm around my shoulders and pulled me in tighter and my nipples spiked and my flesh pebbled. I knew about my nipples because Leroy homed in on them like he had radar.

"Nope. My mistake." I sat my phone on the table and willed Kate to text me to let me know that an arrest had been made for the drug deals and that I could go home, but the screen stayed obstinately blank.

The sommelier finally brought the wine to the table and I barely took time to taste the small amount he'd put in my glass for approval. At this point I didn't care what it tasted like as long as there was alcohol in it. Rosemarie and Leroy were both drinking Maker's Mark, so it was no wonder they were both a little rosy.

"How long have you and Leroy been dating?" I asked once we'd placed our orders.

"About three days. We met at the kennel club. He has a Great Dane too, and we found out we have so much in common."

"It was like kismet," Leroy said, his brown eyes shining. He lifted his arm and put it around Rosemarie, but between his height and her voluptuousness, he ended up smacking her in the ear.

Savage's hand was resting on my shoulder, but I could feel him shaking, trying to hold in the laughter. I looked up at his face and it was completely blank of emotion. I had no idea how he did that. The only reason I wasn't laughing was that I was too busy panicking about being in Savage's arms.

"We like John Holmes movies and bacon. And it turns out we go to the same massage therapist," Rosemarie said.

Leroy's hand still rested awkwardly on Rosemarie's ear and he leaned into her and bit at her bottom lip. My eyes widened and I didn't dare look at Savage.

"We'll have to schedule a couples' massage," Leroy said against her lips, licking them one more time for good measure. My nose scrunched up before I could help it because I knew Rosemarie had probably French kissed her dogs before she left her house. "It'll be so much better to have a happy ending with you there."

I'd chosen that unfortunate time to put a piece of bread in my mouth and I breathed it down the wrong hole. I couldn't draw in oxygen and Savage was slapping me on the back. My eyes watered and I was glad my makeup was waterproof. The bread finally went down and I grabbed my wine and drained it. Rosemarie and Leroy were looking at me as if I were the person at the table who was embarrassing everyone. I reached over to grab the wine bottle to refill my glass and noticed Savage's was empty as well, so I filled them both to the brim and then signaled the sommelier to bring another bottle.

"I'm so glad y'all are finally on a date. It's about time you got back on the horse, so to speak." Rosemarie giggled and waggled her eyebrows at Savage and I took another sip of wine. "You wasted far too long waiting for that no good detective to come back around. What kind of man leaves a woman with a bullet in her leg?"

I'd wondered that myself.

"You've been shot?" Leroy asked, eyes wide. "Do you have a scar? Can I see it? I shot my little toe off when I was fifteen. You probably can't tell by looking at me, but I sometimes walk a little off balance. Sometimes I'll just fall over."

I finished another glass of wine and was feeling pretty

warm all over. Savage's fingers were gliding up and down my arm, and I'd already forgotten the speech I'd given myself about making poor decisions where he was concerned.

Our food was brought to the table and the dinner conversation was pretty much a blur at that point. I watched Rosemarie and Leroy feed each other their food and swap a lot of tongue after each bite, but Savage and I pretty much kept our eyes on our plates and ate as much as we could without gagging.

But the highlight of the evening came when Rosemarie slathered her roll with butter, and we all watched with rapt fascination as the butter slid off and dripped right into the middle of her cleavage.

I grabbed my napkin and was passing it across the table when Leroy said, "No. Allow me." And then he proceeded to put his entire hand between the fleshy mounds of her bosom and bring the butter back to see the light of day. But Leroy didn't stop there. By the time he was done greasing Rosemarie's chest she looked like a turkey about to be put in the oven on Thanksgiving day. "We'll use this later."

"Sweet Jesus," I heard Savage murmur beside me.

Savage and I weren't even a blip on Rosemarie and Leroy's radar anymore. Rosemarie's chest was heaving and Leroy's glasses were fogged. All of a sudden Leroy reached into his back pocket and pulled out his wallet, throwing a bunch of twenties on the table. He grabbed Rosemarie's hand and they ran out of the restaurant like their pants were on fire.

"How do we keep running out of wine?" I asked.

"You keep drinking it all."

My phone buzzed with a text message and I saw it

was the all clear from Kate. Arrests had been made and the car had been impounded as evidence.

"Too bad she couldn't have texted that twenty minutes ago," Savage said. "Let's get out of here. We'll catch a cab home."

My head felt heavy on my shoulders as I teetered unsteadily to my feet. I was guessing Savage had already taken the bill and overtipped the waiter for the sideshow that was Rosemarie and Leroy. I bumped into Savage and grabbed onto his shoulders for balance and felt him suck in a breath.

"You're very hard," I said, poking him in the chest.

"You have no idea. Feel free to poke two and a half feet down."

I smiled sloppily and walked my fingers down his chest. Wine worked miracles on me. I never had anxiety or worried about making the right choices when wine was involved. Savage grabbed my hand and I blew a raspberry at him. He practically hauled me up around the waist and lugged me out of Mambo to the street side.

I breathed in the cool fall air and my head started feeling light again. Then all of a sudden we were in the back of a taxi and everything after that is pretty much a haze.

CHAPTER SEVEN

S*aturday*

THE ALARM WENT off at 6am, and I slapped around on my nightstand until I found my phone and shut it off. It took me a few minutes to remember where I was and how I got there. Then I looked under the covers to make sure I still had all my clothes on. I was still in the red dress but my shoes were sitting on the floor by the bed. Either Savage was trying to be a gentleman or he couldn't figure out how to get the dress off. Either way, I was okay with it.

I laid in bed for a few minutes and stared at the ceiling. My mouth was completely devoid of moisture and my head felt like someone had bashed it with a rock. What I needed was to roll over and go back to sleep, and I was just about to do so when I remember why I was supposed to get up at such a godawful hour on a Saturday. Mrs. Rodriguez liked cranberry muffins.

I creaked and groaned as I rolled out of bed. I needed

coffee in a bad way, but I needed to be out of this dress even more. I tugged at the top and pulled from the bottom, but somewhere during the night the dress had become a part of my body. I found a pair of nail scissors in the drawer of my dressing table, and I cut right up the seam until the dress was nothing but rags on the floor.

I sucked in my first deep breath in almost twelve hours and then padded naked into the kitchen to get the coffee started. I had a moment of panic when I remembered my neighbor with the binoculars, but when I looked at all my windows the blinds were closed tight. Savage must have taken care of it before he left the night before. I caught my reflection in the toaster and grimaced. I looked exactly the same as I felt.

I mixed up the batter for the muffins and put them in the oven, setting the timer above the stove. I took my coffee into the shower and stood there under the spray until I ran out of hot water. When I got out half an hour later I was at least coherent and there was color back in my cheeks. The dark circles under my eyes hadn't disappeared though.

I pulled on a pair of jeans and grabbed the neighborhood watch shirt Spock had left for me the day before. I assumed I was supposed to wear it at the meeting. When I finally got it over my head and pulled down over my chest I realized I it wasn't a shirt meant to be seen in public. It was so tight my breasts were defying gravity, and it was short enough to show my bellybutton.

"Oh, hell no." I tried pulling my arm back through the sleeve to get it off, but I couldn't bend my elbow in the right direction. Someone knocked at the door just as I was eyeing my nail scissors for the second time that morning. I swore and went to answer the door and then I swore again when I looked through the peephole and saw who was standing on the other side.

"Go away," I called to Savage through the door.

"That's not very nice. Especially since I was such a gentleman last night."

"Thanks for getting me home safely."

"That's not what I'm talking about. I'm talking about the part where I want you to be completely sober before I'll take you to bed." There was silence for several seconds. "I take it you don't remember the cab ride home?"

"Umm...no." But now that he mentioned it I was starting to get flashes of memory. I felt heat rush to my cheeks. I was pretty sure there'd been a lot of groping and kissing in the cab. Most of it done by me.

"You know I'm just going to stand here until you let me in, right?"

I sighed and unlatched the chain and then I moved back with my arm over my chest. Savage's eyes widened as soon as he saw me, and I knew from the glazed look in his eyes that the arm wasn't a good deterrent. Savage was like a sexual Batman. He always homed in where it mattered.

"Nice shirt," he said. "It sure doesn't look like that on Mrs. Rodriguez."

Savage was wearing his own neighborhood watch shirt and the sleeves barely fit around his biceps. His jeans molded to him in all the right places and I was pretty sure he had at least three weapons on him somewhere, but I had no idea where he would have fit them and I figured it was best to stay away from that line of thought before I started having hot flashes.

This was the problem with Savage. He was hot. With

a capital H. Any woman would be dead if her hormones didn't go into overdrive the minute she stared at him. The problem was getting my hormones to listen to my brain.

"I'm not wearing this shirt." I started back toward my bedroom. "I guess you'll have to kick me out of the club and have your meetings somewhere else."

Savage stopped me by placing his hand on my shoulder, and I immediately went into panic mode. Savage touching me could only lead to things I'd regret later, so I changed direction and went toward the kitchen so I could put some distance between us.

Savage followed behind me but kept his distance. "I'm pretty sure Spock wouldn't go for that. He seems to think you're exactly what the neighborhood watch needs. He'll probably change his mind once he gets to know you a little better. All in all we're a pretty peaceful neighborhood."

I narrowed my eyes and put my fists on my hips, stretching my shirt across my chest tighter. Savage's eyes widened and he swallowed hard as he took a step forward.

"How do you feel about getting a knuckle sandwich?" I asked.

"I don't mind a little pain. Maybe we should talk about last night?"

"Maybe we should just leave the past in the past. I'm all about living in the moment."

"Hmm. Maybe we should live in the moment tonight and go out again. This time with less wine. I'm okay with the groping."

I breathed out a sigh of relief when I remembered my plans with Nick. "I can't. I've got some wedding rehearsal dinner I have to go to. Maybe some other time."

"Addison—"

There was another knock at the door and whatever Savage had been about to say was shelved. At least for now.

"You'd better get those muffins out of the oven," Savage said, heading for the door as if he owned the place. "You don't want them to burn. Mrs. Rodriguez gets mean if she doesn't have her muffins."

We were going to have to have a serious conversation soon. If he kept at it, I knew he would eventually wear me down. He had a tendency to take charge whenever he was in the vicinity. I liked to tell myself I didn't find the overbearing caveman routine attractive, but I was pretty sure my nipples were hard enough to cut glass, so it would've been a lie.

I pulled the muffins out of the oven as Spock and another man walked through my front door. They both wore their neighborhood watch shirts and Spock had on a black trucker hat that said NAD across the front. Little tufts of his hair stuck out over his ears and beads of sweat dotted his mustache. He took a good look around the house before his gaze settled on me. I was pretty sure I'd never seen anything as disturbing as his inability to blink. His lidless eyes went straight to my chest.

I'd seen the man who'd come in with Spock a time or two as I'd gone on my runs. He owned the house on the corner, and I was pretty sure he was married. He was on the hefty side and only a couple of inches taller than me, but his beard made him seem bigger since it hung halfway to his chest. I stared at him longer than I probably should have because he looked exactly like one of the cast from Duck Dynasty.

"This is Byron," Spock said. "He has binoculars like yours."

"You should remember to keep your blinds closed," Byron said. "You're a woman living alone and you never know who's going to be looking in."

"That's comforting advice," I said.

"Why are you avoiding Agent Savage?" Byron asked, taking a muffin from the basket I'd sat on the counter and bouncing it back and forth in his hands to cool it off. "He hasn't been over to watch a movie in a while, and he didn't stay long enough last night for any of the good stuff to happen. Did you guys have a fight?"

"Agent Savage and I aren't dating. We're just friends. And I've been very busy with work."

He nodded and bit into the muffin so crumbs fell into his beard. I couldn't take my eyes off of it. There was no telling what he had buried in there.

"I only wondered cause you're gettin' to that age. But you probably already know that."

I smiled with a lot of teeth and looked at Savage, but his face was unreadable except for the slight twitch at the corner of his mouth. The cops in my life had a much better ability than me to keep their thoughts to themselves.

"How many people are a part of the neighborhood watch?" I asked Spock. I hoped I had enough muffins. Byron had already devoured two of them and was reaching for a third.

"Six now that we've added you. Ted's got a cold so he won't be here, and Mrs. Rodriguez doesn't move as fast as she used to." Spock swiped his upper lip with the back of his hand and moved in closer.

"Do you want to come over later?" he whispered. "I'm

having a few friends over for a Lord of the Rings marathon. We're roleplaying. I get to be Frodo."

"Congratulations."

"My friend Steve is playing Galadriel, but there's an opening for Arwen Evenstar. Do you have elf ears?"

"I'm afraid not."

"It's okay. I've got extra." Spock was a close talker and I didn't really have anywhere to back up, so I reached for the basket of muffins and shoved them at him before slipping away.

"I wish I could come," I said. "It sounds like a lot of fun. Really. But I have a rehearsal dinner for a wedding to go to tonight."

"Do you need a date?"

"No. I already have one. And one date is more than enough."

Savage's eyebrows raised at my confession. "Busy weekend."

I narrowed my eyes when I remembered Nick had said the same thing the night before.

"Who's your date?" Byron asked. "That guy that dropped you off in the black truck the other afternoon? You didn't kiss him goodbye. Is it serious?"

"What do you do for a living, Byron? Are you always at home?" I asked.

"Pretty much," he shrugged. "I'm a website developer. Not much gets past me."

"Good to know."

"Here comes Mrs. Rodriguez," Savage said.

We all went to stand at the front window and watched as a wizened Hispanic woman walked right down the middle of the street. Her walker had green tennis balls stuck to the bottom and her purse sat in the little basket attached to the top bar.

Cars were stopped on both sides of her, but she pretended she didn't see them waiting for her to move.

"I wish she'd use her scooter," Byron said. "Lord, she's slow."

We all moved in tandem to the front porch as Mrs. Rodriguez finally started making her way up the sidewalk. My first thought was I had no idea how we were going to get her up the stairs and into the house. My second thought was that Mrs. Rodriguez was probably the worst neighborhood watchman to ever exist.

She stopped about ten feet from the house and zeroed in on me. "Did you make the muffins?" Her accent was heavy and her scowl was mean as a snake.

I swallowed and nodded.

"Good," she said, picking up her walker and slamming it back down on the sidewalk for impact. "Don't let *gordo* eat them all."

Her gaze turned to Byron and he dropped the muffin he was eating onto the porch. She let out an impressive stream of Spanish and finished it off by spitting onto my sidewalk. My nose crinkled in revulsion and I backed up slowly, thinking I could just slip back inside the house and lock them all out. This was crazy even by my standards.

I'd barely taken a step when she looked back at me and I froze. There was something about her that struck terror into my very soul. She wasn't even five feet tall and her face resembled a dried raisin. Her eyes were black as pitch and her dark hair was streaked with silver. Her NAD shirt was tucked into black pants pulled up to her armpits and her shoes were orthopedic.

"You!" she called out. Savage put his hand on my shoulder and I leaned into it. I appreciated the support. "You not throw up on my lawn anymore. This is good. You kill my roses and I almost did the voodoo on you."

"S...sorry," I managed to get out. "And thank you for not doing the voodoo on me. I have enough bad luck."

"Sí, I know. It is punishment enough. Now show me your walk."

"I beg your pardon?"

"Show me your walk. What is your song?"

"We haven't gotten that far, Mrs. Rodriguez," Spock said, pulling a piece of paper from his shirt pocket. "I have the agenda right here. First we need to have muffins and coffee, followed by a reading of the minutes. Then we need to discuss old business and what to do about that new man that moved in at the end of the street. I think he's a serial killer, but I can't see him well enough from my house. Ted's the one who'll have to keep watch on him since they're neighbors. Then Savage is going to show us those new martial arts moves. *Then* we can move to new business and give Addison her signal and her theme song."

"I'm sorry," I said. "I think I'm confused. Theme song?" I turned to Savage and he took advantage of the situation to pull me closer.

"Everyone has a theme song that helps them stay focused on the job," he explained. "When you walk down the street on your neighborhood watch rounds you do it to the beat of your theme song. It's very effective at giving you the right attitude."

"Sí," Mrs. Rodriguez agreed. "No motherfuckers mess with me when I'm strutting to my song. Mine is Bad to the Bone." She sang out a few lines. "B-B-B-B-Bad. Bad to the bone."

"That's a good one," Byron agreed. "Mine's Poison. I even learned the dance. I can teach you later." Byron busted into something that wasn't even close to being recognizable as dance moves, and my whole front porch shuddered and groaned under his weight.

"I can't wait to learn it," I said. I could feel my eyes getting bigger and bigger and I was afraid it was going to come to the point where they just popped right out of my head. I turned to Savage and tried to smile. "Can I talk to you for a minute in private?"

Savage kept his arm around me and ushered me back inside the house. Before I knew what was happening he had me pressed against the door and his mouth was hot on mine. My brain cells scrambled and it took me a minute to remember I wasn't going to do this.

"That T-shirt is driving me crazy."

He kissed me again with a lot of tongue and whatever it was that was pressed against my pubic bone felt good enough that my legs somehow ended up around his waist.

"Wait, I can't do this."

"Sweetheart, I'm pretty sure you can. I can feel your heat through a layer of denim. You're hot enough to singe."

I thunked my head against the door several times and he carried me to the middle of the room. Embarrassment scalded my cheeks as I realized my legs were still in a chokehold around his waist.

I pushed against his chest and untangled my legs and he held me steady as my feet touched the floor. My heart was thumping in my chest and my lips and other places on my body tingled from the contact. Savage was a damn good kisser. And we definitely had chemistry. The problem was I'd kissed Nick less than forty-eight hours ago, and as good as the chemistry was between me and Savage, it was about a million times stronger between me and Nick.

Nick and I were over, but it kind of felt like it wasn't completely over, and I didn't want to do anything I'd regret later.

"Listen, you've got to stop kissing me."

"I don't know. I kind of like kissing you. It's going to be hard to stop. And you like kissing me too."

"I know. But I don't like it enough." I sighed and dropped back into one of the overstuffed chairs and closed my eyes. "Listen, Savage. I've got to be completely honest with you. You're not it for me. You're a great kisser, and Lord knows you're nice to look at and could probably rock my world, but we're never going to be anything more than friends. I'm pretty much ruined for all other men."

"Ahh, the great Detective Dempsey. I didn't realize you were back together."

"We're not. But he pretty much trampled my heart to dust. I thought he was it for me, and I'm not up for anything serious at the moment. You either need to accept it and stop with the full court press or I'm going to have Mrs. Rodriguez do the voodoo on you."

"I can accept it," he agreed. "For now. But I figure this is a good thing. Friends hang out, right? We can hang out for a while—watch some movies and find some good places to eat—and then eventually you'll forget all about that other guy and realize it should've been me all along."

I banged my head against the back of the chair several times. "Why do I always find the stubborn ones? It's like I have radar."

"I guess you're just lucky. Are you going to this wedding rehearsal thing with Dempsey?"

"Apparently."

"If he broke your heart, why are you being a glutton for punishment?"

"He's paying me five hundred dollars."

Savage barked out a laugh. "That's my girl. Come on, let's go get your theme song and get everyone out of here before you decide to pull out your gun. I had to start leaving mine at home because the temptation became too great."

"I don't even understand why you're a part of this group. This is insanity."

"It's entertaining for the most part. And the others are so nosy they're actually a pretty good deterrent for theft or vandalism. If anything like that happens they call me on my cell and let me handle it. It's really pretty harmless, and we only meet once a month so it doesn't take a lot of time, though I know the others take turns patrolling the neighborhood at different hours."

I sighed and felt myself being sucked into something I knew could only lead to disaster. "So what's your theme song?" I asked.

His smile was slow and I felt a little flutter in my chest. I had a feeling being friends with Savage wasn't going to be any easier than avoiding his advances.

"What if I told you it was Hot For Teacher?"

"I'd say it's a good thing I got fired."

He pulled me up from the chair and ushered me back to the front door where the others waited.

"Maybe if you ever decide you want to be something more than friends, I'll tell you what it is. Otherwise, I think I'll keep it to myself."

CHAPTER EIGHT

The NAD meeting was adjourned just before noon, and I turned down an invitation to join Spock for lunch. Savage found my case file on Tannenbaum sitting on the bar and the notes I'd made and was now poring over what I'd found.

"Tannenbaum," he said. "I recognize that name."

"I'd think so. I think he owns most of the state of Georgia."

"So what's the deal? He's looking for a long lost son?"

"He was diagnosed with terminal cancer and realized he didn't have any blood relatives to leave his fortune to. The problem is his son is the result of a back alley sperm bank, so it might not be very easy to track him down. Especially with what little information we have. I've narrowed it down to about a hundred women, but I've got to go through each of them one by one so it's going to take a little while."

"I could help you do it faster you know," he said, and I immediately became suspicious at the offer.

"And what would I have to do in return?"

"Nothing," he said, grinning. "Just a friend helping another friend out in his spare time. "Besides, it's the weekend and I've got nothing better to do but work on the deck I'm building in my backyard."

I'd never been to Savage's house, and as long as I had a single working brain cell in my head I'd never step foot across the threshold. It would be a point of no return.

"I've got resources Kate doesn't have. And you could feed me lunch as payment."

I let out a slow breath of relief. For once Savage wasn't flirting and there wasn't any tension between us. Maybe the friends thing would work out after all.

"Deal."

I grabbed my laptop from the desk in my bedroom and came back to join him on the couch. I filled him in on the story Mr. Tannenbaum had told us about Doc Neeley and the extra services he provided out of his clinic. I also told him how Doc Neeley's career ended in flames. Savage's eyebrows raised as the story unfolded, but otherwise he stayed silent. I watched as he went to work on the computer, using the FBI databases to access information I couldn't.

I probably wasn't supposed to be seeing the things he was doing, but Savage had never been one to follow the rules overmuch. Rules were more like guidelines to a man like Savage. Much like the dress code of FBI agents. Savage dressed in a black suit and white shirt with a black tie five days a week. But he wore the loudest, most colorful socks he could find right along with them. He'd once told me if I was impressed by his socks that I should get a look at his underwear, but I'd passed. The thought of Savage's underwear made me have hot flashes.

"That's a little better," Savage said. And just like that my hundred names were narrowed down to twenty-five.

"Maybe I should let Mr. Tannenbaum look through the list and see if anything is jarred loose. It was a long time ago. Surely he knew more than the color of her hair or that her husband was a banker."

"I don't know. Men aren't the most observant creatures. And most men donating sperm for cash don't care about anything but the money in their pocket."

I arched a brow. "Have a lot of experience with sperm banks, do you?"

He grinned. "I'm just putting myself in his place. I'm a professional. It's what I do." He looked up at the clock and closed the computer lid. "If you're going to go see Mr. Tannenbaum before your rehearsal dinner you'd better get busy. I'll let you know if I narrow it down further."

I followed Savage to the door and opened it for him, a little shell shocked from the complete one-eighty our relationship had just taken.

"See you around, neighbor," he said, stepping onto the porch.

"Really?"

"What am I supposed to say?"

"I don't know. Usually at this point you're trying to melt my clothes off with your X-ray vision."

His smile was slow and I felt that damn flutter in my stomach again. "I don't need X-ray vision. That shirt is pretty much a miracle."

IT WASN'T until I'd changed into a black sweater set and pulled on my Uggs that I remembered I didn't have a car. The weather was looking yucky again, and I didn't have enough cash to pay for a cab.

I bit my bottom lip as I contemplated who to call. I could probably ask Savage to borrow his SUV, but he'd probably want to come with me and I didn't want to test the chemistry fates again. It would take my mother too long to get here, and she'd also insist on coming with me. My only other option was Rosemarie, but I had no idea if she was in any shape to go anywhere. She and Leroy had left in a hurry and they'd both had an awful lot to drink.

I gave her a call anyway and was surprised when she picked up after the first ring.

"I've been waiting for you to call," she said in lieu of a greeting. "I've gotta get out of this house. Leroy is still here. I think he's moving in."

"Can you pick me up? I need to go talk to a client about his case."

"I'll be there in ten minutes."

For Rosemarie to make it to my house in ten minutes she had to have her shoes on and already be walking out the door. She'd also have to drive like a bat out of hell, but that never stopped Rosemarie.

Nine and a half minutes later, she squealed to a stop in front of my house. She knocked on the door before I had my purse in hand.

"Can I use your bathroom?" she asked, darting past me and into the tiny half bathroom in the hallway. "I swear that man is a sex maniac. Every time I tried to close myself in the bathroom for a minute of privacy he was there ready and raring to go."

My eyebrows were pretty much stuck in the up position. The last thing I wanted to think about was Leroy raring to go. I heard the toilet flush and the sink running and Rosemarie came back out, her hands waving in agitation. I hadn't had a chance to get a good look at her when she'd first come in. She had whisker burn on her neck and dark circles under her eyes. Her hair looked like she'd stuck her finger in a light socket and her shirt was on inside out. She must have left in a hurry.

We got in the car and I gave Rosemarie the address for Mr. Tannenbaum's house. She was silent for most of the drive, and I was starting to get a little worried. Rosemarie was never silent.

"He didn't hurt you, did he?" I asked. "You seem a little upset."

She fanned herself with her shirt. "I'm just a little kerfuzzled. That man rocked my world. Though I've never had a lover scream like that before during sex. Has that ever happened to you?"

"Not that I can say."

"Hmm. Scared the hell out of me. And then he cried for a good half hour after we were finished. What's the deal with that?"

"What'd you do?" I was fascinated by Rosemarie in the same way I was fascinated by carnies at the Whiskey Bayou fair or hobos I saw riding on the trains.

"I made him a bowl of vanilla ice cream and poured chocolate syrup over the top. Shut him right up. And then he got real creative with the chocolate syrup. I'm not sure I can keep going at a pace like that. You'd never guess it by looking, but Leroy is hung like Harry the Wonderhorse."

"No, I never would have guessed."

"Damned deceiving is what it is. Men like that should come with a label. I'm not as young as I used to be. I'm not in shape to go five times a night. You've gotta stretch and do yoga to prepare for that kind of sex."

I could sympathize with Rosemarie. It sounded like Nick and Leroy had a lot in common. I pretty much had felt kerfuzzled after my first night with Nick too.

We pulled up to Mr. Tannenbaum's house. It was three stories of gray stone. A small garden with creepy statues of little children and their pets was protected by a wrought iron double gate with an ornate T right in the middle. The fence surrounding the property was made of the same gray stone as the house and it was at least ten feet high.

"Lord, would you look at that?" Rosemarie said. "Right next door to the cemetery. You couldn't pay me a million dollars to live in this house. I bet it's haunted."

I pressed the buzzer and gave my name, and the gates opened with a creak. I saw a couple of video cameras as we made our way up the sidewalk and to the front porch. Big flower urns sat on either side of the door and bright red impatiens tumbled over the sides. Another camera sat just over the door, and I figured a man worth as much as Mr. Tannenbaum probably had pretty good security.

The house had one of the old-timey buzzers that you pulled and it screeched like a cat tossed in a bathtub. I expected a butler to answer the door, so I was surprised when Mr. Tannenbaum himself greeted us.

"Good afternoon, ladies. Come in, come in. I have my cook making some tea. We're going to get storms before the afternoon is over, and there's supposed to be a cold front come through."

"Thanks for seeing us, Mr. Tannenbaum." He looked a little better today than he had at Kate's office, but there was still a significant tremble in his hands. "This is my friend Rosemarie. She's helping me out with your case."

"Sure, sure. Whatever it takes to find my son quickly. Do you have any leads?"

"I've narrowed it down to about twenty-five women. I was wondering if you'd mind taking a look and seeing if any of the details jogged your memory about Rose. Maybe her last name?"

"I don't suppose you have any photographs," he said. "I'd remember her right off if I could see her face. She was a looker."

He waited until Rosemarie and I were seated on the ugly green upholstered couch in the den, and then he took his own seat in the matching chair across from us. A massive fireplace took up almost a whole wall, and floor to ceiling windows that looked out at the garden took up the other wall. It was a masculine room that looked like it hadn't been redecorated since 1982.

I handed Mr. Tannenbaum the file with the names of twenty-five women and as much background as I could collect on them in a couple hours time. He went through each page methodically, his hands shaking as he turned from page to page. He paused a couple of times like he wanted to say something, but then he just shook his head and moved on.

"I'm sorry. I don't see anything familiar."

"It was just a shot in the dark anyway. I'm sure we'll narrow it down further once I'm able to do a more thorough background check."

We sat and visited with Mr. Tannenbaum a few more minutes and ate the excellent scones his cook served with the tea, and then we took a tour through the house. It mostly reminded me of a mausoleum, and I was pretty sure Rosemarie was right. The house was definitely haunted. There were enough creepy hallways and creaks and groans to have me practically running out the front door and back to the car.

"I don't know how he sleeps alone in there night after night," Rosemarie said, shuddering. "It gives me the heebie-jeebies."

"Maybe when you're as close to death as he is you don't mind communing with the other side all that much."

~

ROSEMARIE DROPPED me back home and went to go deal with Leroy. I'd spent too much time with Mr. Tannenbaum and now I was running behind. And it had been a wasted trip anyway.

The thunder we'd been hearing all afternoon continued without producing any rain, and the humidity seemed to grow thicker by the hour. If I wasn't careful my hair would be too big to fit through the doors.

I jumped in the shower and jumped out again, and then put on my bathrobe. I put my hair up in hot rollers and went to work on my makeup. I glanced at the clock as I was putting on my eyeliner and poked myself right in the eye. I blinked for a few seconds and swore as my eyes watered. I overcompensated for the red eye by adding more eye shadow and mascara, and after I finished I decided it wasn't such a bad look.

I didn't wear a lot of makeup normally. Usually a couple of swipes of mascara and some lip gloss. I'd been told on more than one occasion that I was more the girl next door type—like one of those Ralph Lauren models sitting out in a field somewhere. I guess being an all-American girl was okay, but I wanted to be a bombshell. Like one of the Bond girls—dangerous and seductive. I was mostly only a danger to myself, and I obviously hadn't had any luck being seductive, but that didn't mean I was going to stop trying.

Back in the day when I could afford extra things I belonged to an underwear of the month club, so I selected the sexiest thing I could find in my lingerie drawer—a black lace bra that helped boost the girls and lacy panties that required a great deal of preparatory waxing. Nick wouldn't know what I had on under the dress, but it would drive him crazy trying to figure it out. And it would sure as hell make me feel better.

The hard part was deciding what to wear. It wasn't easy to find the right balance of classy and sexy, but I ended up pulling out a black dress out that still had the tags on it. I'd bought it last year on clearance and it had still been too expensive. It had been purchased for my honeymoon, and I remembered trying it on and thinking it was the kind of dress that would look terrific crumpled up on the floor after a fit of wild passion. Unfortunately, my fiancé hadn't been all that into fits of wild passion. At least not with me.

The dress wasn't much to look at on the hanger, but when it was on it fit like a second skin in all the right places. It veed low in the front showing just the right amount of cleavage, and the length came to just above the knee and tapered in so my legs looked a mile long. I put on my grandmother's pearls and matching earrings and put just a dab of Cinnabar perfume between my breasts and behind my ears.

I waited until the last second to take out the hot rollers and then finger combed my hair and sprayed it so it was tamed into submission. At least mostly. I put on an extra coat of lipstick and then slipped on a pair of strappy black Jimmy Choos that had never been out of the box. They'd been bought to go with the dress and I figured the bad karma associated with the whole outfit was probably past the statute of limitations by now.

I was nervous as hell, but I was determined not to let Nick fluster me. We were two adults conducting a business transaction. I wouldn't let my emotions get the best of me. I was going to collect my money and eat some free food. And maybe flirt with a couple of the groomsmen just for the hell of it.

There was a knock at the door and I teetered carefully on my heels as I went to answer it. Seeing Nick on the other side dressed in a tux still had the ability to take my breath away. He'd shaved, but he always managed to have a five o'clock shadow.

His eyes darkened as they slowly raked over me from head to toe. I knew that look. If I didn't get the door closed and locked behind me in the next six seconds I was liable to end up flat on my back on the rug. I knew because I'd been in this predicament before.

I flicked the lock and pushed my way out on the porch, pulling the door closed behind me, and I waited for Nick to say something. He wasn't usually so quiet.

"Are we going?" I asked.

"I'm still thinking about it. It seems like a waste for you to be looking like you do just for my brother's rehearsal dinner. Maybe we should skip it and stay in."

"Speaking of your brother's rehearsal dinner, do you have my money?"

"You want your money now?" he asked incredulously.

"Oh, yeah. Payment up front. I know you too well."

His eyes narrowed and never left my face as he

reached inside his jacket for his wallet. He opened it and pulled out five crisp one hundred dollar bills and handed them over. I was proud of myself for being cool as a cucumber. Inside I was elated that I actually had enough to make my rent payment. I slipped the money in my purse and turned my back on Nick as I headed toward his truck.

He touched my arm and I raised a brow in question as I turned back to face him.

"What's going on with you, Addison? You're not acting like yourself."

I widened my eyes in surprise and took a step forward. His swift inhale told me he wasn't unaffected by the closeness. I took it a little farther and brought my hands up to straighten his bowtie.

"I'm just doing what you asked me to do, sugar." I had no idea where the sultry voice that just came out of my mouth came from, but I was damn glad to meet her. "It's just one friend doing a favor for another."

"You're playing with fire, sweetheart."

The heat coming from Nick's body was intense, and the chemical reaction between us was as strong as it ever was. But I smiled and took a step back before turning to make my way to his truck.

"I have no idea what you're talking about, Dempsey. Now lets get this show on the road. I'd hate to have to charge you overtime. Besides, I have to work this evening."

He came up behind me and opened the truck door and helped me get inside. "Anything I want to know about?"

"Not really. Mostly the things I do have a tendency to give you heart palpitations, so I figure it's best not to go into the details. This is the part of our relationship you're trying to avoid if I remember correctly."

If his jaw clenched any tighter I was afraid he was going to break a tooth. "I just want to avoid the parts where you try to get yourself killed. I'm good with everything else."

"I'm the whole package, babe. Take it or leave it."

Nick slammed the truck door and I smiled wide as he made his way around and got in. This was going to be fun.

CHAPTER NINE

I expected it would take a little while to get to Nick's parents house, so I prepared to catch up with Words with Friends on my phone so I wouldn't feel obligated to engage in too much small talk. So you can imagine my surprise to find Nick slowing the truck to a stop less than fifteen minutes later in front of a monstrosity of a house on Gaston Street.

Gaston Street was where old money Savannah lived. The houses started at several million dollars a pop and went up from there, and the house we pulled up to was no exception. The house was like a big Georgian white elephant and took up almost the entire block. Two giant weeping willows flanked each corner and the flowerbeds were ruthlessly organized with white and purple flowers. The house wasn't gated but there was an attendant checking names. Nick was waved through without stopping.

I'd never been to a home on Gaston Street. I'd driven up and down it plenty of times, wondering what kind of people lived in these houses, what they did for a living. I was almost positive none of them were ex-teachers or private investigators, and I was all of a sudden feeling very unsure about this adventure.

"I thought you said we were going to your parents' house?"

"You're looking at it." I could see the tension radiating in Nick's shoulders and in the hard line of his jaw.

"Are you telling me you're rich?"

I was starting to feel more than a little foolish at not knowing this ahead of time. I'd dated Nick off and on for almost four months and I knew virtually nothing about his personal life. I'd never been to his house or met his family. Nick liked to keep his cards close to the vest.

"Not rich. Exactly. I'm what you'd call the black sheep of the family. Being a cop in a family full of high profile attorneys makes for incredibly uncomfortable dinner conversation. I've figured out how to avoid regularly scheduled dinners for the last twelve years or so. I still haven't figured out how to avoid Thanksgiving and Christmas, but I'm thinking of taking a diving trip to the Bahamas. Want to go with me?"

I stared at him with an arched eyebrow. I couldn't believe this was the first time I was hearing about the friction in his family. It's probably what I deserved for letting lust rule instead of common sense. When I didn't say anything he turned to look at me.

"What?" he asked. "I live solely on my cop's salary. My parents cut me off once I decided not to join the family firm. And the only time I've ever had to touch my trust fund was when I bought my house."

"Trust fund?"

"Is that a problem?"

"Not at all," I said. "You think you know a guy and then he turns out to be someone completely different."

"It's not like I'm Ted Bundy. And don't worry. My parents don't like anyone. Their natural temperature is frostbite. Just head straight for the bar. That's what I always do."

"Okay, but next time I'm going to ask for more money."

Nick stopped the car on the semicircle driveway in front of the massive double front doors and the skies finally opened up in a torrential downpour.

"It's like a sign from God," Nick said.

A man in a dark suit opened the car door for me and held an umbrella over me so I wouldn't get wet. Another man was doing the same for Nick. I took the valet's hand and I realized as soon as he dropped my damp palm that I might have been a little nervous. I wasn't prepared for meeting Nick's parents.

What was I supposed to say to them? *By the way, your son is terrific in bed.* Somehow I was thinking that wouldn't put me in the Dempseys' good graces. Though if they were as cold as Nick said, maybe I was overanalyzing the situation.

The foyer of the Dempseys' home was bigger than my whole house. And it was very white. So white I wanted to squint from the brightness. White walls, a white double staircase, white marble floors. Crystal chandeliers hung overhead and the light glared off every surface.

"Jesus," I muttered. "You think this is what heaven looks like?"

"Christ, I hope not. More like purgatory."

"Is the whole house like this?"

"Oh, yes. My mother has very specific tastes."

Nick's hand was warm on my lower back, and I felt sorry for him if this is how his childhood had been. My family didn't have a ton of money when I was growing up, but at least our house felt like a home. And by God, we had color.

"Nicholas, darling." A handsome woman with silvery blond hair swooped in from one of the side rooms and kissed Nick on each cheek. "You're late. We're already serving pre-dinner drinks in the parlor."

"Traffic was bad," Nick lied smoothly. "This is my date, Addison Holmes. Addison, this is my mother, Nina Dempsey."

"Pleased to meet you, Mrs. Dempsey."

She looked back at Nick without acknowledging me and my eyes narrowed. My mother had always said that having money was no excuse for bad manners.

"I thought you were bringing Susan, dear," Mrs. Dempsey said. "She's a lovely young woman, and I did enjoy you bringing her to dinner last month. Is she away on business?"

Mrs. Dempsey turned to me with cruel glee in her eyes. Nick hadn't been kidding about the frostbite, only Mrs. Dempsey had a way of wrapping it up in Southern politeness. "Susan is one of the attorneys in my husband's firm. She and Nicholas make a striking couple."

"I'm sure." I smiled with a lot of teeth.

"What is it you do, Annabeth?"

"It's Addison," I corrected, and I decided then and there that there wasn't enough money in the world to put up with someone like Mrs. Dempsey. It's not like Nick and I were dating or he was bringing me home to meet potential in-laws. "And I guess you could say I'm a jack of all trades. I'm just grateful I met your son.

When he walked into the strip club it was just like magic."

Her eyes widened and Nick's fingers pressed harder into my spine, but I wasn't anywhere near done. I didn't know Susan, but I was pretty sure I was jealous of her.

I thickened my speech so it was syrupy with the Southern drawl I reserved for rude department store clerks or the Jehovah's Witnesses that kept coming to my door. "You see, I was dancing the noon shift and when Nicky walked in I knew I'd found my way out of that place. And then the condom broke and—" I put my fingers over my mouth and widened my eyes in surprise. "Oh, shoot. I wasn't supposed to talk about that."

Two red streaks of color appeared on Mrs. Dempsey's cheeks and if she could have burned me to cinders with her eyes she would've done so in a heartbeat. Nick's grip at my back was almost painful and he was stiff as a board beside me.

"Well," Mrs. Dempsey said, clearing her throat. "I think we need to have a long talk later, Nicholas. But this is your brother's wedding, so I think it's best we keep all this between us until something can be done. Thank God I've got my checkbook with me."

She turned and walked back into the parlor and I felt Nick practically vibrating beside me. It wasn't until I turned to face him that I realized it was laughter.

"Was that her subtle way of telling me she's going to try to buy me off?"

"I'm not sure that was what you'd call subtle," he said, grinning. "Christ, it's never a dull moment with you. And if I'm lucky I'll never be invited to another family event for the rest of my life. Maybe we should get married."

The space between us was electric and we seemed to

be caught in some type of trance. And then I flinched like I'd just been punched in the gut and I took a step back. Nick sobered when his words caught up with his brain and he looked a little pale.

I turned away and straightened my spine. It was just a job. An easy five hundred bucks. I needed to get past all this emotional stuff. It had been two months for Pete's sake. It was high time I moved on. Maybe I wasn't giving Savage a fair chance. The problem was I *was* highly emotional. Being overemotional was a prerequisite in the South. We approached life with lots of laughter and an abundance of tears. My granny had always said hiding your light under a bushel would only give you hemorrhoids.

"Listen, Addison—"

But I interrupted before he could say anything that would make things more awkward between us. "It's too bad you couldn't get Susan to come."

I felt Nick's sigh and he put a hand at my lower back and led me out of the foyer. "She asked for five grand. I'm trying to work on a cop's budget." His answer was deadpan and I gasped before I realized he was kidding. At least I hoped he was kidding.

"I think I need a drink." I wasn't a huge drinker, but in the past three days I'd overindulged three too many times. It probably wasn't a good precedent to set, but I'd been in some unusual circumstances that called for a little numbing.

"I could use one myself, and Lord knows there will be plenty. The Dempseys do everything in a haze of alcohol."

"I definitely should have charged you more."

"Do you think we could call a truce for one night?"

Nick asked seriously. "Coming to family gatherings is pretty much my least favorite thing in the world to do. Can we just pretend things are good just for a little while? I want to be able to take something enjoyable from tonight."

I couldn't deny the plea I saw in his eye. I stepped into his arms and put my head on his chest and just let him hold me for a few minutes. "Just for tonight," I agreed. "But tomorrow all bets are off."

He kissed me once and I could feel his smile against my lips. He pulled back and I could tell he was more relaxed than he'd been when we'd first come in.

"You haven't met my father yet. Just make sure you stay arm's length from him. He's going to love the way you look in that dress."

"Good to know I've still got it."

"From where I'm standing, you've got enough to make me extremely curious what kind of underwear you've got on."

The smile spread across my face before I could help it. I might not have known anything about Nick's personal life, but I sure as hell knew the most basic parts of him.

"I know," I said. "And let me tell you it's spectacular. Too bad you'll never get to find out what it looks like."

"You're a cruel woman, Addison Holmes."

He led me farther toward the sound of muted voices. We stood just at the threshold of the large parlor, no one noticing us yet. This room was also white.

"What would happen if I knocked over that tray of meatballs and got red sauce everywhere?"

"It wouldn't be pretty. I'll pay you an extra hundred dollars if you go through with it."

"I need to make up a fee chart for the next time. I feel

like you're taking advantage of my services. Now lead me to the bar."

"I like that idea. You can never resist my body once you've had a few drinks."

I rolled my eyes. It was true. I was one of those affectionate drunks. I'd always been able to control my urges though before I'd met Nick and Savage. I think the alcohol in my system had some kind of chemical reaction with their pheromones.

"I think you're suffering from short term memory loss. Last time I checked it wasn't me that was trying to resist anything."

"I'm starting to think I maybe made a mistake about that."

"Besides, you've got Susan now. I hope I get to meet her real soon." I fluttered my eyelashes and made a beeline toward the open bar.

"I'll have a whiskey, neat." The bartender must have sensed my urgency because he skipped over the three other people waiting at the bar and got me my drink. Or it could have just been he was enjoying the view of my cleavage since his eyes never made it to my face. I saluted him for the compliment and then knocked back half of the whiskey, not bothering to savor the taste.

I felt Nick come up behind me and order a whiskey for himself. The woman next to us was tall and blond and polished, and dollars to donuts the diamonds draped around her neck were real. She looked Nick up and down twice and then licked her lips. To be fair, Nick was always worth a second look.

I put my empty glass back down on the bar and signaled the waiter. The warmth of the first drink was sliding through my body and it was just enough to take the edge off.

"Don't you think you should slow down on the booze, sweetheart?" Nick asked before the bartender moved away. "The condom broke," Nick whispered conspiratorially to the bartender. The blond beside us scooted closer so she could hear the conversation better. "She's a little upset about it."

I turned to the blond, who was looking at us both with rapt fascination. "Don't be seduced by the pretty face," I told her. "I found out too late he's got kids all over Savannah. And he doesn't pay a dime of child support. How am I supposed to raise this kid, I ask you?"

She shot Nick an angry look and moved away to seek out new prey.

"Very nice, love," Nick whispered against my skin. "If we do this all night my mother will never be able to set me up on another date."

"Another date?"

"Yep. She ambushed me with Susan. She was already here for dinner when I showed up. And then I had to fake an emergency call from dispatch just to escape."

"So what you're saying is we don't need to kill Susan?"

I felt his smile against my neck. "Jealous?" His breath sent chills down my spine and things were becoming rather uncomfortable in my nether regions. Nick had been right. Putting alcohol into my system while he was in the same room wasn't the best idea. I'd have no ability to resist him if he put his mind to it.

"Why would I be jealous? You're free to date whoever you like. Just like I am."

"Maybe we should change the subject. Since you

brought up the story for my mother, I don't suppose there's any truth to the broken condom theory, is there?" he asked.

I choked on my whiskey and Nick slapped me on the back a couple of times. "It's been two months, Nick. I can promise you that if there'd been a broken condom I'd have mentioned it by now." At least I was pretty sure I would've mentioned it. "And I probably wouldn't be swilling whiskey."

"It's been a really long two months."

It had been an eternity. Mr. Incredible wasn't cutting it anymore. I needed Nick in a bad way. His finger trailed up my arm and around the neckline of my dress. My nipples spiked to hard points and I think I stopped breathing.

It's a good thing we were interrupted by Nick's father, otherwise I was about thirty seconds from grabbing Nick by the hand and heading to the nearest closet.

An hour later, all my amorous feelings had disappeared. Nick's dad looked a lot like Nick and Nick's older brother David. The Dempsey men were all built like runners, with long, lean lines of muscle and broad shoulders. Nick's dad had the same stunning blue eyes and dark hair, only his was just graying at the temples. Very distinguished and handsome for a man who had to be in his early sixties. That's pretty much where all similarities stopped.

My granny always used to say that all assholes came in different shapes and sizes and some were just smellier than others, but I'd never met an asshole as big or smelly as Charles Dempsey.

"Nicholas," Charles said, coming up next to us at the bar. He ordered another gin and tonic and I could tell it wasn't his first. Probably more like his fifth. "Introduce me to your lady friend."

"This is Addison Holmes. And she's armed, so watch your hands."

"You always go for the feisty ones. I hear you're an exotic dancer." Charles completely ignored Nick's warning and leaned in close. "How much do you charge for private showings?" His hand landed on my knee and was going straight for the money pot when I grabbed his thumb and bent it back all the way to his wrist.

Charles screamed like a girl and went down to his knees. I'd been faster reacting than Nick and by the look on his face it was probably a good thing. I was pretty sure I'd never seen Nick as angry as he was now. And he'd been angry at me a lot. Everyone in the room was looking our direction, but no one came over to see what was wrong. Apparently they were used to this kind of scene.

Nick grabbed his dad by his tux lapels and hauled him to her feet. Charles swatted Nick away and straightened his jacket. He was white as a sheet and his face was clammy with sweat. "You bitch. Do you know who I am?"

"A man who managed to sire a decent son despite being a misogynist asshole?"

Nick stepped between us and I couldn't see the look on Nick's face, but his dad paled even more. "Go drink some coffee and sober up. I'd hate to have to arrest you for sexual assault, but I'd do it in a heartbeat."

Charles stood up straight and gathered as much dignity around him as he could. "You've never been anything but a disappointment to us, Nicholas. We gave you a future that you squandered. Joining the military and running off to do God knows what. Then coming back home and deciding to be some piss-ant cop. Two hundred years of Dempseys are rolling in their graves because of you."

"It's probably good for them to get a little exercise," Nick said, moving aside and helping me up from the barstool.

I'd decided the best thing I could do would be to shrink away and pretend I wasn't listening in on what should probably be a private conversation between father and son. Charles clapped his hand on Nick's shoulder and held tight so we couldn't walk away.

"I'll drop the lawsuit if you'll agree to sign the money over to the company. No judge with a lick of sense is going to side with you over this. Your grandfather wasn't in his right mind when he left everything to you. It was always agreed upon that the money would go back into the firm."

"Take your hand off me." Nick's voice was deadly and Charles must have gotten the hint. "As far as I'm concerned, grandfather was the only Dempsey who has ever been in his right mind. Now if you'll excuse us, I need to go congratulate my brother."

I didn't say anything as Nick led us through the crowd and away from his father. In all honesty, I didn't know *what* to say. And I wasn't about to ask what that last bit had been about with the lawsuit, though I was curious as hell.

"Do you see my brother anywhere? I've made it about as long as I can."

I hadn't officially met David yet, but Nick had pointed him and his fiancée out to me. They looked like a very nice couple, and I was starting to recognize that polished look of the really rich. Their bones were different. High cheekbones and high brows. They didn't have a lot of facial expressions and they all looked the same. There was no one with any character in the whole bunch, and I was looking hard to try and find some.

Nick had those upper crust bones too now that I looked closely. But Nick's perfection was marred by a previous broken nose and the slash over his eyebrow. Not to mention his eyes had more living in them then everyone in the room combined.

Nick and I were back at the double doors and a waiter stood just to the left of us and rang a tiny bell signaling dinner. This must have been a hungry group, because they filed out of the parlor and into the dining room like a herd of cattle.

We followed behind everyone else, but we were halfway across the foyer when something caught my eye. I knew Nick had noticed it too because he stopped dead in his tracks. His brother David had broken out of the herd with a brunette I didn't recognize and slipped through the door under the stairs. Considering his pants were unzipped and his hand was already up her dress I was guessing they weren't having a quick business meeting before the rehearsal dinner.

"What room is that?" I asked.

"Half bath." Nick's jaw was locked again and the little veins were bulging in his forehead. I was starting to think being around his family was probably not good for his health.

"Hunh. Maybe it's not what we think. Maybe she needs help with her Spanx to go to the bathroom. Sometimes they're hard to maneuver and you've got to have a friend help you out."

His smile was tight and I could see his disgust. "My brother is definitely a professional Spanx remover. If anything, David's holding tight to the family legacy. They don't take a lot of stock in saying vows before God. In the Dempsey world of law, there's always a loophole somewhere."

Nick led me away from the dining room where everyone was being seated and back toward the front door so we could make our escape. But the hall doorknob rattled and we sprinted back to the parlor where the party had just been.

David slipped out of the bathroom, straightening his clothes as he went to join the others in the dining room, and a minute later the brunette followed.

"Well, I'm certainly glad you didn't inherit that quality from the men in your family," I said.

"Infidelity?"

"Premature ejaculation."

Nick laughed and some of the tension went out of his shoulders. "What do you say? Want to have dinner in here? We've got an open bar and trays of spicy meatballs and little quiche."

"You sure know how to show a girl a good time."

"You ain't seen nothing yet, babe."

Oh, boy.

CHAPTER TEN

S*unday*

THE THING about drinking good liquor is that it doesn't cause a hangover. So I woke up the next morning bright-eyed and bushy-tailed. Only not in my bed.

Nick and I had gorged ourselves on spicy meatballs and thrown back a couple of more drinks, and while we were doing it we managed to have a pretty decent conversation. I told him about the neighborhood watch and caught him up on what was happening with my mom and Vince, and he talked about sports and told me he was thinking of buying a boat.

Nick never talked about work because apparently that was a no-no, though I'd suggested more than once that he might get some new ideas if he talked it out loud. Mostly I was just nosy and wanted to know what he was working on. I also understood perfectly well now why he'd never talked about his family before. If I had a family like that, I'd want to pretend I was an only child too.

We'd filched a bottle of single malt from behind the bar and snuck out the front door when we heard people start moving around the house again. But then we realized we were both entirely too drunk to drive home and we ended up calling a cab.

Somewhere between Nick's parents' house and my place, Nick decided he wanted me to look at his new kitchen cabinets and help him decide on a paint color for his breakfast room. Now I didn't fall off the turnip truck yesterday, so I figured this was his way of trying to get me into bed. It turns out he really wanted me to look at his kitchen cabinets and pick out paint. I'm not sure that's saying a lot for me. In fact, I was more than a little peeved he didn't try to make a move on me at all. I was wearing my best lingerie to drive him crazy, and I'd made up an entire speech in my mind I didn't even get to use.

"So what do you think?" he asked.

"About what?"

"The paint. I can't decide what looks best with the cabinets."

I was still trying to come to terms with the fact that I was standing in Nick's house. I had no idea where we were. He lived way outside of Savannah. I remember the cab heading toward Whiskey Bayou and wondering briefly if he was going to drop me at my mother's house. And then the cabbie turned off the highway about halfway there and took a one-lane road through a bunch of trees that I never would have found even in the daylight.

And then all of a sudden a little clearing appeared along with a house that looked like Frank Lloyd Wright on steroids. I couldn't see it all that well, but I could see enough to know that it was the kind of house that couldn't be bought on a cop's salary.

"You seriously want me to pick out a paint color? That's why you brought me here?"

His eyes sparkled with devilment and his mouth quirked in a smile. "Sure, why else would I bring you here?"

I narrowed my eyes and looked at the rows of different color test paints on his breakfast room wall. "I like the yellow. It's cheerful. Why aren't you trying to take my clothes off?" In my head I knew I'd regret this conversation in the morning. But I was maybe a little more than drunk, and drunk Addison didn't have a lot of filters.

"You could probably seduce me pretty easily right now," I went on. "And I like the look of you in a tux." Something alarmingly close to a giggle escaped my lips and I saw Nick's mouth twitch. I was starting to think maybe he held his liquor better than I did. I was mostly a cheap date.

I stalked him so he was backed up against the kitchen table and I walked my fingers up his chest. He'd stopped smiling and his eyes turned so dark they were almost navy.

"Addison—"

"What? You said it's been a long two months. It's been a long two months for me too. And I'm afraid Mr. Incredible is going to short out he's getting so much use."

"Not that I don't appreciate the offer, but I'd prefer you sober. The next time I'm inside you I want you to remember it."

I was so turned on I was afraid my clothes were going to melt, and I pressed against Nick and nipped at his bottom lip. I wasn't only an affectionate drunk, I was also an honest drunk. "I'm pretty sure you should take advantage of me now. When I'm sober I'm probably going to be mortified about my behavior and never want to see you again. Also, I'm pretty mad at you still, so this situation probably won't help things."

Nick grinned at my confession and I might have giggled some more, but it was all starting to get hazy. All I knew was that Nick wasn't totally unaffected by the way I was pressed against him. Either he'd started carrying his gun in the front of his pants or he was really happy to see me.

"Why don't I show you to the guest room?"

"Why don't we skip that and use this table? It looks sturdy enough. You look good enough to eat." I licked my lips and Nick sucked in a breath at the implication.

"Jesus. I'd better get massive points for this."

"Oh, it's massive all right." I waggled my eyebrows and went into another fit of laughter. And then I gasped as Nick picked me up and threw me over his shoulder and ran for the stairs like a bat out of hell. The rest of the house spun around me, and I was starting to think hanging upside down might not be the best idea considering all I'd had to drink.

Then all of a sudden I was flat on my back in the middle of a large bed. The sheets were cool against my back and the ceiling fan spun lazily above my head.

"Be back in a minute," Nick said.

"I'll be waiting." I got up unsteadily and stripped out of my dress so I only wore the black lace contraption and my high heels. I figured Nick was going to get protection and then we'd get down to business. I was having a sexual crisis. It turns out two months was a long time for me too, though I'd never thought so before when I was only having bad sex.

Nick appeared a minute later with a stack of what looked like clothes in his hands, but he promptly dropped them as soon as he got a look at me.

"Sweet holy mother," he said. The bulge in the front of his slacks looked to be at Hulk proportions.

"What do you think?"

"I think I deserve a fucking medal." He scooped up the clothes he'd dropped on the floor and handed them to me. "The bathroom is through there if you want a shower. There's an extra toothbrush and other toiletries if you need them. I brought you one of my shirts and some sweatpants." And then he shut the door in my face and left me in the room all alone. I stood there like a dummy a few minutes with my mouth hanging open before I realized he wasn't coming back.

I'd just been rejected by Nick. Again. I dropped back on the bed and tried to decide how upset I was but everything was blurry. I kicked off my shoes and pulled the comforter over me. Nothing wore a good buzz off faster than reality. And I'd just had a good dose of it.

DESPITE THE FACT that I woke up without a hangover, I wasn't in that great of a mood. I'd tossed and turned all night, switching back and forth between complete mortification and wondering what Nick was doing only a room or two away. I hoped he'd had as miserable a night as I had. It was the least he deserved.

I'd ended up showering about three in the morning in hopes that the hot water would be soothing and finally put me to sleep, but mostly it had just made me experiment with the adjustable shower head. I checked the brand when I got out so I could have one installed in my own bathroom. I put on the sweats and shirt and crawled back into bed.

At five-thirty I was still awake and birds chirped an annoyingly cheerful tune outside my window. I finally rolled out of bed to see what all the fuss was about. The sky was still the hazy gray of night turning to day. The birds sat just outside my window on a tree limb I could've touched if the window was open, and they sang and warbled as they bathed in the water that dripped from the leaves from the storm the night before.

I pounded on the window. "Hey, shut up out there. Not everyone has had their coffee yet." I startled them enough that they stopped for just a second and then they started again with even greater fervor.

Thoughts of coffee made me wonder if I was having a hallucination because I swore I could smell it wafting from under the door. Nick was an early riser, but not usually that early. And especially not on a Sunday. I took a second to use the bathroom and splash water on my face and then I grabbed my phone and checked my email as I followed the smell down the stairs.

My behavior from the previous night was in the forefront of my mind, but I was determined to pretend like nothing had happened. We were both adults. No big deal. I'd grab a cup of coffee and call a cab to take me home, and I'd forget all about Nick Dempsey and move on with my life. I wasn't going to be the kind of woman to keeping pining over a man who didn't want her. That was for reality TV shows and people like Mrs. Messer who'd lived down the street from us when I was a kid. Her husband ran off with a hooker he met on a business trip, but Mrs. Messer waited for him to come back for the next twenty years, sure he'd come to his senses.

I didn't take the time to snoop around Nick's house. I needed to get out of there and fast. Though I couldn't help but notice a few things. The house was modern in style. All the rooms had floor to ceiling windows, letting in lots of natural light, and each room flowed into the next so there was lots of open space. I stopped where the living area turning into the breakfast room and kitchen and just stared.

The sight of Nick first thing in the morning made my mouth water and my lady bits sing. I was pathetic. With a capital P. I wished like hell my heart had the common sense my brain did. He stood facing the stove with his legs braced apart as if he were waging war with the omelet he was cooking. He only wore a pair of jeans, his feet were bare, and his hair was slightly mussed.

I needed to get a grip. I'd get my coffee, call a cab, and disappear to my room until it came for me. I headed over to the coffeemaker and grabbed a mug hanging from the hook just above it. I inhaled once before I took the first rehabilitating sip.

"Hangover?" Nick asked. "I've got some aspirin in the cabinet there above your head."

"Nope. No hangover. Your parents know their liquor."

"I guess that's one thing they have going for them. I should probably apologize for their behavior. In hindsight a date like that was probably worth way more than five hundred dollars."

"I'll send you a bill for damages." I hadn't made eye contact with him yet, but I could feel his gaze on me and my cheeks heated with embarrassment. I stared at my phone, trying to remember what I was going to do.

Oh, yeah. A cab.

I looked up the number, took my coffee, and started back out of the room. I was just about to hit the dial button when Nick stopped me again.

"Hold on a sec," he said, sliding the first omelet on a plate. He walked over and handed me the plate, and I put my phone down and grabbed it out of reflex. "Have some breakfast. We didn't really have dinner last night, so I figured you'd be hungry."

I finally found the courage to meet his eyes and we both froze for a minute, the plate caught between us. His face was scruffy with his morning beard and he looked as tired as I did.

"Did you sleep well?"

"Like a baby," I lied and took my plate to the table.

"Really?" His mouth quirked. "I could've sworn I heard the shower running in the middle of the night. Must have been my imagination."

I decided no response was the best response. I had fond memories of his showerhead and I wondered if he'd heard anything else. He brought his own plate to the table and sat across from me. We ate in silence for a few minutes.

"So how'd you like the showerhead?"

I pushed my plate away and moved to run out of the room, but Nick caught my hand.

"Let me go. I need to get home. I've got work to do today."

"I don't think so. You know how hard it was to stay away from you? I thought about you all night, wanting nothing more than to slip into bed and slide right into you."

My mouth dropped open and I started to stutter. I couldn't remember how to form words. He tugged at my hand and pulled me between his thighs. I tried pulling away, but there was no way I could out-muscle him.

"Let me go, Nick. I mean it. You had your chance last night and decided you didn't want me."

"You were drunk."

"So what? I knew what I was doing."

"Yeah, but I didn't want to take any chances that you'd regret what you were doing. Not to mention I wanted to make sure you'd remember every detail of what I plan to do to you."

I was starting to panic a little bit. Being with Nick was an emotional rollercoaster.

"Guess what, babe?"

"What?"

"You're sober now." His hand found its way beneath my shirt and his fingers skimmed up my ribcage and rubbed the underside of my breast. I whimpered before I could help it and I shook my head to try to shake some sense loose. I pulled against him and a sob broke free when he didn't let me go.

"Why are you making this so hard? We can't keep doing this." A couple of tears had broken free and I was on the verge of hysteria. It wasn't fair for him to keep bringing all the feelings I had for him to the surface all the time. "Maybe someday we can be friends, Nick. But now is not that day. I need you to stay out of my life. All the way out. I deserve to have a chance at something else."

"With Savage?"

"Maybe. I don't know."

"It's not going to happen, babe." And then he tugged me so that I fell against his chest and into his arms. His mouth was hot on mine, and I kissed him back. I unleashed all the pent up frustration from the night before, my fingers tangling in his hair and each of us fighting for possession.

He tugged my shirt over my head and my sweatpants somehow ended up on the table. It was a good thing I wasn't wearing underwear. I'd saved him a step. Nick kissed his way down my neck, suckling and nibbling until he reached my nipple. I groaned at the pressure and tore at the button on his jeans. Before I knew what was happening I was flat on the table and Nick was taking his mouth south.

"Looks like the table is as sturdy as you thought," he said. "All I could think about last night was what you said about being good enough to eat. And baby I'm starving."

The thing about Nick is that he knows his way around a vagina. I think he studied for a lot of years before he met me. I was about two seconds away from the orgasm of a lifetime. My muscles were tight and vibrating. Sound had condensed so I only heard buzzing in my ears and my erratic pulse.

He pulled away and I grabbed for his head but I couldn't reach him. And then I heard why he'd stopped.

"Wha—" I shook my head and tried to come back to reality. And then his phone rang again.

"Fuck. It's the station. I've got to take it. I'm on call."

"Don't you dare stop! I swear to God I'll kill you first."

He kissed the inside of my thigh and adjusted his jeans and then went to grab his phone off the counter. I was still sprawled on the table like a Thanksgiving spread.

I lay there for a couple of seconds to try and get my brains unscrambled while Nick took his call.

I rolled off the table and pulled my clothes back on. I had a feeling there was probably egg in my hair, but I wasn't going to take the time to shower. I headed toward the stairs and left Nick in the kitchen to deal with whatever crisis had arisen. I stripped out of Nick's borrowed shirt and sweat pants and put on my dress from the night before. I dumped my jewelry in my handbag and was back downstairs before Nick had finished his call.

I knew as soon as I walked back in the kitchen he had to go. I avoided his dark stare as he answered in one syllable words and grabbed my phone off the counter to call a cab. I hoped the driver had change for a hundred because that was all I had.

"I'll drop you at your house," Nick said as he hung up.

"Not necessary. I'll call a cab. You don't want to waste time getting to the scene." Nick worked homicide, so this wasn't the first time a call had interrupted our personal lives. I'd pretty much gotten used to it when we'd been dating.

"I've got time to drop you. The body isn't going anywhere, and the scene is still fresh. There aren't even uniforms on site yet. Housecleaner called it into the station."

Nick ran upstairs and got ready. When he came back down he looked as presentable as someone could at a little after six. His weapon was strapped securely to his side. I ignored him about giving me a ride because I remembered we'd left his truck at his parents' house the night before.

I was on hold with the cab company when he took my phone and ended the call. He took my elbow, dragged me outside, and locked his front door.

"Excuse me, Mr. Caveman, but you left your truck at your parents' house. And honestly, even if it was here I'd still want to take a cab."

"I like the ice queen routine. Very sexy." He hit the remote on his garage, tossed me over his shoulder again and dropped me inside a sporty little black Audi that looked like something Batman would drive. It had leather seats and smelled like Nick's cologne.

"I recognize that stubborn look on your face," he said, getting in and cranking the engine. "I'm taking you home and that's final."

I was still trying to wrap my head around the whole car thing. "Nick, you did not buy this car on a cop's salary."

"It was a gift from my granddad a couple of years ago. My dad had tried to bribe me into going to law school and joining the firm with just about everything you could imagine. He also called the governor and the police chief and tried to have me fired. When that didn't work he had internal affairs start an investigation to see if they could dig any dirt that way to find grounds for release.

"I don't think I like your dad."

"I'm sorry to say, I don't like him all that much either." I could tell by the sadness in his voice that he really was sorry. The rift between Nick and his parents was obviously painful for him.

"I pretty much told dad to go to hell after I'd found out about the investigation. Granddad found out what dad had done and he put a stop to it. He said anyone that wouldn't buckle under the Dempsey pressure was someone he could be proud of. Then he gave me the car, changed his will so I'd inherit most of his wealth, and then he died two weeks later. My dad has been protesting the will and keeping things tied up in legal red tape ever since then. I have my trust fund, which he can't touch, and that's what I used to buy the house with."

"I'm sorry about your family," I said. "And I wish you would have told me all of this before when we were together. But I meant what I said. You're going to take me home and then I don't ever want to see you again. If you see me on the street I want you to turn the other direction, and if you see me at the agency I want you to pretend I don't exist. I can't keep doing this."

"It's not going to happen, sweetheart. When I get finished with the case I'm going to come get you and we're going to finish what we started."

"Over my dead body." I was so angry I could feel the roots of my hair sizzling. Angry at myself for not having more willpower. Angry at Nick for not letting me come. Angry at whoever died and interrupted us. And angry that Nick *did* have the willpower to stop.

"I mean it, Nick. No more. You're the one who called things off. And I'm not in the market for a fuck buddy. If I wanted that I have plenty of other options. As far as I'm concerned you're just being cruel at this point."

"Well, maybe I was an idiot for calling things off." He was speeding like a demon through the Savannah streets and I was glad there was no traffic. "It's been a miserable two months. I want us to give it another chance."

"Are you fucking kidding me?" I opened my handbag and dug around for my gun. "Where the hell is my gun? This one has real bullets in it too. I'm not letting you get off with a puny tranquilizer dart this time." A couple of months before I might have accidentally shot Nick in the backside with a tranquilizer gun when I caught him standing outside a motel with another woman. How was I supposed to know she was an informant?

"Why are you so angry? We obviously still want each other. I thought this was what you wanted. Women," he said, his exasperation clear.

"What I wanted was for you not to dump me in the first place. And now you're ready to get back together because you haven't had sex in two months and I happen to be convenient? So I'm supposed to just roll over all because *you're* ready to get back together."

"Jesus, is all this anger just because you didn't come? Because really, I'll only be a few hours."

"I haven't needed you to come for the last two months, and I didn't need you to come all the years before you met me."

Nick slowed in front of my house and I had the door open before he stopped completely. "We're not through, Addison. I'll be back and we're going to talk about this. I made a mistake leaving you before and I admit that, but I'm pretty sure I love you more than I'm afraid for you and the crazy stunts you pull. Maybe think about that before you start looking for real bullets."

He drove away and left me standing there with my mouth hanging open. Savage came out of his front door about the same time, ready to go on his morning run, and his brows rose at the sight of me still dressed in the clothes I'd worn the night before. I should have been embarrassed that he'd caught me like that, but I was past the point of caring.

"I'll be ready to run in ten minutes," I called out. "I'm ready for some serious training this morning."

CHAPTER ELEVEN

Two hours later I was sprawled on my back in the middle of my living room floor. I didn't have the strength to make it to my bathroom to shower and change.

"You need to get up and stretch before your muscles get tight."

"What I need is for you to just shoot me in the head."

When I'd told Savage I was ready for serious training he'd taken me at my word. He hadn't asked me why I'd been dressed in yesterday's clothes and he hadn't tried to find out if I'd rekindled with Nick. He could tell something was wrong and he let me simmer and use the anger to drive me to have a better workout. We ran a couple of miles and we somehow ended up at a hole-in-the-wall gym that had a bunch of serious body builders and no women in brightly colored leotards. I was the only one, and after the third man dropped his weights I was told by the owner I had to put on a T-shirt. Savage had an extra in his locker and let me borrow it. And then we got down to business.

It turns out I was going about my exercise routine all

wrong. Savage said if I did exactly what he said then I'd be in the best shape of my life long before I had to take the physical portion of the test, and that if I didn't pass with flying colors he'd personally make sure I never ate another hot fudge sundae for the rest of my life.

"Seriously," I said when I tried to roll over. "I don't think I can get up. At least not for three or four years."

Savage came over to where I was sprawled on the floor and hauled me up from under my armpits. Then he put another one of his smoothie concoctions in my hand.

"Drink this and go get your shower. I've narrowed down your search for Tannenbaum's son."

An hour later, I was clean and mostly had full control over my arms and legs again. I wore black leggings, a royal blue cashmere sweater, and my black Ugg boots because the temperature had started to drop. Savage had showered and changed too and was wearing old jeans and a Harvard sweatshirt.

I was riding shotgun in Savage's SUV and I had the information he'd found for me spread out on my lap. He had it narrowed down to three Roses. It was a hell of a lot more information than I'd managed to find.

"It says here that Rose Parker is still alive. Maybe we should go talk to her first."

"Where does she live?"

"Charleston." Charleston was only a couple of hours from Savannah. We could go talk to Rose Parker and be back by the end of the day. "The file says she gave birth to a son, James Parker, on April second of 1942. She was eighteen years old. I can't imagine a woman that age being dragged to a back alley sperm bank by her husband. It seems skeezy."

"Times were different then. Especially in the South.

I've been here long enough to know that lineage is about the most important thing to all of you. Where you came from and who's worth noting in the family tree. I'd think a man might see it as a weakness if he wasn't able to get an heir in a timely fashion."

"It couldn't have been that timely. She was only eighteen for Christ's sake. Anyway, the dates certainly line up with the information Mr. Tannenbaum gave us. Rose gave birth to a daughter six years later, and she lives with her daughter and son-in-law now. James is now deceased, as is his own son. There's a grandson listed here who is nineteen and also living in the house with Rose. If this Rose was able to have more children with her husband, maybe she's not the one we're looking for."

"We'll check it out. Process of elimination, babe. The most exciting thing about police work."

I hoped Savage was being sarcastic, but sometimes it was hard to tell. Mostly I hated the process of elimination. It was about as exciting as watching paint dry. I much preferred the stakeouts and catching people in the act of doing something they shouldn't. Other people's mistakes were good for my own self-esteem.

The Dragnet theme filled the car and I dug around in my purse until I found my phone. The theme song belonged to Kate.

"What's up?" I asked.

"I just heard over the police scanners that Mr. Tannenbaum's body was found this morning. Looks like homicide."

"Shit. I just spoke with him at his house yesterday."

"You might want to let the investigating officer know that before they find your prints."

"Let me guess. Nick's the investigating officer."

"Right the first time."

"Fuck."

There was silence on the other end of the line and from Savage as well. He'd pulled to the side of the road instead of taking the turn off to head to Charleston.

"Is everything okay?" Kate asked. "I can relay the message if you want me to."

"I don't want to talk about it. And it's probably best I relay the message myself. I'm not armed at the moment, so I can't shoot him."

"As your friend I'd advise against it. The paperwork would be a bitch."

Kate hung up and I gave Savage the news about Tannenbaum. "Let's take a detour and drive by the scene. I need to let Nick know I was there yesterday before he goes ballistic when he finds my prints."

"I was under the impression you and Dempsey had patched things up. You seem a little hostile for someone who was wearing yesterday's clothes this morning."

"It's not what you think," I said, and then I remembered it had started out being exactly what he was thinking. "At least not really. I mean, I was drunk and sometimes alcohol makes me a little...amorous. So I probably would have but Nick turned me down. And then I would have again this morning because apparently I'm a sex addict with no willpower, but then he got called to a crime scene and my brain started working again before I could do something stupid. Now I'm just mostly pissed. I'm not much for casual sex. And apparently I'm a big fat loser without a modicum of self-control because I can't seem to tell him no."

"Hmm. Maybe you should pretend he's me. You don't seem to have a problem telling me no."

"It's complicated."

"Not really. You had feelings for the guy and then he dumped you. That's not something that's easy to get over, and it's understandable you might slip up now and again if he shows interest in you. Maybe all you need is to get him out of your system once and for all."

I gave Savage an arched look.

"I was a psychology minor," he said, shrugging.

"So you think I should sleep with him one last time? Like a cleansing?"

"Possibly. Then you'll be free to move on to something better."

It was my turn to *hmmm*. I could read between the lines there. I was almost positive that Savage would be miraculous in bed. Like an oversexed Captain Kirk, exploring uncharted territory. But Savage was the kind of man who probably wasn't good for a woman's self-esteem. And believe me, after being left at the altar for a Barbie doll and then left again while stuck in the hospital with a gunshot wound, I definitely had some self-esteem issues. Savage was larger than life and just a tad scary. I had a feeling that being in bed naked with Savage would bring all my insecurities to the surface. He certainly wasn't a comfortable man.

Nick, on the other hand, was handsome in an approachable way. Unless he had his cop face on, then all bets were off. His body was a work of art and he had that aura about him that made men want to drink beer with him and women want to rip their clothes off. But when we were in bed together I never wondered if I looked stupid or if I needed to lose five pounds. If I ever went to bed with Savage, I'd never be able to just enjoy myself.

It didn't take long to get to Mr. Tannenbaum's house.

He lived over on Hall Street not far from Nick's parents. The street in front of the house and to the side was cordoned off and a couple of police cruisers and Nick's truck blocked it so traffic couldn't drive through.

Nick must have picked up his truck from his parents' house before coming to the crime scene. Probably it wasn't a good idea for a public servant to drive around a car that cost six figures.

"Why don't you just badge us through?" I asked.

"Because it's always good for the local police not to hate your guts on sight. I might have to work with them again, and cops have long memories."

"If I had a badge I'd use it for everything. Cutting in line at the Piggly Wiggly and to get discounts on movie tickets."

"Everyone who has a badge uses it for that stuff. Sometimes you've just got to be more circumspect when dealing with the local cops. They have badge envy."

"Is that like penis envy?"

"It's the same principle."

I broke out in a smile and got out of Savage's SUV. "I'll give you a hundred dollars to say that to Nick."

"Not while he's armed."

Savage and I waited just outside the perimeter while the uniform went inside to get Nick. I popped my knuckles a couple of times and realized I'd chewed off my lipstick. Nick wasn't going to be happy with me. But I figured it probably served him right because I sure as hell wasn't happy with him.

Nick walked out of the house and I could already tell it wasn't going to be a pleasant conversation. He still wore the same worn jeans and thin charcoal sweater he'd put on that morning, and if it wasn't for the weapon at his side and the badge clipped to his belt most people would never place him as a cop. Unless they looked at his eyes.

"Agent Savage," Nick said, nodding.

"Detective Dempsey," Savage nodded back.

I could feel the testosterone pumping between them and I looked back and forth a couple of times just to make sure they weren't going to jump at each other's throats in the middle of the street.

"I won't assume you guys were just in the neighborhood," Nick said, his brow arching.

Nick had issues with Savage. Most of those issues had to do with Savage's interest in me. I knew Nick's jealousy was legitimate. I wasn't so sure about Savage's. Sometimes I had a feeling that Savage's interest in me had more to do with winning and Nick than it actually had to do with me.

"We're working."

"I didn't realize Kate was hiring off duty FBI agents now."

"Savage is doing me a favor."

"Just make sure the price isn't too high." Nick directed those words right at Savage, and I watched as Savage smiled. It wasn't a reassuring smile.

"I guess it's a good thing I have an extra five hundred dollars in my pocketbook." My eyes narrowed to slits and I felt myself getting angry again at the way things had gone between us the night before. "Besides, this is all your fault. If you'd told me this morning you were the primary on Mr. Tannenbaum I could have done all this sooner."

Nick growled and his fingers twitched down at his side like a gunslinger.

"I think I'll wait in the car," Savage said. "The temperature here is dropping pretty fast."

Now that he mentioned it, I was starting to feel the cold. My anger had kept me warm before. I hadn't brought a jacket with me, and I crossed my arms over my chest and shivered as I explained my connection with Mr. Tannenbaum to Nick. He stood perfectly still as I relayed the information. Nothing but blank cop's eyes looked back at me.

"Do you know if he was successful at getting his will changed?" Nick asked.

"I have no reason to believe otherwise. He had an appointment with his attorney to sign the papers the afternoon he came to see us. His plan was to leave his entire fortune to his child or any grandchildren if that child was deceased. The step-children were the ones getting cut from the money."

"They're on my list of people to talk to. Two of them were at the rehearsal dinner last night. The stepdaughter is a bridesmaid and the stepson is a groomsman."

"Small world."

"When people have as much money as Mr. Tannenbaum and my parents, then yes, it's a very small world. What makes it even better is Tannenbaum's attorney on record is none other than Charles Dempsey."

I winced and couldn't help feeling a little sympathy. Things were likely to get very ugly as this investigation progressed.

"What was cause of death?" I asked.

He ran his fingers through his hair like he did when he was agitated. "Blunt force trauma is my first guess. I'll have to wait for the ME's report before I can be sure. The murder weapon still hasn't been found, so I've got uniforms canvassing the neighborhood. Where are you going with Savage?"

"I've narrowed down the list of possible Tannenbaum heirs and we're going to talk to a lady named Rose Parker." Technically Savage had been the one to narrow it down, but I figured it wasn't in my best interest to mention Savage at the moment.

"Fine, but why are you going with Savage? Why not Kate?"

"He's been helping me out lately. Besides, I don't have a car at the moment and needed a ride."

"I'm going to be a few more hours, but as soon as I'm finished I'm coming to your house and we're going to finish what we started."

I thought about what Savage said and getting Nick out of my system. "Maybe it's for the best," I nodded. "Like closure."

"The last thing I have in mind is closure. If I have to prove it to you all night long then that's what I'll do. I'm going to leave such a permanent imprint on you that you'll start walking funny every time you think of me. We're going to settle this between us once and for all tonight."

I gulped at the threat. I knew he wasn't bluffing. "I don't know when I'll be home. Maybe you should just come tomorrow." So I had time to move out of the country.

Nick pressed his lips together and turned and headed back toward the house. I had my hand on the door handle when he turned around and called out.

"Oh, and Addison? Next time you need a ride take the Audi. I don't need a psych minor putting ideas of closure in your head."

"You ran a background on Savage?" I asked, shocked that he'd pegged the situation so quickly. Mostly I was shocked because I hadn't thought to do a background check on Savage myself. I *had* had the forethought to run one on Nick, but I couldn't dig out anything more than the basics.

"Of course I did. Just like he ran an in-depth check on me. Be careful with him, babe. He's a dangerous man."

Nick walked back into the house and I stood next to the car, debating whether or not I should get in. I finally did because I couldn't feel my fingers from the cold. I knew deep down that Savage was a dangerous man. Just like I knew that the persona he'd adopted on the surface probably wasn't the real Savage. It was hard to say what the *real* Savage would be like. But it would pay to remember that in Savage's line of work he had to learn how to read and manipulate people to get the results he wanted. I could never let my guard down around him. I finally got in and buckled up.

"I was wondering for a second there if you were going to walk to Charleston," he said. His dark eyes were unreadable and I tried to use my woman's intuition to see deep into his soul. How dangerous was Savage? I was thinking my safety probably wasn't an issue. He was way more dangerous to my libido. I had a brief moment where I wished I'd start my period so I'd have an excuse to send both Savage and Nick away, but unless there was divine intervention that wasn't going to happen.

"I was thinking about it," I confessed.

"Let me guess, Dempsey told you he ran a check on me. He told you I was dangerous and that you should be careful. That my methods are sometimes unconventional and about that hostage that almost died when I was assigned to the Miami office."

I stared wide-eyed at Savage, wondering what the hell

happened to the hostage in Miami. "Yep, that's exactly what he told me."

"Sometimes you've got to take chances to bring the bad guys down. That's what it's all about. Making this world a little safer so there's room for more of the filth on the streets to multiply."

"That's a little depressing."

"It's a dark world, sweetheart. Dempsey and I just do our jobs and hope at the end of the day we make it home. That's all we can really ask for."

Jesus. I knew men like Nick and Savage put their lives on the line on a daily basis, but it was almost a periphery thought. I was used to it. I'd grown up the daughter of a cop and I'd watched my dad put on a weapon and fight the good fight for almost thirty years. I was probably pretty good material to be a cop's wife in all actuality because I understood the long hours and the frustrations. But part of how I coped was not thinking about the possible situations the men in my life might be getting themselves into. Just like it was probably for the best if they didn't think about the situations I was getting into on a daily basis.

We drove to Charleston in silence and Savage turned the radio on classic rock. I had two hours to think about my life, but thinking is pretty hard work so I dozed off at some point. Savage woke me once we crossed over the river and into Charleston.

Rose Parker lived with her daughter and son-in-law in a little row house on Wentworth Street. Savage pulled into the driveway behind a beige Cadillac that was at least ten years old, and four people had just gotten out of the car and were staring at us as they waited to see who we were.

"Crap. They're just getting home from church." I was mostly Southern Methodist, but lately I'd been paving the pathway to hell by sleeping in late on Sundays and fornicating outside of wedlock.

The older man, who I assumed was Rose's son-in-law, wore a gray suit. The woman next to him wore a tasteful navy pinstripe dress and pearls. The young man who had to be James Parker's grandson, and Rose's great-grandson, stood watchful with his hands in the pockets of his khakis and the top button of his golf shirt undone. He was still thin and gangly with youth. His hair was dark auburn and swooped low on his forehead and his face was baby smooth.

The last woman wore a dress of neon pink that made my eyes bleed and zebra striped shoes that made me dizzy. She had a handbag to match the shoes. I had a feeling I was looking at Rose Parker. Her bones could barely support the weight of her clothes and her skin was so loose it looked like someone had zipped her up in a flesh colored body bag and dunked her in the river.

"You get pretty uptight about church. You need to relax."

"You don't worry about going to hell?"

"I figure that's where all the good stuff is happening. Besides, I spent most of my summers on the reservation. We don't believe in hell."

"Must be nice."

We got out of the car and went to introduce ourselves, but I let Savage take the lead. This was the part where him having a badge was pretty handy.

"Are you Rose Parker?" Savage asked the woman in the hot pink zebra. Her hair was white and fluffed around her head like a dandelion puff and her eyes were a vivid blue.

"I am." She looked him up and down a couple of times and I was starting to wonder if she was going to start stuffing money in his pants. Savage had that effect on women of all ages.

"I'm Agent Matt Savage with the FBI and this is my associate, Addison Holmes. Would you mind if we ask you a few questions?" He flashed his badge and she read it over carefully.

"You don't look much like an FBI agent," she said. "I don't see a gun. And you've got on jeans and a sweatshirt. What kind of sweatshirt is that? My eyes aren't so good anymore."

"It's my alma mater. Harvard."

My mouth dropped open in surprise. I didn't actually think Savage had gone to Harvard. You could buy Harvard sweatshirts at Walmart for crying out loud. I figured it had been an old girlfriend's or he'd found it at a rummage sale. I still had an old NYU sweatshirt I'd gotten from an old boyfriend. The shirts of our past weren't supposed to actually *mean* anything. Hell, I even had an FBI T-shirt I'd bought online to wear while I watched X-Files every week during college. My whole closet of advertising paraphernalia was a lie.

"Hmm," Rose said. "I guess that's pretty impressive. How come you're just an FBI agent if you went to Harvard?"

"I went to law school. I like being an agent much better than I liked being an attorney."

"Attorneys are bloodsucking assholes."

"That was pretty much my thought too."

"Well come on in," Rose said. "This is my daughter, Caroline, and my son-in-law, Richard. And the young'un here is little Jamie. He's my great-grandson," she said proudly. "That means I'm really old. Caroline put in a nice roast before services this morning. You want to eat with us?"

"I appreciate the offer, but we'll pass. We've got to get back to Savannah this afternoon."

"Savannah? I haven't been to Savannah in thirty years."

We followed Rose into the house and my stomach immediately growled. The roast reminded me of every Sunday morning I'd ever had growing up in my house. My mother would put it in the oven before we left for church and then we'd come home to the whole house smelling like meat. Of course, since it was my mother the roast was always dry as a bone and hard as a rock, but it still smelled good enough to make my mouth water. I was willing to bet that Rose Parker's daughter didn't have dry roast.

"Can I get y'all something to drink?" Caroline asked.

Niceties always had to be seen to first in the South. I knew the drill. Eventually we'd get around to what we came for, but there was an order of etiquette to be observed. I looked over at Savage and saw he was impatiently tapping his fingers against his thigh. I hadn't known Savage long, but these rituals seemed to confound him. I'd always figured Savage was a Yankee through and through, and the Harvard thing pretty much confirmed my suspicions.

"I'm fine, thank you," I said. Savage and Rose declined the offer, and Rose's daughter disappeared back into the kitchen and left us alone for privacy.

"This is a lovely room," I said.

Rose had led us into a formal living area done in soft creams and golds. Two off-white microfiber sofas faced each other and a coffee table sat in the middle. An upright piano stood against the wall with family photos on top and little lace doilies sat out on the end tables. The house wasn't huge by most standards, but it was tasteful and homey.

"My daughter has lovely taste," Rose said proudly. "Now take a seat and tell me what this is all about. Am I a suspect in a crime? Are you going to handcuff me? You've got to be careful of my bones because they'll snap like a twig. Except for my hips and my knees. Those are pure titanium."

I could see Savage was trying not to smile as he took a spot on the couch. I sat next to him and immediately sank in his direction. I was pretty sure I'd never sat on a couch that soft. Savage didn't seem to be having any trouble at all remaining upright, but I had to prop my foot against the coffee table to keep from rolling into his lap. I was starting to reach that point in my life where I wondered if I'd ever be able to do anything right. A little Yorkie came into the room and jumped onto Rose's lap.

"No, you're not under arrest," Savage said. "We're conducting an investigation and your name came up."

There was a little bowl of mints at one end of the table and I grabbed one as a pretense to scoot farther away from Savage. I was practically sitting in his lap as it was. I popped the mint in my mouth and teetered on the very edge of the sofa.

"You were born and raised near Atlanta, correct?"

"That's right. And lived there a good number of years after I was married as well."

"Your husband was a banker?" I asked.

"Sure. Edgar and I were married more than fifty years when he finally passed on. He was bank president at First National on Peach Street. That's him on the wall there." She pointed to a man who reminded me of an egg—an oval face, shiny head, and no neck. "He was as ugly as homemade sin but he was a good man. That counted for something back in those days you know. Now all women want are rippling muscles and monster schlongs. I read all about it in *Cosmo*. Those kind of men are good for an affair but not for the long haul."

I breathed the mint in my mouth and all air was blocked from reaching my lungs. I grabbed my throat as I choked and gasped for air and pounded at my chest. Savage finally whacked me on the back and I ended up swallowing the mint whole.

"Are you all right, dear? You don't look so good."

"I'm fine." I sucked in a couple of big breaths and could feel the mint lodged somewhere in my esophagus. I assumed it would end up in my stomach eventually. Either that or it would just stay there and collect little stray bits of food and grow bigger and bigger until I finally just keeled over from lack of oxygen. "Carry on," I told Savage.

"Are you familiar with a Doctor Horace Neeley? He had a clinic down in Savannah in the early forties."

Her brow crinkled as she thought it over. "I'm afraid it doesn't ring a bell. But I'm not surprised by that. I had the same doctor in Atlanta for a good part of my life. He delivered both of my children. Why don't you just spit it out? I can tell you're trying to be delicate about something. I haven't got time to be delicate. At my age it's best to just get everything out as fast as possible before I die."

"Was Edgar the father of your son?" Savage asked.

Two streaks of color appeared on Rose's cheeks and her lips tightened into a straight line. She clutched her hand to her breast and seemed to collapse back against the sofa. She was so still I wondered if she'd died from the shock.

I smacked Savage on the arm. "That was maybe a little too blunt. Look, you've killed her."

"No, I didn't. I can see her chest moving. Are you all right, Mrs. Parker? Do you need some water?"

"No, I'm not all right. Don't you know I'm an old lady? I can't take too much excitement. I went to one of those naked shows once where the men dance on stage and they wear the socks on their privates. I got so worked up I had an angina attack and the doctor told me my heart couldn't take it anymore. Getting old is for the birds, let me tell you."

I already knew this, but it was good to have her reaffirm my suspicions. "You did tell us to be blunt," I reminded her.

"Yes, but I didn't think you'd know about James. No one knows about James. I never told Edgar when he was alive and I never told James either. I never even told the man who fathered the child I was pregnant. What I want to know is how the FBI found out."

My adrenaline was pumping along with the excitement running through my veins. I never got this lucky when I was out on my own. It must be because of Savage. I was surprised to hear she mentioned the biological father. Mr. Tannenbaum never mentioned that he knew her more than just in passing.

"So you did make the trip to Savannah to Doc Neeley's clinic?" I asked again. "Your husband didn't know you were being inseminated?"

"Inseminated?" Her eyes widened and her mouth formed a little O. "I told you I don't know a Doc Neeley, and I sure as hell was never inseminated."

"I think I'm confused then. You said James wasn't Edgar's son."

"Yes, but I still conceived him the old fashioned way. I had an affair with one of Edgar's clients at the bank. Lord, that man was handsome. Lots of muscles in all the right places and he knew just what to do with the one between his legs too. He died in a car crash before I found out I was pregnant and I never had the heart to confess to Edgar. He would've been devastated. I never regretted what I did though, and I'll take whatever punishment God decides to give me. Every woman deserves to have a man like that at least once in her life, don't you think?"

CHAPTER TWELVE

We stopped and grabbed lunch at a shrimp shack that sat right on the water. It was a little hole in the wall joint that had a scarred plastic table, fresh shrimp served in metal buckets, and sweet tea by the gallon. My mouth started watering as soon as we walked through the door.

We each ordered a pound of shrimp and I got a side of hushpuppies and coleslaw, and then we found a corner booth and waited. Savage was an enigma. He seemed to adapt to whatever situation he was in as if he'd always been there. He peeled shrimp like a local and only grimaced a little at the sweetness of the tea. And I knew if I asked he could tell me every detail of anyone sitting in the restaurant without looking. He and Nick had that constant awareness in common.

"So what do you think?" he asked.

I'd been thinking about what Rose had said ever since we left her. *Every woman deserves a man like that at least once in her life.* Maybe I was going about my dilemma with Savage entirely the wrong way. Maybe *he* was the one I needed to get out of my system. Because Savage definitely fit that once in a lifetime mold Rose had been talking about.

"I don't know," I said, peeling all of my shrimp so I had a big pile right in front of me. "Maybe just once. And maybe we could leave the lights off. It's not like I'm in a relationship, so it wouldn't be cheating. But it still doesn't seem right. It's a moral dilemma. I need to think on it some more."

Savage's hand froze just as he was dipping a shrimp into cocktail sauce, and I looked up to see him staring at me with his brows raised. "I meant what do you think about Rose and her denial of knowing Doc Neeley? Did it feel legit to you?"

"Oh." I felt my cheeks heat and stuffed a shrimp into my mouth. "Yeah, but it sure is a coincidence about her son being illegitimate. What do you think?"

"I think she was lying about something, but I don't know what. She's had a lot of years to come up with a cover story. I don't think we should rule her out."

"If she's lying, that would mean that Jamie is the only Tannenbaum heir. Why wouldn't she want him to collect his inheritance?

"Who knows," he shrugged. "But Jamie is legally an adult. I didn't see him leave the house or I would have asked him if he'd be willing to take a DNA test. You can hunt him down later and ask him for it."

We ate our shrimp in silence until I couldn't take it anymore. "How long have you lived in the South?" I asked. Curiosity had finally gotten the best of me.

"Three years."

"You like it?"

"It has its perks." His eyes darkened to black fire and I

watched the sensual curve of his lips as he licked a little sauce from his thumb. I didn't particularly want to hear what the perks were so I dedicated myself to eating.

We finished and Savage left a tip on the table on our way out. The wind had picked up off the water and the chill in the air had turned bitter. Shrimp boats were tied to the docks and the sky was overcast. I was really regretting not bringing a jacket along and I shuffled from foot to foot as I waited for Savage to unlock the door of the SUV.

He came up behind me, shielding the wind from my body as he opened the passenger door. His hand rested on the curve of my hip and I felt the heat of his fingers through layers of clothes. I froze where I was, and all of a sudden thoughts of being cold vanished. I was hot enough to burst into flame.

"Why just once?" His breath was warm against my ear and I shivered. I knew exactly what he was asking. He turned me slowly so I was facing him and I hoped I didn't start to hyperventilate. My heart thudded in my chest and I was having trouble making eye contact.

I licked my lips once before I answered. "It seemed like a good number at the time. You know, the whole cleansing thing you were talking about."

"So I'm the one you want to get out of your system?" His smile was challenging.

"You're the kind of man Rose described. Great for an affair but not good for the long term. I'm looking for the long term."

His thigh worked its way between my legs. He was hard. Everywhere. His hand had worked its way beneath my sweater and his fingers touched the underside of my breast and I felt my eyes roll to the back of my head.

"Maybe what you should do is try to convince me to

stay for the long haul." He whispered a lot of suggestions about how I might go about that and spots flashed in front of my eyes.

"I think I'm having a little trouble breathing. Maybe it's an allergic reaction."

His mouth captured mine and stars exploded behind my eyelids. Our bodies were pressed together and somehow my legs ended up wrapped around his waist. Warning bells clanged in my mind that I was in way over my head. I wasn't the kind of woman who'd be a good match for Savage. He didn't need a clumsy quasi-P.I. who threw up when she got too much exercise. He needed someone like Catwoman.

That knowledge didn't stop me from enjoying what the man could do with his mouth though. His thumb skimmed across my nipple and I felt the caress all the way between my legs. If I didn't get control of things I was going to have an orgasm in the middle of a parking lot. The good thing was we were in another state so my mother probably wouldn't hear about it.

Savage pulled back just as a cop car pulled up beside us and blasted his sirens. "Break it up and get a room," he said through the car speaker.

I thunked my head against Savage's chest as the loudspeaker drew the attention of everyone in a quarter mile radius. I realized Savage couldn't move until I untangled my legs from the chokehold I had on him. Not that it was probably a good idea for him to move at the moment. From what I could tell his pants weren't fitting all that well. Probably everyone else would be able to tell too.

I launched myself into the car and slammed the door closed, hunching down in my seat. Savage got behind the wheel a few seconds later and we took off. Everyone else went about their business.

Kissing Savage was apparently as exhausting as a good workout because I fell asleep again before we got out of Charleston. When I woke up again it was dark and we were just making our way into Savannah.

"There was a bad wreck on I-17. They had the whole road shut down because of a tanker explosion. It put us a little behind schedule."

A little was an understatement. It was going on ten o'clock and I'd been asleep for several hours. I cracked my knuckles as we turned onto our street and I wiped my damp palms on my leggings. Savage stopped right in the middle of the road.

"What's it going to be, babe? My house or yours?"

Little spots danced in front of my eyes and I started having a breathing problem again.

"I'm not Catwoman," I blurted out. He looked a little taken aback and a lot confused. "Never mind. Take me to my house."

I jumped out of the SUV as soon as he pulled to a stop. "Thanks for the ride. And the lunch. Have a safe drive home."

I mentally smacked myself in the head. Of course he was going to have a safe drive home. He only had to drive twenty feet to get there.

The look he gave me was unreadable, but he opened the car door and started to get out and I realized he was going to walk me inside. I was pretty sure that would be the point of no return. I reminded myself again that I wasn't Catwoman and that I didn't have any condoms in my nightstand drawer. I was on birth control, but I figured

Savage needed the extra protection. He looked like a man with good mobility.

"You don't have to walk me to the door," I told him before he could get all the way out. "I left the light on and I'm sure Spock and everyone else had things under control while we were gone."

Savage looked like he was going to argue with me, but he finally nodded and got back in the car. "I'll be here at six in the morning so we can go running and get in some gym time before work."

My mouth dropped open. "But we did that this morning. Are you saying we have to do that hellish workout every day?"

His mouth quirked and he shook his head. "See you in the morning."

I slammed the door shut and headed up the sidewalk, digging for my key. The porch light next door came on and Spock stuck his head out. He was dressed like Obi-Wan Kenobi and held a plastic light saber in his hand.

"That detective in the black truck was here earlier," he called out. "He didn't look happy."

"Good to know," I said. "Anyone else?"

"A lady showed up in a green Jaguar. She didn't look happy either. You must be really good at your job to piss so many people off."

"Yep. That's exactly what it is. Well, good night."

"Wait! Do you like those microwave pizza rolls?"

I had the key in the lock and the doorknob half turned. I looked back over my shoulder and saw Savage was already parked and getting out of his truck. If his smile was anything to go by he was hearing every word of our conversation.

"Sure, everyone likes pizza rolls. But I'm on a diet. Savage is trying to get me into shape."

"You've been doing pretty good too. We've all been watching in the mornings. You hardly ever throw up anymore. Maybe I should get in shape too. Maybe I'll join you for a run in the morning."

"Sounds great." I couldn't help but smile. Savage would *not* be happy if Spock showed up for our workout in the morning, but his interference would probably keep me from making any bad decisions.

I waved good night and closed the door behind me, locking the deadbolt and fastening the chain. It was chilly inside. In fact, it was downright cold and I went to the thermostat to turn the heat on.

My house is shaped like a box. Living room and dining room in the front corners, kitchen in the back right, two small bedrooms and a bathroom in the back left. The backyard was fenced with six-foot wooden panels that would probably blow over with the next strong wind. I never went in the backyard. I didn't have a pet or a pool and the only reason it wasn't overgrown with weeds was because Savage was nice enough to keep the lawn trimmed for me.

I kicked off my Uggs and tossed my purse on the bar. I grabbed my laptop and the files on the remaining two prospects I needed to talk to and headed toward my bedroom. The door was closed to the guest bedroom, but the air coming from under the door was colder than usual. My bedroom door was open and I stuck my head in to see if there was a draft in there as well.

I laid down my stuff on the bed and went back to the guest room. I was going to be pissed if there was something wrong with the central heat unit. It felt like the air conditioner was on full blast. I opened the guest room door and flipped on the light switch. And then it took a minute for my brain to catch up with my eyes. Someone had smashed the window in. The white curtains I'd hung floated out from the wall with the breeze and shards of glass were scattered across the floor.

I took an automatic step back and bumped into something solid. A hand clasped over my mouth before I could scream and I was dragged back into the hallway. By the size and bulk of my attacker I knew it was a man. He smelled like sweat and fried onions. My foot went back to try and connect with his knee, but he dodged the blow and instead jerked my hair hard enough to rip some out by the roots.

My eyes watered and I couldn't seem to think. I'd taken self-defense courses, but it's different when you don't have time to prepare. I went into panic mode and started flailing arms and legs and trying to bite his hand. I must have made contact somewhere because all of a sudden he pushed me hard enough into the wall that my head bounced off and I saw stars. A nice framed picture of me and Kate at the beach fell to the floor next to me and the glass shattered.

"Who are you?" I asked, trying to get my wits back enough to get to my feet. I needed to stay moving, to put as much space between us as I could, and hopefully get to the door and escape. My chances seemed pretty slim.

"Doesn't matter," he said.

I tried to place his voice but I didn't recognize it. I didn't recognize him. He was a couple of inches taller than me with pockmarked skin, beady black eyes, and a nose that looked like it had met a lot of fists. "All you need to know is that Johnny Sakko knows who you are. You messed up a big deal last night, little girl. And Johnny's decided you owe him for the trouble."

I'd managed to scoot my way down the hall to the living room and I was getting ready to propel myself to my feet and jump through a window if I had to. At least, that's what I was planning on doing before he pulled a gun from his coat pocket.

I'd been on the receiving end of a gun before. It wasn't an experience worth repeating. Getting shot hurt like hell. My skin turned cold and clammy and my teeth chattered. I couldn't take my eyes off the end of the gun, and any second I was expecting to die.

I finally decided if I was going to die I wasn't going to do it like a coward. I stood slowly to my feet and watched the gun raise with me.

"I was just doing my job," I said. "Maybe next time Johnny should be more careful."

"Johnny wants you to do a job for him. He thinks it's the least you owe him."

"I'd rather just pay him back. Will he take a payment plan?"

"Sure," Smash Nose said. "I can start putting bullets in your body. Knees first. Then feet. I can cut out your tongue and slice off your ears. Does that seem like a good payment plan to you?"

"I've heard better."

"And don't even think about getting the police involved. Johnny has so many cops in his pocket you'd be dead before they could set up another sting. Believe me, someone is already paying for letting you get the draw on us the other night."

There was a knock at the door and Smash Nose and I

both jerked. It was well past ten o'clock and I'd never had a visitor this late.

"Answer it, but don't let them in or you'll be digging a hole in your back yard to bury a body."

My head was throbbing and my hands were shaking and I hoped to God it wasn't Nick at the door. I looked through the peephole and saw Spock and then I answered the door, leaving the chain on so it didn't open very far.

"Are you okay?" he asked. "I thought I heard some weird noises."

"I saw a mouse," I lied. "I'm fine. You must have pretty good ears."

"Not so much. I have this super sensitive equipment that picks up all kinds of things. Just part of the neighborhood watch job."

He backed down the porch stairs, giving me an odd look, and I wondered if my lie hadn't been convincing enough.

"You should call an exterminator. We don't want a mouse infestation in the neighborhood. The last time that happened they chewed right through my life size cardboard cutout of Leonard Nimoy."

"I'll call first thing in the morning." I closed the door before he could give me any more advice and I turned back to Smash Nose.

"Someone will be in touch regarding the job. And if you fail to deliver, I promise you won't get out easy with a bullet to the head." He grabbed his crotch and rubbed enough for me to see everything was in working order down there, and then he laughed when he saw the revulsion on my face. "You're a pretty piece. I almost hope you fail."

Smash Nose went to my back door and kicked the

chair I kept pushed under the doorknob. He slipped out into the dark backyard and disappeared like smoke.

My knees gave way and I crashed to the floor. It was then I noticed the little droplets of blood dripping to the hardwood. I'd hit my head harder than I'd thought. I wheezed between sobs as I crawled to the back door and closed it again. Not that it made much difference. My window was still broken. I didn't have a car so I couldn't drive to my mom's house. I didn't want to get Savage because I didn't know him well enough to know how he'd handle a situation like this one. I couldn't call Rosemarie because she was probably fornicating with Leroy.

I only had one person I could call.

CHAPTER THIRTEEN

I answered the door with my gun in hand when Nick arrived. I hadn't explained things in detail over the phone. I was afraid he'd call in a uniform to come take a statement and that was the last thing I wanted. I'd just told him I needed help and that he needed to be discreet.

"What happened to your head?" he asked, shutting the door behind him.

I'd mostly gotten the bleeding stopped and I'd placed a giant ice bag on top of my head to help the knot go down.

"It got slammed into that wall over there." I pointed to the head sized dent in the wall and Nick took in the shattered picture. His eyes turned pure cop and then they focused back on me.

"Shit. This isn't a joke is it?"

I narrowed my eyes. "Of course it's not a joke. I told you I needed help."

"Yeah, but I thought you were just trying to get me over here to finish what we'd started earlier. Maybe next time you want to say you've been attacked. Christ, Addison. I could have called it in and already had a team here taking prints."

"Which is exactly why I didn't tell you. I can't report this to the police."

Nick ran his hand through his hair in frustration. "You want to run that by me again? Did someone break into your house and attack you or not?"

"Maybe you should let me explain and get off your high horse. My head is pounding."

"It looks like you're missing a little hair too."

I gasped and reached up to touch my head. Sure enough, there was a bald spot just above my ear. My eyes welled with tears and a couple leaked out before I could help it.

"I'm bald," I sniveled.

Nick went into panic mode at the sight of tears. "You're not completely bald. I bet a good hairdresser could fix it. Maybe you should sit down."

He led me to the dining room table and I sat in one of the hardback chairs, and I laid my head on the table and readjusted my ice pack while Nick went exploring through the house.

"What time did you get in?" he asked.

"A little after ten. There was a bad wreck on the highway so it took longer than it should have to get back from Savannah."

"Savage didn't walk you to the door?" Nick growled Savage's name and I could tell he was less than happy with Savage.

"My fault. I told him not to bother. The neighborhood watch is good about knowing who's coming and going. I already knew you'd been here to see me before I got to my front door."

"This guy slipped in the back. Tell me who he is and why I'm not putting out an APB on him."

I explained about Johnny Sakko and the police he supposedly had in his pocket. Also that Nick should keep his eyes out for a missing cop. His jaw clenched tighter at that but he didn't say anything. I also explained about the job Johnny wanted me to do for him to make up for the money he'd lost the night before. By the time I was finished Nick's lips were pressed tight and his eyes were cold as ice.

"How do you do it?" he asked. "I don't understand how things like this keep happening to you. It's amazing you've lived to the age of thirty." He rummaged around in my kitchen until he found a bottle of extra strength Tylenol. He set three of them down in front of me with a glass of water.

"I think maybe I've been cursed or something. Like maybe Veronica Wade sold her soul to the devil or one of those voodoo shamans and put a bad luck hex on me."

Veronica Wade was my archenemy and an all around supreme bitch. She'd been the one caught doing the nasty with my fiancé on our wedding day. That had been the icing on the cake on years and years of torture she'd hurled my way. I hadn't seen her since she'd sued me for damaging her person and causing her extreme distress when her breast implant popped during a doozy of a fight we had. My mom told me she'd heard Veronica had joined a convent in Miami to do a little soul searching. I don't know if I believed that. More than likely, Veronica was giving blow jobs in the confessional.

"Yes. I'm sure that's what happened," Nick said, rolling his eyes. "Or maybe it's just that you kamikaze through life without thinking first."

That was probably a better summation.

"Pack a bag. You can stay with me tonight and decide what you want to do tomorrow. I'll have someone come fix your window first thing in the morning."

I was too tired and too depressed to argue. Nick was providing a safe haven and I was going to take it. I grabbed my laptop and case files and tossed clean clothes and underwear into a duffle bag. I taped a note to the door for Savage letting him know something had come up and I wouldn't be able to run the next morning. With the way my head was pounding, I might not be running for another week or two.

Nick was silent on the way to his house. I had no idea what he was thinking. He hadn't given me a hug or any kind of sympathy. If he had, I would've broken down into tears, but still I was feeling a little unloved. Not that that wasn't to be expected. Nick had told me once that he *thought* he loved me. His feelings for me since then are a little ambiguous.

Twenty minutes later we pulled up in front of Nick's house and we shuffled inside. No one had followed us as we'd left my house. Nick had taken a couple of detours on the way to make sure.

I dropped my duffle in the foyer and headed toward the couch. I was done. All I needed was a flat surface to crash until morning. I didn't even care if it was a bed. I was too tired to walk up the stairs and to the guest room anyway.

"The bed's upstairs," Nick said.

"It's okay. The couch will do. Too tired."

Before I knew what was happening the world spun around me and I was cradled in Nick's arms. "I'm sorry he hurt you." He kissed my temple softly and then carried me up the stairs. I was too tired to argue so I just laid my head against his chest. On a normal day, I would have been impressed by his manly show of strength. Today, I was glad he still cared just a little. Fucking pathetic.

He walked past the room I'd stayed in previously and down to the end of the hall. My head was swimming and I hoped I wouldn't be sick. Nick laid me down on the bed and pulled my shoes off, and then he systematically undressed me until all I wore was my underwear. He pulled one of his T-shirts over my head, stuffed my arms in the sleeves and then covered me up to my chin.

I planned on telling him thanks, but I fell asleep before I could get the words out.

CHAPTER FOURTEEN

M*onday*

I WOKE the next morning to the sound of buzzsaws working away in my head and something hard prodding my backside. An arm was thrown over my waist and a hand cupped my breast. Since I'd woken up like this several times over the past months I wasn't completely alarmed, but it was still a little disconcerting considering the current standing of our relationship.

"You'd better still be asleep," I said, removing his hand from my breast.

He placed a kiss at the nape of my neck and moved his hand back. "How's your head?"

"It hurts like the devil."

"I don't suppose you've changed your mind about pressing charges. I've got a couple of guys I trust in vice I could hand this over to."

"Let me think about it."

"So just how bad does your head hurt?"

The nightstick pushing against my bottom flexed at the same time Nick did something magical with his fingers across my nipple. Probably an orgasm would help my headache go away. I read in a magazine once that orgasms cured a lot of ailments because of the endorphin rush.

"You're making things complicated," I said, moving away from the nightstick. My head swam when I sat up on the side of the bed and I put my head between my knees until the nausea passed.

"Not from where I'm standing. I'm trying to fix things. You're the one making things complicated."

"You're trying to fix things with sex. Sex always makes things complicated."

"Are you sure? Because I've always found it makes things a lot clearer. I'm thinking you should try things my way for once."

I grunted and moved toward the bathroom. We both knew it was only a matter of time before I gave in. My hope was I could get some kind of clue as to what Nick wanted out of a relationship before I let him unleash his nightstick.

I stood under the hot shower until I was pruny. Nick's hot water lasted a lot longer than mine. I washed my hair as carefully as possible and felt around the bump on my head. Then my fingers ran across the bald spot and I started crying again.

When I got out of the shower I found clean towels and my toiletry bag sitting on the countertop. I dressed in a pair of jeans and a red sweater that drew attention to my breasts instead of the bald spot on my head, and then I followed the smell of coffee. Nick handed me a cup as soon as I walked into the kitchen.

He'd used the other shower and his hair was still damp at the collar. He was dressed for work in gray slacks and a white button down shirt. His tie hung around his neck but wasn't tied yet.

"I want you to stay here for a while."

"How long?"

"I don't know. Maybe forever."

I bobbled my cup and spilled hot coffee on my hand. I cursed and sucked at the burn. "That seems like a remarkably bad idea."

"Give me a good reason why you shouldn't."

"Well, my mother would have a fit for one thing. Living in sin is right up there with getting drunk on the communal wine or using the pages of your bible to practice origami." Both of which I'd done, but I figured it was best not to mention it. "Also, we're not in a relationship. I don't need a roommate. It would make dating awkward."

"Not if you're not dating anyone else."

"Do you know how old I am?" My voice had risen in pitch with every word spoken. "Of course I'm going to date. You think I like being alone when all my friends are married and starting families. Do you think it's fun to know the chance I had at marriage disappeared like smoke because I have rotten taste in men?"

"You don't have rotten taste in all men. I'm a pretty good guy. I can do my own laundry, and I know just where to touch so you make those little sounds in the back of your throat. What more could you ask for?"

"The fact that you're even asking that is reason enough for me to decline your oh so generous offer." Talking to Nick was as good as bashing my head against the wall, though not quite as painful. I rinsed my cup in the sink and located my purse, laptop, and files.

"Going somewhere?"

"I need to go into the office and talk to Kate." It was then I remembered about Mr. Tannenbaum. I'd forgotten all about him with the excitement from the night before. "Anything new on finding Mr. Tannenbaum's murderer?"

"I questioned two of his step-children. The third is on a yacht somewhere down in the Keys. We're checking to make sure he was really there at the time of the murder. The two I questioned were well alibied for the night, but something is off there. They both denied knowing about the change in the will, but they were lying. They're the only ones I can see who have motive at this point. The killing was up close and personal, and whoever did it had a lot of rage."

"It seems pointless considering the man had only weeks to live anyway."

"Was that common knowledge?" Nick asked.

I shrugged. "I don't know."

"I've got to check in at the station." Nick rinsed his own cup and then strapped on his gun and clipped his badge to his belt. My mouth watered at the sight of him. Lord, that man was hot. "Take the Audi today." He took a set of keys from the hook and handed them to me. "And let me know the second you hear anything from Johnny Sakko. I can put some feelers out without sending out any signals. He's not someone you want to get tangled with."

"If he's so bad, why isn't he behind bars?"

"Nothing but circumstantial evidence. The FBI was running a tax evasion case against him but that went up in smoke too. Word is Sakko had the judge in his pocket. Just be aware of your surroundings and let me know if you need any help."

He kissed me goodbye with a lot of tongue and a couple of well placed gropes and then he was out the door. I took some more aspirin and then I put on eyeliner, mascara, and lip gloss. There wasn't much I could do about the hair so I pulled one of Nick's black toboggans down low over my ears so it covered the bald spot. I pulled on my Uggs and was out the door. The Cabriolet sat in the garage and the door was already up. It was black with black leather interior, and the wheels were solid black as well. It was a car the devil himself would drive.

I slid into the leather seat and breathed in deep. It smelled of leather and Nick and it hugged my butt like a glove. It made me miss my Z. I revved the engine and then backed out of the garage slowly until I got a good feel for the car. And then I sped down the long private road that led back to the highway.

Driving a car like this with a bald spot would be a sin, so I decided the first thing I needed to do was see if I could get a hair appointment somewhere. It would be a miracle if the hairdresser managed to cover up the bald spot and avoid the lump on my head, but I was willing to give the pain a shot for the sake of vanity.

It was barely nine o'clock by the time I got downtown, and the mall wasn't open yet. There was a little barbershop on Broughton Street that seemed to do a brisk business, so I headed that direction. I figured if customers kept going there they must not be all that bad.

I was in luck. An OPEN sign flashed in the window and I managed to find street parking. A woman named Jules greeted me at the door. She had piercings all the way up both ears and her hair was dyed pink and spiked in a Mohawk down the center of her head. She wore black leggings, a sweater that had moth holes eaten in it, and hot pink Chucks. And she didn't have an early morning appointment.

I kept my eyes closed the entire time she was cutting because I told myself I wanted to be surprised. She put some stuff on my scalp to help with the tenderness and amazingly enough the soreness around the lump and where my hair had been pulled out didn't hurt so bad anymore.

Snip, snip, snip went the scissors, and the weight of my hair became lighter and lighter.

"Cool," Jules said, cracking her gum and whipping off my cape. "You asleep?"

"Do I want to look?"

"It's going to be a shock. You had a lot of hair. You can only see the bald spot now if you pull it back. The layers cover it."

"That's good." No bald spot was what I came in for. If she accomplished that then I shouldn't care about the rest. Only I did care. How was I supposed to drive a sexy car around if I looked like I'd gotten a haircut from Edward Scissorhands? I cracked my eyes open one at a time and then stared at the stranger in the mirror.

The first thing I noticed was that my eyes were huge. More exotic. And my cheekbones were sharper. I looked edgier. If you could get over the fact that all my hair was laying on the floor and all that was left was a chin-length bob parted on the side.

I was so relieved I didn't have a matching Mohawk I almost wept. I wasn't hideous. I could drive Nick's car without slinking down low in the seat. I paid the girl and tipped her with my roll of quarters I'd been saving for emergency ice cream, and then I headed to Kate's a couple of blocks away.

I couldn't find street parking so I parked at the courthouse and cut across Telfair Park to get to the office. Lucy didn't bother to glance up when I walked in. She was too busy filing her blood red nails into sharp points.

It was early enough that there were still pastries on the sideboard. I grabbed an apple fritter as I made my way back to Kate's office.

"Whoa," Kate said as soon as she got a look at me. I went over to her Keurig and put in a pod for a cup of coffee.

"What do you think?" I asked.

"I like it. You look more sophisticated."

"Hmm...I was hoping for younger or sexier."

"Next time go for the shorn prostitute look. It worked for Anne Hathaway in Les Mis."

"If I remember right she looked neither younger nor sexier in that movie. I'm not sure the tuberculosis look is what I'm aiming for." I took the seat across from her desk and bit into my fritter. "You have anything new for me?"

"Because finding Tannenbaum's heir isn't enough for you to do?"

"I'm working on it. I've got a couple of people to talk to today. I was just hoping you had something extra. It's been a while since I've had a good adultery case."

"I've got one for you. I was going to give it to Carl since you're working the Tannenbaum case, but he's still not a hundred percent after his surgery. He's more use to me now doing computer work in house."

I took the file and stuffed it in my bag and then I filled Kate in on how things were going with finding Tannenbaum's heir. She stayed silent as I explained about Rose Parker and the son who didn't belong to her husband.

"You know what this job has made me realize?" I asked.

"That you're accident prone and have a tendency to daydream?"

"I knew all of that beforehand," I said, waving my hand in dismissal. "It makes me realize how rare a faithful marriage is. I don't even know why people bother anymore. Maybe I'd be better off forgoing the man altogether and just going to a sperm bank when I'm ready to have children."

"You've been watching Kathie Lee and Hoda again. I can always tell because you start talking about how you can do everything for yourself and you're responsible for your own orgasm kind of bullshit."

"Hmm." Maybe she was right. But I wasn't going to completely rule out the sperm bank if one day I woke up and was somehow almost forty and without a man. "How come when I do a background search on Nick nothing comes up?"

Kate snorted out a laugh. "Jesus. You tried to do a background on Nick?"

"He never talks about himself. I was just curious."

"Law enforcement officers have encrypted files. You don't have the clearance to pass through them. Whenever we're working a case against another cop I have to get a court order to dig very deep."

"Huh. Wish I'd known that ahead of time."

I grabbed my bag and waved bye to Kate, and then I headed back to the car to plan my next course of action. I had two possible heirs to check out. The first was a man named Norman Hinkle. He was in his early seventies and was an only child. He'd never married, and as luck would have it, he was a full-time resident of the Summer's Eve Assisted Living center.

My phone buzzed on the console and I remembered I'd turned it to silent when I'd gone to bed. Nick's number showed up in the caller ID so I answered.

"What's up?"

"A glass repairman will be by to fix your window in about twenty minutes. Can you meet him there?"

I looked at my watch and shuffled the things I had planned for the day around a bit. "Sure. Thanks for taking care of it."

"You can pack some more clothes while you're there. We found the cop you mentioned this morning. Or at least pieces of him. He worked property crimes. The good news is IAD had already been looking at him for being involved with Sakko. The bad news is we're going to have a hell of a time tying Sakko to this murder."

"Is this your case too?"

"I'm assisting. Homicides are up so we're all doing double duty. Be careful out there. This guy didn't die pleasantly."

"On that happy thought—"

"You want me to bring dinner tonight?" he interrupted.

Normally, I liked to cook. I've found it's a good way of relieving stress. But I'd be cutting it close if I got everything done on my list today.

"Sure. Surprise me."

I hung up and realized we'd had a normal conversation without any arguing or raised voices. Maybe my haircut *had* made me more mature.

I turned the car on and blasted the heater and then

punched buttons on the dashboard until I found the heater in the seat too. My buns were warm and tingly when my phone rang again. I used the Bluetooth in the car since I was pulling out into traffic. Nick was going to have a hard time getting this car back from me if he didn't take it soon. I was in love.

"Hello," I said.

There was no answer so I repeated it again.

"Hope you're having a good day. I like the haircut."

I recognized the voice. It belonged to Smash Nose. I slammed on the brakes and looked in my rearview mirror and then I looked on the sidewalks to see if I could spot him. My palms were sweaty and my heart rate had accelerated to dangerous levels.

"What do you want?"

"I just wanted to let you know you can't hide from Johnny Sakko. I watched your cop boyfriend help pick up the pieces of one of his colleagues this morning. It was real entertaining."

"You're sick." Cars were lined up and honking behind me so I drove a couple of times around Orleans Square.

"I just enjoy my work. Can't wait to see you again."

He hung up and I somehow managed to navigate my way back to my neighborhood. I'd known my share of fear over the last several months, but Smash Nose took the cake.

A pickup truck was waiting in front of my house when I pulled into the driveway and I got out and let the workman get busy on repairing my window. I couldn't see any of my neighbors since they were tucked away inside their houses, but I could feel several sets of eyes on me. I remembered Savage had the day off since he'd taken a long weekend, but I didn't see his SUV parked in the driveway.

I made myself a sandwich while I waited for the window and drank it down with another cup of coffee. I was thinking I should probably lay off the coffee a bit. My hands were shaky. Or it could have just been the terror.

The theme song from *Grease* made me jump and a little squeak might have escaped my mouth. The window repairman popped his head out of the bedroom with his eyebrows raised and I gave him a thumbs up before I answered the phone. It was Rosemarie and not another call from Smash Nose.

"Hey," I said.

"I need to go shopping and thought you might want to come with me. I might need an outsider opinion. I've got a hot date with Leroy and I want to make sure I knock his socks off."

I was thinking Rosemarie probably didn't have to worry about dressing special to knock Leroy's socks off. Leroy seemed pretty self-sufficient in getting himself in the mood.

"You don't have school today?"

"I called in sick. Leroy pretty much wore me out this weekend. It'll probably be Wednesday before I have the strength to go back and face all those teenagers."

I winced in sympathy. I remembered the feeling. You needed a *lot* of energy to deal with some of those kids.

"I don't know if I've got time to shop today. I need to follow up on a couple of things for a case I'm working on. Plus I don't have a lot of money to shop with."

After I paid my rent I'd have exactly a hundred and twelve dollars left to live on until I got an unemployment check. Kate paid me under the table every two weeks so I wouldn't have to give up my unemployment benefits and she wouldn't have to pay extra taxes, but that was a secret between the two of us. I wasn't due for another payment from Kate until the following Friday.

"I'll just come with you for whatever case you're working on and then we can go shopping afterward. It'll save time."

I was silent for a couple of seconds. Telling Rosemarie no about anything was the equivalent of kicking a small puppy. It was impossible to do. I sighed and knew I might as well give in.

"I'll pick you up in an hour. I'm waiting on a repairman at my house."

"What's the dress code today? Are we spying on adulterers? Should I wear my trench coat?"

"We're visiting the old folks' home. Just try to blend in."

I disconnected from Rosemarie and went to check my new hair out in the mirror again in hopes that it would brighten my spirits. The hair looked pretty good. But the rest of me needed an overhaul. I was sporting some monstrous bags under my eyes and my skin still had that clammy pallor of being scared shitless. I needed concealer. A lot of it. And maybe some ice cream.

I said goodbye to the window guy and got back in Nick's car. There was a Dairy Queen two blocks from our neighborhood so I went through the drive-thru and ordered a strawberry shortcake sundae since I felt like I needed the fruit to balance things out.

I'd perfected the art of driving and eating with a spoon by using my knees to steer, so I hit the highway and headed toward Whiskey Bayou. I'd been born and raised in Whiskey Bayou, and it was like the entire town was stuck in a time warp. Nothing ever changed. The street signs were all the same, the lone grocery store was still run by the same family, and the teenagers still went out to the swamp to make out.

I passed by the sign that said *Welcome to Whiskey Bayou, The First Drink's on us!* and crossed the bridge next to the railroad graveyard. Once I hit Main Street I immediately became the center of attention. There weren't very many people in Whiskey Bayou who drove expensive cars, and the one I was driving was unrecognizable so everyone watched as I passed by.

Mrs. Meador was washing the windows of The Good Luck Café and gave me a steely stare until she recognized me behind the wheel. Then her eyes widened and she pulled out her cell phone. I ducked down in the seat as I passed the fire station and then the whiskey distillery the town had been built around.

I meant to go straight to Rosemarie's, but I ended up turning into the residential area and heading toward my mom's house. I don't know why I did it. Familial guilt more than likely. My mother would no doubt get a phone call letting her know I'd been seen driving a fancy car through town, and then she'd get her feelings hurt if I didn't come to visit.

I parked in the driveway next to my mom's 1969 Dodge Charger that was an exact replica of the General Lee from the Dukes of Hazzard. She'd bought the car with the insurance money she'd gotten after my dad's death, and I was pretty sure she had stronger feelings for the car than she ever had for my dad. They'd loved each other in their own way, but my dad was pretty straight-laced about things and my mom...well...my mom was more of a free spirit forced to become a respectable member of the community once she married and gave birth to me and my sister.

I hadn't realized how much she'd been strangling under the weight of the whole respectability thing until recently. Her new husband, Vince, had been my dad's former partner and they'd known each other for years. My mom seemed happy, but I never knew what she was going to say or do, and it was like a total stranger had taken over her body.

My mom was standing with the door open by the time I got out of the car, and I knew she'd already received a phone call. She wore yoga pants, a red sport tank, and her hair was piled high on her head in a ponytail. If it wasn't for the few lines around her eyes we probably could've been mistaken for sisters.

"You're just in time for yoga and meditation," she said as I crossed the threshold into the house I'd been raised in.

It was a house filled with memories and one bathroom that had been the bane of my existence during high school. It smelled like whatever she'd managed to burn that morning for breakfast and lemons. My mother had never quite managed to learn how to cook. Fortunately, Vince had a cast iron stomach and was good about bringing home takeout.

"I'm in a rush so I'll have to pass on the yoga. I was just in the neighborhood, so I thought I'd drop by."

"Well, isn't that sweet. And look at you! You've done something different." My mother wasn't the most observant woman in the world. There were times when I was a child that she drove away from a store without me or my sister. Eventually she'd remember and come back to pick us up, but my mom wasn't so good with short term memory.

"I cut my hair."

"I see it now. You look older."

"How much older?" I'd almost rather deal with the bald spot that look older.

"Maybe older is the wrong word. More sophisticated. Like a real adult."

It made me wonder what the hell I looked like before. Though I guess I hadn't had a different hairstyle since my freshman year of high school.

"I just wanted to drop by and say hi."

"This is so exciting!" She clapped her hands and bounced on the soles of her cross trainers. "I get two surprises in one day. That doesn't happen very often."

I was just about to ask what the other surprise was when my sister Phoebe came out of from the back of the house where the bedrooms were.

"Oh, my God. I didn't know you were coming to town," I said, wrapping her in a hug.

The last time I'd seen Phoebe had been at my non-existent wedding. We'd celebrated my wedding night with several bottles of champagne, a wedding cake for 200 people, and a Nora Ephron marathon. Then she'd disappeared the next day with one of the groomsmen who traveled the country in his rock band, and I hadn't seen her since.

This was pretty normal for my sister. She'd inherited the free spirit gene from my mom. She'd also inherited a flaky gene because on her best day she could barely remember to tie her shoes, and time was more of a suggestion than an actual thing you were supposed to keep track of. When she wasn't being a rock band groupie she was a painter. Not the house kind but the artist kind. And she was good enough that some of her work was displayed in galleries, so I assumed she wasn't exactly a starving artist. She always managed to have sweet cars and funky clothes.

Phoebe pretty much looked exactly like me and my mom, only she had hot pink streaks in her waist length hair and she sported a tiny diamond stud in her nose. She wore jeans with the knees torn out and a Black Sabbath T-shirt that had paint spatter on it.

"Paul decided he didn't like the rocker lifestyle anymore, and I was getting antsy to paint for a while. I'm staying here until I can find a place to live. Maybe I'll look at some property in downtown Savannah. I've been thinking about having a permanent studio."

My mother's phone rang in the kitchen and she hurried off to answer it. I was sure it was someone else calling to let her know I was here.

"You've got to help me get out of here," Phoebe hissed as soon as my mom left the room. "I've been looking everywhere for an apartment, but I can't find anything. I don't think I can stay here another night. Mom and Vince are *loud*."

I winced because I knew exactly what she was talking about. I'd had the same experience of trying to sleep in my childhood bed while my mother and her lover went at it like animals in the next room. I'd rather have needles poked in my eyes rather than ever have to listen to that again.

"And when did she start wearing yoga pants and start getting all these crazy ideas? This morning she told me she's getting in shape so she can go to spy school and learn how to tango and make martinis. Is she on drugs?"

I actually didn't think the spy school idea was a bad one. I'd always wanted to learn how to tango. "Not that I know of. I think she's starting to find herself. Or maybe it's menopause."

"Well, whatever it is, it's creeping me out. If I ever get like that you should probably just shoot me."

I pressed my lips together and elected not to say anything. The three of us were cut from the same cloth. I didn't think menopause or drugs had anything to do with it. We just had lots of imagination and nowhere to use it.

Mom came back in and said, "That was Loretta Grueber. She just wanted to let me know she saw you drive through town. She wants to know if you're selling drugs since you're driving that car."

"It's not my car. I borrowed it from Nick."

Her face lit with joy at the mention of Nick. She *loved* Nick. Probably because she saw him as my last chance at a husband. And then her smile turned into a frown.

"Is Nick selling drugs? Your father was a cop for a lot of years, and he never had a car like that."

"It turns out he's independently wealthy."

"Oh, well then. That's convenient. You should invite him to dinner tomorrow night. Now that Phoebe's here it'll be nice to have a family meal with everyone at the table again. And it would be wonderful if you could find Phoebe a date too. I don't want her feeling like a fifth wheel."

I hmmmed noncommittally because I figured Nick wouldn't come to another dinner unless he was dragged kicking and screaming. The last time he'd been here he'd had to eat two helpings of burned Cornish game hens while he'd been asked what he thought his chances were of getting me pregnant.

"I hate to have to leave you girls since you just got here, but I've got a yoga class and I don't want to miss it."

"When did you start doing yoga classes?" I asked.

"About a month ago. I got a coupon in one of those booklets they send through the mail and I signed up for a whole year. I never realized yoga could be so empowering. I tried to get Vince to go with me, but he's shy about taking his clothes off in front of other people."

Her cheeks pinkened and she lowered her voice to a whisper, though I had no idea why since we were the only ones in the house.

"I guess I could understand why a man might not want to be naked out in public. It's not like they can hide it when they get affected, if you know what I mean. And he doesn't like to go anywhere without his gun, and there wouldn't be a place to put it now that I think about it."

"Why in God's name would Vince have to take his clothes off?" Phoebe asked.

"Because it's naked yoga. They turn the heat up in the room to about a hundred degrees and everyone strips down to what God gave us. It's a very spiritual experience. And by the end you've got sweat dripping from places best left unmentioned so it's not like it's sexual in any way. You hardly even notice you're naked. Though I've started getting there early so I don't have to put my mat next to Leon Gardello. He's got bushy black hair on every square inch of his body and his balls hang clear down to his knees. I've never seen them that big before. Makes me wonder how he sits down. It's distracting."

Phoebe grabbed my hand and started squeezing. "I think I have to go now," I said, backing toward the door. "I've got to pick up Rosemarie and do some legwork on a case."

"I'll come with you." Phoebe was desperate. She grabbed her purse and we both hustled out to the car before we could be scarred any more by the visual images my mother had a talent of painting.

"Christ, I need a drink," Phoebe said once we got in the car. "I've got to find another place to live. I'm having a car delivered today so I can start looking around the city."

"You really want to move to Savannah? I thought you hated it here."

"I don't know," she shrugged. "I'm getting older and I've decided there probably isn't a man out there for me. I've tried a lot of them on for size. In the books that's always what happens when you get old and your body starts to shrivel. You move back home so you can die where your family is. That way they don't have to spend a lot of money shipping your body back home."

"It's been a while since I've seen you, but you don't look all that shriveled to me." Phoebe looked like a badass in her ripped jeans and concert T-shirt. She was a couple of inches shorter than me and she had an intricate tattoo on her muscled biceps.

"Sometimes my knees pop when I go up the stairs now. It's fucking depressing."

"You're welcome to stay at my place until you find something. I have an extra bedroom." Though once I mentioned it I regretted issuing the invitation. My house wasn't exactly a safe haven as of late.

"I'd appreciate it. I won't stay but a couple of days. Only until I can find a place of my own."

I headed to the other side of town where Rosemarie's duplex was located and I honked the horn once I pulled in front.

"Holy mother of God," I thought I heard Phoebe whisper.

Rosemarie barreled out of the house in a lavender jogging suit and white tennis shoes. The pants were so tight her camel toe had a camel toe, and I wouldn't be surprised if the zipper of her jacket didn't leave teeth marks on her skin. Her hair was curled in tight Shirley Temple spirals and her eyes were lined with dark purple liner.

I realized we had a problem as soon as she reached the car. There was no way Rosemarie was fitting in the back seat, so Phoebe crawled into the back and Rosemarie dropped down into the seat next to me. I introduced Rosemarie to Phoebe and by the time we made it out of Whiskey Bayou and to Summer's Eve Assisted Living, the two of them had compared tattoos and Rosemarie was considering getting a nose ring.

I checked myself in at the gate and parked to the side of the house again.

"This place is creepy as shit," Phoebe said. "I might need to paint it. But maybe I'll add zombies. And more blood." Phoebe's art was an acquired taste.

Vicki answered the door for us again. "Welcome back to SEAL," she said smiling. "I didn't know you were coming back. Did you bring your grandmother with you this time."

"No, but I brought my sister along." Vicki's eyes kind of bugged out of her head when she got a good look at Rosemarie, so when she was faced with Phoebe and pink hair and a nose ring she looked almost relieved. "We'd love to do another walk-through and maybe talk to some of the residents to see how they like it. We just want our grandmother to have the best experience she can in her remaining years."

Phoebe absorbed my lie as if it were truth without batting an eyelash. I was a pretty good liar, but Phoebe was champion. I'd pretty much been the good girl of the two of us growing up. I was the honor student and the one who never managed to get away with anything without getting caught. I'd tried being bad. Really I had. I just wasn't terribly good at it.

Phoebe, on the other hand, was the wild child. She was two years older than me and was Miss Popularity. She spent more time in detention than in the classroom, and she *never* got caught sneaking out of her bedroom in the middle of the night to go meet her boyfriend or smoking in the bathroom at school. I'd always wanted to be just like Phoebe when I was growing up, but now that she was having problems with creaky knees I was starting to rethink my goals.

We made our way to the activity room and it was then I realized why Rosemarie had dressed like she had. I'd told her to fit in and that's exactly what she'd tried to do, though I wasn't sure Rosemarie really fit in anywhere. At least four other old women were wearing the exact same lavender jogging suit as Rosemarie, their hair rolled in tight curls on top of their head. It was good to know that Rosemarie took the whole sidekick thing seriously.

I found Deloris back at the ping-pong table talking trash to a different man who seemed to be holding his own pretty well against her. Deloris took her ping-pong seriously and I didn't want to interrupt. Mostly I was scared of Deloris. The last time I'd visited and we'd partaken of a couple of bottles of wine, she'd showed me the knife she kept strapped in her garter. I didn't want to give her cause to use it, so I waited until the match was finished.

"Do you know where we can find Norman Hinkle?" I asked her.

"What do you want with old Norm? He get into trouble again? Norm likes to lift things from the sundries shop over in the lobby. Sticks them right down the front of his pants. When he first moved in here he had to fight the women off with a stick. Then they figured out he didn't have much down there but Slim Jims and those little bottles of wine."

I saw Phoebe's mouth drop open out of the corner of my eye. Phoebe had a lot of life experience, but she had no experience when it came to my life. I was an experience all by myself.

"It's not nice to deceive ladies like that," Rosemarie said, shaking her head. "Men have it easy. They pretty much know what a woman's going to look like with her clothes off right off the bat. We women have to wait until that critical moment when the clothes come off to know whether the man is going to be worth anything. It's not like you can just get up and leave if he doesn't have much to speak of."

"It'll get easier as you get older," Deloris said. "I don't have time to waste on those little ones. I could die tomorrow. That's not the last memory I want to take with me. But I gotta tell you, after they get to a certain age those special parts shrink a little unless they've got professional help. Myron Wilkes over there has one of them pumps. He pumps that pecker twenty-four hours a day. It's not natural. And if you sit next to him during dinner all you can do is watch his napkin go up and down in his lap. It's damned hard to enjoy a pot roast with that kind of distraction."

"I can see how hard that would be." Rosemarie was wide-eyed and nodding furiously. "I'd hate for anything to distract me from a pot roast."

"This time of day Norm's probably out in the greenhouse. He's a horticulturist. Or at least he was before he retired. He's got a real green thumb. We all have beautiful fresh arrangements in our room because of Norm."

I thanked Deloris and we all followed her pointed finger to the French doors that led into the garden, and what I assumed, would eventually lead to the greenhouse.

"This place is pretty nice," Phoebe said. "I could live here. And it looks like they get good light through the windows. You think there's an age limit?"

"I've got a pamphlet at my house. I'll let you look at it."

The gardens were beautiful. There were lots of evergreen shrubs, and the red roses and white chrysanthemums were in full bloom. A couple of huge weeping willows provided shade for anyone who wanted to sit at the picnic tables and a cobblestone pathway curved like a serpent toward the greenhouse.

I knocked on the door first and then stuck my head inside. The heat and humidity immediately dampened my face and I was afraid to see what it would do to my new hair.

"Yoohoo," I called out. "Mr. Hinkle?"

"Close the door! You'll kill them." He mumbled something else, but I couldn't make out what it was. I assumed the person yelling at us was Mr. Hinkle, so we shuffled inside and closed the door.

"Holy shit," Phoebe whispered.

I realized why she'd said it once I got a good look around. I'd never seen so many marijuana plants in one place before. Summer's Eve Assisted Living had a hell of a crop. I pushed plants aside as I made my way to the back of the building.

"Mr. Hinkle?"

"You still here? You're interruptin' my work schedule."

The closer I got to the voice behind the plants the more I realized what kind of work Mr. Hinkle was doing. The smell of weed was so strong my eyes watered and I got a little light headed.

Norman Hinkle was sitting on a stool, hidden behind his precious plants like a lazy jungle cat. He wore a plaid button down shirt in green and orange, a pair of khaki shorts, brown dress socks pulled up to his knees, and loafers. Round glasses were perched on his nose and they were fogged from the smoke of his joint. He was bald except for a fringe of wiry gray hair over his ears.

"My name is Addison Holmes. Do you mind if we join you for a bit?"

"It's a free country. Pull up a stool."

There were old wooden crates against the wall and we each grabbed one and made a circle with Mr. Hinkle. My eyes widened as he passed the joint to Rosemarie. Her Shirley Temple curls looked like they'd been attacked by mutants and frizzed around her flushed face. She stared at the joint for a couple of seconds, shrugged, and then put it to her lips and inhaled. She immediately went into a fit of coughing and Hinkle pounded her on the back.

"You gotta pace yourself, girl. This is the good stuff. You see this plant here?" We all turned as one and looked at the plant. Hinkle was touching the leaves like he'd caress a lover. It had purple blooms and sat in a ceramic pot that said Doris painted on the front.

"This is purple haze. But sshhhh...it's a myth. It's supposed to be extinct, but I'm crafty like that. I've been cultivating this baby since 1969. Doris never fails me."

Rosemarie took another puff and passed the joint to Phoebe. I was having trouble remembering why I was even here. This was like my worst nightmare come to life. I'd never actually done marijuana before. I was always the girl at the parties everyone made fun of because I wouldn't try it, but I figured I had enough problems stumbling through life without adding pharmaceuticals to the mix.

"I'd like to ask you a little bit about your mother, Rose Hinkle," I started.

"Oh, yeah? She's dead. Been dead for almost sixty years. Shot herself in the bathtub when my daddy ran off with her best friend. The realtor said she was real considerate because the cleanup was pretty simple. Took awhile to sell the house though because no one wanted to live in a place where a woman shot herself. I thought it gave it character."

Mr. Hinkle had obviously been spending way too much time with his plants. He talked about his mother's suicide like he would a grocery list. Or maybe he was just too relaxed to care.

"Umm..." I wasn't quite sure what to say next, but Phoebe caught my attention. She took a quick puff and passed it on to me. Phoebe had never particularly cared for marijuana, but she was the girl who'd do just enough so everyone could see she fit in. Phoebe never got made fun of.

I took the joint from her and stared at it. Then I looked up and met three stares. "I...umm...I had to quit. It makes me paranoid." And then I passed it back to Hinkle. I mentally thunked myself in the head and rolled my eyes. It was high school all over again. And I pretty much hated high school.

"Why do you want to know about my mama?" he asked.

I told him about Doc Neeley and that there was a possibility his father wasn't really his father. He seemed intrigued but not altogether surprised. When I told him about the money he agreed to take a DNA test to see if there was a paternity match with Mr. Tannenbaum.

"You got any chips?" Rosemarie asked after another puff. Her makeup had wilted a bit and her mascara was smudged under her eyes.

"Nope. They get stuck in my dentures. Besides, it's about snack time. They got a real nice spread inside. Too bad y'all don't live here. You could have a snack."

"I'm thinking about moving in," Rosemarie said.

"Let me know if you do. I'll share my Slim Jims with you."

WE SHUFFLED BACK to the car, Rosemarie and Phoebe giggling the whole way. I hadn't done anything wrong, but I was the one paranoid that a cop was going to pop out and ask us what we'd been up to.

"You know what we need?" Rosemarie said. "We need a snack time like they've got at SEAL. I'm pretty hungry. I'd like some nachos. Or maybe one of those chocolate dipped bananas with the sprinkles on top."

"Nachos sound pretty good," Phoebe said. "It'd be even better with a margarita."

"Now you're talkin' my language." Rosemarie and Phoebe booty-bumped and then got in the car.

I drove us all to a Mexican restaurant on the outskirts of town that had low lighting and plastic tablecloths. The floor was sticky and it was probably best it wasn't too easy to see, but they had the best salsa around and margaritas so strong it would kill any germs.

"You gotta relax, Addison," Rosemarie said, cramming tortilla chips in her mouth like it was her last meal.

"I've been telling her that for years." Phoebe sucked down her margarita and then ordered another. "She's always afraid she's going to get into trouble with the police. Pot is legal now, you know."

"Not in the state of Georgia," I said. "You've been hanging with the west coast crowd too much."

"I sometimes forget that this place is like Mayberry." She took another sip and looked a little forlorn. "This conversation is totally putting a damper on my high. Can we talk about something else now? Like root canals or pelvic exams?"

"Maybe you should stay away from the pot," I said. "It makes you a real Debbie Downer."

Big tears welled in Phoebe's eyes. "I know," she cried, slapping both hands over her face. "I don't want to be a Debbie Downer." She was sobbing in earnest now and other people were starting to look in our direction. "I want to be a Susie Sunshine. But I'm a criminal. I've been trying to be good and be more like you. And now I smoked pot in Mayberry and I'm going to go to jail." Her voice had escalated to a high-pitched whine.

"You're not going to go to jail," I said, starting to panic. I didn't do well with tears.

"Yeah, Addison's not going to let you go to the pokey," Rosemarie said. "She's got an in with them now that she's sleeping with a grade A hunk of detective."

"We're not sleeping together. Not exactly."

"Well, that's your problem right there. No wonder you've got such a stick up your ass about doing a little recreational smoking."

"Excuse me?" I said, eyes narrowing. I was almost positive I didn't care for a high Rosemarie. She was a mouthy broad.

"I think you should do something dangerous and illegal so Nick has to arrest you. Then you can do it in the back of the police car. I saw a porno like that one time. Only it turns out the woman he arrested was really a transvestite and she had dangly bits under her skirt."

Phoebe had stopped crying and she and I were staring at Rosemarie with our mouths open.

"I think maybe my Leroy might've spent some time in the big house. He seems to know a lot of things a more law abiding man wouldn't." Rosemarie got a faraway look in her eyes that had nothing to do with the pot and everything, I was afraid, to do with her sexual experience with Leroy.

"How come no one told me you were dating a detective?" Phoebe asked.

"We broke up. Besides, it's complicated."

"The best things always are."

I paid the check with some of the money Nick had given me and left a generous tip considering the conversation our waiter had been privy too. He still looked shell-shocked.

"Please don't take me back to Mom's," Phoebe said, before we got up to leave. "I can't take another night like the one I had last night. She and Dad were never so... vigorous. It's embarrassing."

I bit my lip and worried about putting Phoebe up in my house for a while. Johnny Sakko could use her to get to me. On the other hand, if it was me in Phoebe's position, I'd take a chance on death just to not have to listen to my mom having sex in stereo. What I *could* do is ask Savage and the neighborhood watch to be more vigilant while she was there.

"Okay, but you're not going to have room to paint."

"That's okay. Being back home has pretty much dried up my creative juices. I think I need an exorcist."

"Maybe you should try naked yoga. It sounds like that might get your juices flowing just fine."

CHAPTER FIFTEEN

I dropped Rosemarie home and swung by my mother's house so Phoebe could grab her suitcase and leave a note that she was staying with me for a couple of days.

We drove back to my place in silence. Phoebe was asleep in the passenger seat and I was thinking about the final potential heir on my list. I looked at the clock and wondered if I still had time to make a visit to Jacksonville and visit Walter Price. Probably not. But I could leave the next morning and be back home before I had to show up at my Mom's for dinner.

I pulled into the driveway of my house and saw a green Jaguar parked at the curb. I remembered the night before that Spock had said a woman in a green Jaguar had stopped by. It looked like she was back.

I nudged Phoebe awake and we got out of the car and headed to the front door. My brows raised in surprise when Nick's mother got out of the green Jag and met us at the porch.

"Mrs. Dempsey," I said.

"Ms. Holmes." Her gaze landed on Nick's car and her

eyes turned to steel. "I assume you can find time in your schedule to meet with me?"

"I've got a few minutes."

Phoebe's brows raised at the open hostility, but she didn't say anything. I put the key in the lock and had my other hand on the gun in my purse. I was a little nervous about going inside after what happened the night before. I felt eyes on me and looked over to see Spock looking out his window with his binoculars.

I didn't feel a disturbance in the force after we crossed the threshold, so I left Mrs. Dempsey cooling her heels in the living room while I showed Phoebe where to put her stuff. When I came back out Mrs. Dempsey was sitting at one of the bar stools looking through her purse.

"My time is valuable, Ms. Holmes, so I'd prefer we get this finished quickly. You obviously have some sort of plans for trapping my son into marriage, but I can assure you that's not going to happen. Nicholas is the heir to one of the oldest and wealthiest families in Savannah. You might be fun to play with, but you're certainly not long term material. Now what's your price?"

She had her checkbook open and her pen poised and ready to write a lot of zeroes. I bided my time by making myself a cup of coffee and wishing I'd bought an extra praline at the restaurant. I needed a hit of sugar.

"This seems like a conversation you need to be having with Nick," I said. "I don't want your money."

"Oh, believe me, I'll be having a long discussion with my son. Will fifty thousand do? Who shall I make the check out to?"

I almost choked on my coffee at the amount. It was more than my yearly teacher salary, that was for sure. Phoebe chose that moment to come back in and I could tell she had no problems with eavesdropping on the conversation.

"Like I told you, Mrs. Dempsey. I'm not interested in your money. Nick and I aren't even really dating. We work together if you want to know the truth."

"I seriously doubt the truth is anything you're familiar with. I could see the way he looks at you."

I walked back to the front door and opened it for her, hoping she'd get the hint, but she just stared at me with that steely gaze.

"My sister is here visiting, and we have an appointment this afternoon," I fibbed.

Phoebe put on her company smile and came the rest of the way into the room. "I'm Phoebe," she said. "And your plastic surgeon is just fabulous, darlin'. But you might want to have him take another nip the next time you see him. You're sagging around the eyes a bit."

Mrs. Dempsey sucked in a breath and two splotches of color appeared on her cheeks. I had to bite my lip to keep from laughing. This was why I loved my sister. She didn't take shit from anyone. And when she was around she did a hell of a job looking out for her baby sister. The problem was it was like the blind leading the blind.

Mrs. Dempsey tucked her clutch under her arm and walked past me and out onto the porch. "I'll not make another offer."

"It'll save us both time then," I said.

"You realize my husband and I can make a lot of trouble for you, Ms. Holmes?"

"You're going to have to get in line. Trouble is my middle name." I shut the door in her face and turned back to Phoebe.

"What a bitch," she said. "Do you have an X-Box?"

"No. I have a box of crossword puzzles and Pictionary somewhere in the top of the closet." I went to collect my coffee cup and realized my heart was pounding like crazy. "I think I need to lay off the coffee. I'm getting heart palpitations."

"I'm pretty sure that woman would give anyone palpitations."

"I've got some more work to do this afternoon. How are you going to get around if you need to leave?"

"I just called the rental place and told them to deliver the car here instead of Mom's. My car won't be here until next week. I did one of those customized car orders on the Internet. Apparently, they're having to ship it from somewhere in Oregon."

"You ordered a car on the Internet?" I asked.

"Yeah, I got to customize it and everything. My initials are even going to be embroidered on the seats."

I was guessing the painting business was going better than the private investigator business.

"I'm going to go take a nap. Weed makes me sleepy. I'm out of practice. Haven't done it since college."

"It might not have been such a good time to start up again."

"I figured once wouldn't hurt. I'm an artist. I'm supposed to be on drugs. It would ruin the image if people knew I wasn't. Perception is half the battle."

I wasn't sure which half of the battle she was referring to, but clearly Phoebe had her life figured out. I couldn't say the same. Phoebe was the kind of person who was usually underestimated. She was really smart, but the artistic side of her lended itself well to general flakiness and living in her own world all the time. No one ever questioned it when Phoebe did something the tiniest bit stupid. It was just artistic temperament.

There was a knock at the door and before I could answer it Nick came in and closed the door behind him.

"Leaving the doors unlocked?" he asked.

"I just had an unexpected visitor. I forgot to lock it back."

He looked like he'd put in a hard day. The sleeves of his shirt were rolled up and his tie was stuffed in his shirt pocket. He froze when he saw Phoebe and raised his brows in question.

"This is my sister, Phoebe. She's staying here a while. Phoebe, this is Nick."

Phoebe let out a long whistle. "Is this the cop you're not sleeping with? Because I have to say that's probably a mistake."

"That's what I've been trying to tell her," Nick said.

"Both of your opinions are duly noted. What are you doing here?"

"I brought Chinese."

"Then you can stay."

Nick looked at Phoebe again and he deflated a little bit. I could tell she'd definitely put a kink in his plans. By the smug smile on her face, I could tell she knew it.

"Was your visitor Johnny Sakko's man?" The question was casual but I could tell he was in full cop mode.

"No, your mother. She's a lovely woman. Really."

Nick smiled and dumped a bunch of plastic bags on the dining table. "How much did she try to offer you to leave me alone?"

"Fifty thousand."

"Good job holding out for more. She offered my first wife five times that."

"Whoa," I said, eyes widening at that bit of information. "You never told me your first wife left you because your mother paid her off."

"It didn't seem like a good conversation starter."

"This is pretty exciting stuff, but I'm going to crash," Phoebe said. "It was good to meet you, Nick. You're a much better choice than that asshole she was going to marry. Have you thought of seducing her with ice cream? I've seen her do a lot of things when ice cream is involved."

Nick opened up one of the plastic sacks he brought in and pulled out a pint of Haagen Daas chocolate ice cream. "That was my hope."

"I'll put my headphones on in case you two kids can't control yourself." Phoebe headed to the guest room and closed the door behind her.

"I like your sister," Nick said, opening up cartons of Chinese. I got a couple of plates and joined him at the table. "But I think she's doing drugs. It smells like pot in here."

I pulled my shirt up to sniff it and realized he was right. I reeked of pot. "It's a long story. I'll explain it to you some day."

"So how good do you think her headphones are?"

"Not that good or she'd still be staying with my mom and Vince."

Nick's shoulders shook with laughter. "Vince for the win. I want to be just like him in thirty years."

"It's not funny. Do you know how embarrassing it is to know your mother is having more sex than you are?"

"We can remedy that at any time. And I'm a desperate man. I'm to the point I don't really care who's listening."

"Hmm." I grabbed a couple of beers from the fridge and we dug into the food. "How are things going in the world of law and order?" I asked.

"They've been better. We still don't have a murder weapon for the Tannenbaum case. I've got a muddy footprint in a size 12 athletic shoe and the housekeeper says there are things missing from his personal desk. A couple of rare coins, a sweater that he kept over the back of his chair that he used when he got cold, and an umbrella from the stand just by the front door. The place had been ransacked pretty good, so she's not sure if anything else is missing. His papers were scattered all over his desk and office and she didn't have access to them so she wasn't able to tell us if anything was missing there."

"No one saw him leave the house?"

"The weather's been bad. No one's out on the street when we have storms like we have been. The medical examiner is putting time of death between ten P.M. and midnight. The alarms were turned off. We think Tannenbaum opened the door for his killer since there was no sign of forced entry."

"No one else was in the house?"

"He doesn't have live in staff. He has a housekeeper and cook that come in daily and various outdoor staff for his yard and the pool in the back. What about you? Any word from Sakko?"

I told him about my phone call from Smash Nose and that he had someone watching me. Nick's mouth tightened and I caught a flash of anger in his eyes before he damped it down. Nick knew how to keep hold of his temper.

"Smash Nose has a name," Nick said. "I did a little checking today after you described him to me. His name is Anthony Franco, but everyone knows him as Tony Hatchet. You want to stay far away from him. There's a reason he has that nickname." I shuddered and drank down the rest of my beer. Nick leaned back in his chair and crossed his hands over his abs. "He did some boxing during some time spent in prison, which explains the nose."

"What was he in prison for?"

"He got caught with a stolen car. Not only that, but there was a trash bag in the trunk that held various body parts. The murder charge didn't stick, but he spent a year in the cage for the stolen car and for assaulting an officer when he was arrested. He's managed to not get caught ever since then, but we've looked at him several times for various things. I don't like that he's got eyes on you."

"I'm not exactly thrilled either."

We cleared the table and loaded the dishwasher. I'd just closed the dishwasher when Nick came up behind me and pressed me into the counter. He kissed the back of my neck and I could tell he was *very* happy to be kissing me.

"I don't suppose I can talk you into pretending your sister isn't here." His teeth nipped at the sensitive spot just under my ear and my eyes crossed with the pleasure. His hands were becoming very involved under my sweater.

"That probably wouldn't be a good idea. Besides, I've got some work to do tonight. Speaking of, would you mind if we traded cars? It's not exactly a good car to be invisible in."

He sighed and gave me his truck keys and took back the keys to the Cabriolet. "I'm going to need the truck for work in the morning, so stop by on your way home and we'll trade back." A long, silent look passed between us and I licked my lips. The tension was thick and I could almost taste the anticipation of what that one smoldering look promised.

He let himself out since I was pretty much frozen to the spot, and I looked down and noticed my nipples were as hard as rocks. I knew for a fact if I went to Nick's house again tonight under the pretense of trading cars that I wouldn't be walking out of there until the next morning. And I'd probably be walking bowlegged at that. Nick had that effect on a woman.

CHAPTER SIXTEEN

I grabbed a quick shower and changed into clothes that didn't smell like cannabis. My head was still tender so I took some more aspirin, but my hair looked great. If I ever saw Jules again I might be tempted to kiss her square on the mouth.

My plans were to do some early surveillance on the new case file I'd picked up from Kate. We'd been hired by a guy named Hugh Mathis who was convinced his wife, Carly, was cheating on him. Truth be told, Hugh was probably correct in his assumptions. In my experience, once the spouse moved from denial and started looking at the clues, the signs of adultery were usually there. By the time they hired us, they knew what was going on and just wanted the proof.

I put on jeans and I tucked a stretchy black long-sleeved T-shirt into the waistband and added a black belt. I knew from experience I might end up climbing trees or hanging from rooftops, so I passed on the Uggs and laced up my black sneakers. I grabbed a black zip up hoodie and a raincoat just in case and headed back into the kitchen.

My gun was in my purse along with other tools of the trade that came in handy on occasion. I was ready to roll.

Nick's truck was big and black with bug-eyed headlights and lots of buttons and other things on the dashboard that didn't come in normal cars. I knew he had a Kojak light in there somewhere, and if I could have found it I would have used it just to see what it was like.

Carly worked at a Chase bank over in Thunderbolt, and it said in her paperwork she had step aerobics every Monday and Thursday after work at the local gym. I could catch her there if I hurried.

I saw Spock looking out the window and went over to talk to him before I left. He had the door open for me before I could knock.

"Who's the new girl?" he asked. "Does she like Dr. Who?"

"My sister is staying with me for a couple of days. I have no idea if she likes Dr. Who, but you should ask her." If Phoebe spent time hanging out with Spock I wouldn't have to worry about her while I was gone. "Can you do me a favor and keep an eye on my place? I had a break-in last night. I'm afraid someone will come back."

Spock sucked in a deep breath and his eyes that never blinked seemed to get bigger until I thought they were going to pop right out of his head. "NO," he exclaimed. "It can't be. I was on watch last night and I saw no one. I can't have failed. I'll be open for challenges. I had to fight hard to win my place as president."

"You had to fight?" I knew I shouldn't have asked, but the words had already left my mouth.

"Oh, yes. This is a very coveted position. Agent Savage graciously bowed out of the fights because obviously he was our first choice as leader. But he already has too many commitments saving the world, so the torch fell to me. I almost didn't make it though. Mrs. Rodriguez gets awfully violent with that walker."

His eyes were rolling around until I was starting to feel dizzy. I know he had lids. Every person had to. But I'd yet to see them. "There was nothing you could've done. The person came through the backyard and broke a window."

"That explains it. Your backyard is a blind spot for me. You should consider taking down your fence." He snapped his fingers and pulled a giant Android phone from his pocket. "I know just who to call. My friend Walter lives in the house directly behind yours. He's got a second story. I'll have to deputize him for the night."

"I'd appreciate it." And I'd remember to make sure my blinds were closed in my bedroom from now on.

I went back to the truck and dialed Savage for backup. Spock was good in the nosy department, but he didn't really have the muscle to back it up.

"You owe me big time," Savage said when he answered the phone. "Spock showed up for the workout you ditched this morning. I don't suppose you want to explain that?"

"He wants to get in shape. I figured you'd save time by doing both of us together."

"You just don't want to be alone with me because you're afraid you're going to give in."

"That too. I have a favor to ask."

"Does it involve Spock?"

"No, it involves my sister. I had a break-in last night." I explained what had happened with Tony Hatchet the night before and how I was supposed to keep the police out of it when he contacted me for the job he wanted me to do.

"You should have called me first instead of Dempsey. I'm in a better position to help you. And we don't have as many leaks. I heard about the cop that was found this morning. You need to be careful."

"So I've been told. I'm out doing a job for Kate, but I'd appreciate it if you could keep a closer watch around the neighborhood while my sister is there. I don't want her getting caught in the middle."

"Got it covered." He disconnected and I stopped at a four-way light getting ready to turn on Victory. I was in the right hand lane and there was someone in a blue Toyota in front of me who didn't believe in turning right on red. I honked a couple of times but they didn't move. And then all of a sudden the passenger door was jerked open and Smash Nose slid into the truck with me.

He had a gun in his hand and a duffle bag at his feet. The car in front of me moved forward. "Follow the car while we have our little chat."

The spit had dried up in my mouth and I had a hard time concentrating on the road with the gun pointed at me.

"You have a lot of cops in your life. I hope you've been keeping our talks to yourself. I'd hate for your detective or FBI friends to end up like the cop they found this morning. Johnny isn't too fond of the boys in blue."

I was pretty sure the boys in blue weren't too fond of Johnny. "I haven't told anyone. What do you want?" Sometimes I was impressed with my ability to look like I was staying cool under pressure, but I was sweating like a pig under my hoodie.

"You're going to go to the extended hours care clinic

over on Bayonette and you're going to take this duffle bag with you."

I knew which clinic he was talking about. It wasn't in the best part of town. It was a low roofed white brick building that treated a lot of meth heads and prostitutes that got on a john's bad side. It was the area of Savannah no one liked to admit existed and where cops frequently patrolled, not that it did a lot of good.

"When you get there, you're going to go up to the check-in station and you're going to say, "I'm here to see Doctor Blackbeard. I have the shingles again."

"But aren't they going to know I'm lying since I don't have shingles?"

"Don't worry about it. Just make sure you say it exactly how I told you to. They'll take it from there. You're going to give this bag to Blackbeard and he's going to give you a briefcase in return. If you look in either of the bags you're going to become intimate friends with my hatchet."

I blacked out for a second and had to swerve around a car to keep following the Toyota.

"What do I do with the briefcase?"

"I'll let you know once you have it. We'll be watching." The Toyota pulled into the right hand lane at another stoplight and I pulled behind it. Tony hid his gun back in his jacket pocket and put his hand on the door handle.

"Wait! If I do this, am I off the hook with Johnny?"

"If you do this without screwing up, he'll put you on the payroll so you can work off the debt. If you screw it up I'll be back to visit and I'll bring along my favorite toy. I saw your sister this afternoon. It's been a while since I've done a twofer."

Smash Nose smiled, flashing a gold tooth. He had soulless eyes, so even when he smiled, I couldn't see anything inside that gave me hope for getting out of this mess. He got out of the truck, walked up to the blue Toyota, and got inside. They sped away and I was left sitting there in a daze. A horn blared behind me and I automatically put the truck in motion.

I checked the time and circled around so I could hit Bayonette without hitting all the town traffic. I'd missed my window of opportunity to check out Carly Mathis. I'd have to get her another day.

It was getting dark and the streetlights were flickering on. At least the ones that hadn't been shot out. The buildings on this side of town were ramshackle at best—a lot of rusted tin siding and broken out windows. There was a 7-11 that had bars on all the windows and I'd been told the clerk kept a sawed off shotgun under the counter. He liked to shoot first and ask questions later. It was probably a smart philosophy to go by.

I don't know if God was on my side today or what, but a parking space opened up on the opposite side of the street from the clinic and I moved into position to parallel park. The problem was I wasn't such a good parallel parker on a good day with a small car. I was even worse in a truck. It was like docking a boat.

By the time I was finished a couple of homeless men sitting on the sidewalk were staring at me wide-eyed. I got out and surveyed the job. The back tire was up on the curb and I'd knocked over a trashcan.

"Better watch out, lady," one of the homeless men cackled. "You knocked over Harry's house. He's gonna be pissed."

"Harry lives in a trashcan?" I asked.

"Sure does. He likes it because he gets first dibs when people throw their food away. Harry's pretty smart like that."

"Where is Harry?" I looked up and down the street. There was a drug deal taking place in the alley up ahead and a hooker was working the corner behind me. I didn't see anyone that might resemble a Harry.

"Sometimes Harry likes to hump things. He's got a sickness. It's not natural."

"You better hope Harry never finds out you said that," the other homeless guy said. "I seen him hump a man to death before. Harry gets goin' and he doesn't know how to stop. If he finds out you knocked over his house he'll probably hump you too."

I wrinkled my nose in disgust and hiked the duffle bag on my shoulder. I locked the car, not that that would keep anyone from stealing it in this neighborhood, and hoped God was still hanging with me long enough to keep watch over Nick's car.

I looked both ways before I crossed the street and entered the clinic. The doors were propped open with cement blocks. Probably to let whatever the godawful stench was escape. The waiting room was filled with plastic orange chairs and a whole lot of people. There were a couple of babies crying and a woman crying in big gulping sobs in the corner. Addicts sat slumped over in their chairs and other couldn't sit still at all so they paced around.

I saw the check-in counter towards the back and a big-boned woman the color of dark chocolate manned the desk with a righteous hand. She was doing eleven things at once and talking on the phone, and she still managed to keep patients in check when they started yelling for the doctor to hurry up.

I tightened my grip on the duffle bag and made my way to the counter. She held out a finger and pushed a clipboard and pen in my direction. She hung up the phone and fanned herself with one of the clipboards. It had to be ninety degrees inside the clinic.

"Fill that out and take a seat. You might have to come back tomorrow though. We close at midnight and we're bursting at the seams."

I licked my lips nervously and hoped I remembered the exact saying Smash Nose gave me. "I'm here to see Doctor Blackbeard. I have the shingles again."

She pursed her lips together and put her hand on her hip. "We ain't got a Doctor Blackbeard here. What kind of stupid name is that? Fill out the form and Doctor Lester will see you if he sees you."

"I'm here to see Doctor Blackbeard. I have the shingles again." I said it louder this time.

About the most used up prostitute I'd ever seen in my life clucked her tongue. She was white as a ghost, weighed ninety pounds soaking wet, and she wasn't wearing underwear under the table napkin she called a skirt. Several of her teeth were missing and her wig was vibrant blue. It sounded like she smoked a carton a day.

"I hate them shingles," she said. "Got 'em all over my privates one time. Really did a number on my business. I had to make sure the lights were turned out before I let 'em go at me. Otherwise they'd just pick up their drawers and run out."

I took a careful step back from the woman and turned my attention back on the nurse behind the counter. If I were her I'd make sure I Cloroxed the hell out of the chair that hooker was sitting in. I could tell the nurse was about to tell me to sit down again when another nurse came up beside me and took my elbow.

"I got this one, Hildie," she said. She took me back to the treatment area to a bunch of catcalls and boos. It sounded like things were about to get pretty rough out there. I'd just cut in front of a room full of hos and crack heads. And probably they weren't the most patient of people.

The nurse led me to a little room at the very end of the hall. It seemed clean enough. White walls, scarred linoleum floor, small table with white paper on top. There was a sink and all the countertops were cleaned off. Probably they couldn't even leave a tongue depressor out in the open or it would get stolen.

"Doctor Blackbeard will be with you shortly," the nurse said and left. She didn't close the door all the way so I moved so I could see the traffic coming and going down the hall. Hildie from the front desk cornered the nurse who took me back and gave her what for. I could hear the dressing down all the way down the hall, and probably everyone in the patient rooms could too.

The door across from me opened and I stepped back a little. It looked like an office of some sort. I could see a TV and a desk that had papers piled high. There was a file cabinet and a folding chair. A man in a white lab coat came out with a briefcase in his hand and turned around and locked the door before closing it. *Paranoid, much?* I thought.

I was leaning against the exam table, still holding onto the duffle for dear life when he came in. Doctor Blackbeard was about five foot ten and he had naturally curly dark hair and a salt and pepper goatee. He had brown eyes and wore round glasses like Harry Potter. He was also sweating like a whore in church. And I didn't think it had anything to do with the temperature in the building. He looked scared shitless.

"I hear you have shingles," he said, nodding at the bag in my hand.

"That's what they tell me." He sat the briefcase down beside me on the table and I handed him the duffle bag.

"Tell our mutual friend my interest payment is included. I don't want any misunderstandings."

"No problemo." I took hold of the briefcase and hugged it close and followed him to the door. He went directly to his office, looked both ways and unlocked it. He went in, unlocked the file cabinet, and then put the duffle bag in the bottom drawer.

I didn't wait around. I needed another shower and maybe a bottle of wine. I went back through the waiting room and several people threw little paper cups at me they'd gotten from the water dispenser.

When I got outside I breathed in as much fresh air as was possible in this part of the city and started back across the street to Nick's truck. I stopped and stared as soon as I stepped foot into the street. The truck was rocking from side to side in a steady rhythm, but I couldn't see anyone inside or in the bed of the truck from where I stood.

I heard the beat of drums and a small crowd had gathered on the other side of the truck. I crept across the street and watched in slackjawed amazement as, who I assumed was Harry, humped the shit out of Nick's truck. He was going at it right on the front tire and the two men I'd been talking to earlier were laying down a good humping rhythm on the bottom of Harry's trashcan.

Harry was about a hundred years old and he wore

nothing but a blanket wrapped around him like a diaper. I could count his ribs and his beard hung down to his chest. I didn't know if it was all Harry in the diaper or a summer sausage, but I wasn't about to look closer to find out.

I hit the car alarm and the drums stopped. About a dozen people turned to look my direction and I opened the door and put the briefcase inside, ignoring the stares.

"What you doin' bitch? Can't you see Harry was windin' up for the finale?"

"Guess he'll have to finish up on that Honda in front of me."

The truck started rocking again and I jumped onto the side step and held onto the door for dear life.

"I can't hump on no Honda," Harry called out. "You see those tires? Hardly got any tread on 'em at all. These tires are just right for Harry. They got real deep grooves."

The drums began again and the humping started in earnest. I kept losing my grip and couldn't hoist myself the rest of the way into the truck. Harry had really found his rhythm. I finally managed to get into the driver's seat and slam the door shut just as the crowd broke into applause and the truck stopped moving.

I revved the engine and I might have run over a foot as I sped out of there.

CHAPTER SEVENTEEN

I was halfway out of Savannah and I'd been debating going through a car wash or Dairy Queen. I was having trouble making up my mind. I was probably going to settle on Dairy Queen. Nick could get the truck washed in the morning, and I needed a hit of something real bad. A hot fudge sundae seemed like the right choice.

I left the line at Dairy Queen and went to pull back onto the road when a familiar blue Toyota pulled up next to me. Smash Nose got out and rapped on the passenger side window. He tried the door handle, but I'd learned from my mistake the first time. It was locked. I rolled down the window a crack to hear what he was saying.

"Did you get the case?"

"I've got it." I leaned down to get it from the floorboard and when I came back up Smash Nose had a gun pointed right at my head.

"Hand it over."

"Are you going to shoot me?"

"Yes, but I'll do it in the head so it's fast."

"Well that's comforting." I started to hand the case

over and then at the last second I shoved it at him. A shot went wild and pinged of the edge of the truck door and I laid pedal to the metal. I squealed out of the Dairy Queen parking lot and felt another bullet ping off my bumper. Nick was going to be pissed. He really liked his truck.

I'd almost gotten my breathing back under control by the time I hit the highway and the single lane road that led to Nick's house. Smash Nose hadn't followed me. At least not that I'd noticed.

I checked in with Phoebe and she said all was quiet around the house and that she'd been invited to a Dr. Who party the following night. I reminded her we were expected to eat dinner at home, but she said the party didn't start till after ten. She also wanted to let me know a scary looking dude that said he was FBI kept knocking on the door. She was afraid he was there to arrest her for smoking pot with Norman Hinkle.

I assured her Savage was a neighbor and not really all that scary once you got to know him. And probably the FBI didn't care all that much that she'd been smoking pot with Norman. They were probably much more interested in the fact that Norman was growing enough pot to make the entire state of Georgia high as a kite. I hoped to God Summer's Eve Assisted Living never burned to the ground. We'd all be in trouble.

I hung up with Phoebe and pulled into Nick's driveway. The garage door was closed and I assumed the Cabriolet was tucked away inside. A few lights were on in the house, and I took a deep breath before I found the courage to get out.

"Just trade keys and then get out. Easy as pie."

I knocked on the door and Nick opened it a second later.

"I was just about to call you. It's going on ten o'clock."

"I had a little detour on the way to bust Carly Mathis for cheating on her husband." I filled him in on Smash Nose getting in the car with me and the exchange made at the clinic.

"I've got to call that in," he said, pinching his thumb and his forefinger at the bridge of his nose. Nick wasn't happy. In fact, he was down right furious. "Why didn't you call me as soon as he gave you the duffle? We could have intercepted the drop."

"He said he was watching. And he was. By the way, your truck might have a couple of bullet holes in it. It turns out Johnny Sakko didn't want me to work for him on a full time basis after all and Smash Nose got a couple of shots off. Also, you probably want to run your truck through a car wash in the morning. It got humped on a little."

"You must have parked by Harry's house." Nick went to the phone and dialed into the station, and he relayed that he got an anonymous tip that a deal had taken place at the clinic on Bayonette earlier tonight. He made a few notes and then hung up the phone.

"We can at least get the ball rolling and find out the background on the clinic. Go through it one more time with as many details as possible and I can start running backgrounds."

By the time we were finished, it was after one in the morning and I could barely keep my eyes open.

"I need to get home and get some sleep. I have to drive to Jacksonville in the morning."

"It's probably a good thing you're going to be out of the city for a while. We can maybe make some headway without anyone trying to shoot you."

I got up and headed toward the door, and Nick stuck his finger in the waist of my jeans and pulled me backward until he was pressed against my back. "You might as well stay here for the night." He kissed the back of my neck and all of a sudden I wasn't so tired anymore.

"I—uhh—didn't bring any clothes with me."

"That's okay. You're not going to need any." And then he was kissing me and my brain short circuited.

I'm not sure how we made it to the second floor and Nick's bedroom, but by the time we got there we were both completely naked and I'd stopped worrying whether or not I'd worn my good underwear. He hadn't taken the time to look at them anyway.

I was about foreplayed out. It seemed like we'd been leading up to this for days, so I had no complaints when he slid home right off the bat. Everything after was a blur of one sensation to another, and when I finally dropped from complete exhaustion the sun was just coming up.

CHAPTER EIGHTEEN

T*uesday*

IT WAS nine o'clock when my alarm went off and I dragged myself to the shower. There was no part of my body that had gone untouched, and I'd be walking funny for days.

Nick had gotten up for work just as I'd fallen asleep, and I remembered him kissing me on the head before he left. I got a look at myself in the mirror and almost screamed. Black mascara smudged under my eyes and my hair looked like it had been brushed with a hand mixer. I had beard burn on my neck and chest.

I showered and wrapped a towel around myself as I went to find my clothes. My jeans and underwear were on the stairs, my shirt was draped over a lamp, and my socks and shoes were by the front door. I had no idea where my bra was.

I looked around for a few minutes and gave up hope

of finding it, so I put my clothes on minus the bra and prayed my mother never got word of it. Though the way she'd been acting lately, maybe she was all for going without a bra.

Nick had left the keys to the Cabriolet next to the coffee pot with a note that said we should talk later. I had no idea what that meant. Was it the good kind of talk or the bad kind of talk? I thunked my head against the kitchen cabinet and ran out the door, locking the door behind me.

I drove into Savannah and turned onto 53rd Street to head into my neighborhood. It was a workday, so there weren't many cars parked in driveways, but I knew every member of NAD had their binoculars pointed in my direction when I pulled in front of my house. A bright red Corvette sat in the driveway so I couldn't park there.

I sat in the car for a few minutes and thought things through. They'd notice I was wearing yesterday's clothes and no bra right off. Well, probably Spock wouldn't notice but Mrs. Rodriguez and Byron would for sure. And they'd tell Savage. There was no way they wouldn't. I didn't really know how I felt about it. I liked Savage a lot and I didn't want to hurt his feelings, but he wasn't the man for me.

I grabbed my purse and ran to the front door with my arms over my chest. I unlocked the door and found Phoebe in the kitchen standing over the coffee pot. She wasn't normally a morning person. In fact, I'm not sure I've ever seen her up before noon.

My phone rang just as I set my stuff down and my eye started twitching. I knew it had to be my mother.

"Addison, this is your mother," she said, when I

answered the phone. "Why aren't you wearing a bra? Are you back together with Nick?"

"Dammit." I went to the front curtains and looked out. "Who's the snitch? I just walked in the front door for crying out loud."

"Mothers never have to reveal their sources. Someday when you're a mother you'll find this out. I wanted to remind you about dinner tonight. I'm making stuffed shells. I got the recipe off Pinterest."

"Sounds great. I don't know about Nick though. He might have to work."

"He's got to eat sometime. This is why you always get the ring on your finger before you give away the goods. He's got no surprises left with you. How are you supposed to keep him this time?"

"Someone's knocking at the door," I lied. "I have to go now." I hung up and thunked my head against the wall some more. I was probably going to develop a permanent lump in my forehead if I kept it up, but it was better than putting a rifle in my mouth.

"That must have been Mom," Phoebe said. "You always get that twitch in your eye when she starts talking about marriage."

Phoebe was dressed in another ripped pair of jeans, a white stretchy shirt, and a black leather biker jacket. She had on black studded boots with four-inch heels.

"You're up early."

"I've got a couple of appointments to check out some studio space with a realtor. Tell me about the guy across the street. Are you doing him?"

I could tell by the look in her eyes she was interested and a light bulb went off over my head. This was perfect.

"I'm not doing him. He's a friend. He's also an FBI agent. Go for it."

"I caught sight of his socks as he was walking back across the street. Kinky." She rinsed her cup in the sink and grabbed an oversized leather bag she slung over her shoulder. "I'm interested, but I don't know if I could sleep with him. I've never had sex with someone who looks like a superhero before. You think he has special powers in bed?"

"Most definitely. The superhero thing was pretty much my hang-up too. It's fucking intimidating."

Phoebe left to go studio hunting and I headed to my room to change clothes. I was feeling a little vanilla after standing next to Phoebe. Which was pretty much the story of my life. I put on my best red push-up bra and matching thong, tight jeans, and a red sweater that showed a lot of cleavage. I put on matching suede boots with sky-high heels that I'd regret wearing in a couple of hours. I took extra time on my makeup and then stood back and observed.

I thought about getting a streak of color in my hair or a nose ring like Phoebe but that was a little outside of my comfort zone. Maybe I should try for the tattoo instead. Somewhere where no one would see it.

I called Rosemarie as I went back into the kitchen to grab my stuff.

"Are you still skipping school today?"

"I'm not skipping. I'm taking mental health days. Leroy is a machine."

Leroy didn't look like a machine to me. Leroy looked like The Penguin. "Is he still there?"

"Nah, he's at work. He's going to pick me up for dinner with his parents. I'm a little nervous."

"I'm sure it will be fine." I was lying of course. It was going to be a disaster of epic proportions. Probably as bad as dinner with my family. "Do you want to drive to Jacksonville with me today? I need to talk to someone for one of my cases."

"Can we stop at the outlet mall on the way back?"

I mentally juggled the money in my checking account and added up how much room I had on my credit card. "Sounds good."

I disconnected from Rosemarie and immediately dialed Nick.

"Couldn't go without hearing my voice, huh?" he said.

"What would it take to get you to have dinner with my mom and Vince tonight?" There was silence on the other end for a couple of minutes and I thought he might have hung up.

"How do you feel about anal sex?"

"Does it have to take place in the anus?"

More silence. "I can't think of a good enough payback for dinner right now. I'll go, but then you're going to owe me big time."

I disconnected and worried briefly about what I'd just agreed to. I clenched my butt cheeks and then headed out to the car. The blue Toyota was parked next to it, the engine running and the passenger window rolled down.

I froze as Smash Nose brought his finger up like a gun and went *Bang!* He smiled and then the car drove off down the street. I realized I'd been standing there a while when Mr. Walner came out from next door to get his mail and he let out a wolf whistle.

"Nice rack, chickie. Don't see 'em made like that very often."

I did a half smile, half grimace and hurried to the car.

My cell phone started ringing as soon as I turned over the engine and I knew it was my mother. I let it go to voicemail and looked across the street at Jemimah Blaze's house. She was standing at the window holding the curtain back so she could see.

Damn carnies.

~

I DID a quick swing by the agency to see if any new information had surfaced about the Tannenbaum murder. I could have probably asked Nick but he'd distracted me with the whole anal sex thing.

I found an open parking meter and scrounged at the bottom of my purse for nickels and dimes. I was fresh out of quarters.

Lucy wasn't manning the front desk when I walked in. I was pretty sure vampires never had to go to the bathroom, so my second best guess was she was in the filing room. Kate's office door was open and she was behind her desk, her face buried in the papers she was going over. I closed the door and headed to my usual chair.

"What's new?" I asked.

"Jerry Missner has decided to retire so I'm about to be short an agent, all this rain has caused a leak in the upstairs conference room, and I think I'm pregnant. Other than that things are peachy."

My mouth dropped open and it took a second for my brain to catch up with the words. "You're pregnant?"

"I *think* I'm pregnant. I haven't found the courage to buy one of those little tests yet." And then Kate burst into tears. Kate never cried. I mean *never*. Not when she broke her arm in two places when we were in the fourth grade and not when her date to the senior prom stood her up for the head cheerleader.

A couple of months ago, she'd been convinced that her husband Mike was cheating on her and that was one of the only times I can remember that she cried. It turns out Mike just had a bit of a gambling problem, but since then he'd been going to counseling and things seemed to be good between them. I couldn't tell if these were happy tears or ones of pure panic.

I hopped up and went behind the desk. Her head was down on the papers she'd been reading and she was soaking them through. I patted frantically at her back and looked around the office in panic for some inspiration. I wasn't sure what to do. Kate was always the one who could handle anything.

"Are you excited or not excited about having a baby? You've got to help me out here. Have you told Mike?"

"I—" sniffle, "Don't—" sniffle, "Know."

"You don't know if you told Mike?" I asked, confused. "That seems like a conversation you might remember."

"I don't know if I'm excited." She wiped her face with her hands and I was glad Kate hardly ever wore makeup or she'd be in a real fix right now. "What do I know about babies? I've never had one before. Suppose I do it all wrong."

"You'll be an awesome mother. You've got lots of common sense and you're good at keeping people out of trouble. You've been doing it for me for years."

I pulled a couple of Kleenex's from the box on her desk and put them in her hands, and then I went to the sideboard and grabbed a chocolate éclair, which was Kate's favorite. "You probably shouldn't have coffee," I said and rummaged in the mini fridge for a bottle of water. "Drink this. You don't want to get dehydrated."

I put my hands on my hips and paced back and forth in front of her desk. "Here's what we're going to do. You need to take a test so you know for sure."

"I don't have time today. I've got nothing but meetings. And I can't do it once I get home because Mike will be there."

"I've got to do dinner with my mom and Vince, but I can pick one up for you and you can take it at my house. You can come with me to catch Carly Mathis in the act so you don't have to lie to Mike. Just tell him you're helping me with a job."

Kate's tears had started to dry up and she inhaled the éclair. "I can do that. I'm glad you stopped by. I feel better now."

"That's what friends are for, babe. Have you heard any rumblings about Johnny Sakko and the free clinic over on Bayonette Street?"

Kate's eyebrows raised so high I thought they were going to shoot off the top of her head. "More than rumblings. They've got bad business happening over there. The cops have been sniffing around there for months, but they haven't come up with anything. Word is that Sakko is a silent partner in the clinic and it's one of his fronts for the drugs he pushes through the city."

"I got the word from my guy we set up the sting with the other night at Mambo. They caught the valets red handed using the car to pick up a pretty large shipment of marijuana from the docks. More than half a million dollars in bricks were confiscated. The cops couldn't get either of them to rat on Sakko though. The FBI came in and took over at that point and the two valets went into a safe house."

I narrowed my eyes. "Are the FBI and Savannah PD working on this together?"

"That's the rumor. They're keeping everything pretty close to the vest. That cop they found the other morning was in Sakko's pocket, so they're keeping the inner circle pretty small on this one."

I had a feeling I knew exactly who belonged to that inner circle.

ROSEMARIE WAS WAITING OUTSIDE for me when I pulled up in front of her duplex. She was back to her normal wardrobe, thank God. She wore a denim skirt, a white cableknit sweater, and brown boots. Her cheeks were back to apple dumpling pink and her hair was back to Farrah Fawcett. She had on a complete set of wooden jewelry made of alphabet blocks. She was in teacher mode today, which I thought was odd considering she was taking the day for mental wellness.

Nick's car had Sirius radio, so we fiddled around with it and decided it was a nineties kind of day. Rosemarie spent most of the two-hour drive to Jacksonville snoring in the seat next to me. As soon as I crossed the border into Florida the gray clouds were gone and there was nothing but sunshine.

Eugene Woods lived in a condo on Oceanfront Street in Jacksonville Beach. It wasn't anything to write home about, but it was a decent place to live for a single guy and it was well maintained. The condos were cookie cutter white stucco. The lawns were well manicured. And everyone had access to the beach.

I nudged Rosemarie and she swatted at my hand. "Not now, Leroy. I'm tired. I've got a headache." She gave another indelicate snuffle and went back to sleep.

I rolled my eyes and nudged her again. "Wake up. We're in Jacksonville."

Rosemarie popped up in the seat, wild-eyed and out of breath. She patted herself down and then gave a sigh of relief.

"I was just making sure my clothes were still on. Ever since Leroy started staying over I've been going to bed fully dressed and waking up butt ass naked. I don't know how it happens and I can't really remember anything except for pieces of crazy dreams. It's just like that movie."

"What movie? *Field of Dreams*?"

"No. *Rosemary's Baby*. Except this time it's Rosemarie's Baby. But I like *Field of Dreams* too. I always thought James Earl Jones would make an excellent lover."

To each his own I guess. I'd always thought Indiana Jones would make an excellent lover, but what did I know.

"I think maybe I need to find a man with less of a sex drive," she said, opening the car door and leveraging herself out. "That can't be normal. Sex morning, noon, and night, and then selfies in between."

"Maybe you should send him home for a while so you can recuperate. Maybe it's been a long time for him and he's just trying to catch up."

"Hmm."

We made our way to the front door and rang the bell. My information showed that Eugene was a computer programmer and worked from home. He was divorced, and his ex-wife and teenaged son lived in Chicago. He hadn't remarried and it didn't look like he was seeing anyone serious.

A man answered the door and I looked up several inches and into the face of a god. His hair was burnished gold, his eyes an odd turquoise-blue, and his lips were sensual and made for kissing. I knew his age was thirty-eight. He was shirtless and only wore a pair of sweat pants that hung low on his hips. He was the kind of man who should never put on clothes.

Rosemarie and I stood there slack-jawed and motionless for a good two minutes while he waited to see what we wanted.

"Can I help you ladies?" he finally asked. He asked the question to my cleavage and I high-fived myself for picking today to want to be like Phoebe.

I handed him an agency business card and introduced myself. "Do you mind if we come in for a few minutes. This won't take long."

"Sure. Sorry about the mess. I'm working today and haven't gotten around to cleaning."

I looked around the spotless room and wondered why women weren't camped out on his front lawn. The condo was a good size—bigger than my house. The living room had beige Berber carpet and creamy walls. Oil paintings of seascapes hung beneath special lighting and the sofas were cream colored leather with turquoise and dark brown pillows to continue the whole beach theme he had going.

I could see the ocean and a large deck from where we stood and a kitchen done entirely in white wainscoting, even the refrigerator and other appliances. It was a great space, and I was thinking I wouldn't mind living at the beach.

"Have a seat," Eugene said.

I looked over in time to catch Rosemarie taking a photo of him with her iPhone and I went into a coughing fit in hopes he wouldn't notice.

"Are you okay? Do you need water?" he asked.

"I'm fine. Just a tickle." I'd learned from the last couch I'd sat on with Savage and decided to opt for one of the chairs this time. Eugene took the other one and Rosemarie made herself comfortable on the couch.

I explained I was working for the agency in looking for the Tannenbaum heir.

"You're saying my Grandma Rose went to a back alley sperm bank to conceive my father and now my biological grandfather, who's been murdered, has left a heap of money to whoever is left of his bloodline."

"Pretty much."

"That was a real good summary," Rosemarie said. "You could get a job writing Cliff's Notes."

"Wow," he said. "I'm speechless. Nothing good ever happens to me."

"Maybe that's because you got your lump of good stuff when you were born," Rosemarie said. "I don't mean to speak out of turn, but you don't look much like a computer programmer."

His smile was blindingly white and a dimple winked at the corner of his mouth. "My ex-wife told me that all the time. She didn't like how much time I spent on the computer. She thought I should've been making more money considering the kind of jobs I could do. She never liked Florida anyway. She moved with my son back to Chicago a few months after we divorced."

"What kinds of jobs do you mean?" Rosemarie asked. She flipped through several magazines on his end table, not trying to be subtle about poking around.

"Hacking jobs. I'm really good at it. My wife thought I should've gone independent and broadened my market to the international level. I've got a sealed juvie file for hacking into the Pentagon when I was a teenager. I do a lot of government contract work now so I make out okay, but I could be living the high life, if you know what I mean. But if there's something you want to know about somebody, then I'm your guy."

He winked and I had that awkward teenager moment where you stutter and stammer as soon as the cute guy at school pays any attention to you. Not only was he handsome, but he was smart too. I couldn't deny I was tempted to have him run a full background check on Nick. He hadn't told me about family, so who knew what other secrets he was keeping.

"Your son sure does live far away," Rosemarie said. "That must be hard."

"I miss him for sure." Eugene's smile spoke of genuine affection for his son. "He's thirteen now and already wearing a size twelve shoe like me. I have a feeling they're not going to stop growing any time soon. He comes for the summers and a couple weeks at Christmas. And I'll fly up to Chicago whenever I can to catch a ballgame or something."

I gave Eugene the information on where he could do the DNA testing and then Rosemarie and I left.

"Mmm, mmm," she said, shoehorning her way back into the Cabriolet. "That man is about as close to perfection as you can get. If it was him trying to wake me up in the middle of the night you can guarantee I wouldn't say no."

"There's got to be something wrong with him," I said. "Nobody is that perfect. His wife left him for some reason."

"Maybe he leaves the toilet seat up. Or maybe he's a hummer. My daddy used to hum all the time. Drove my mother crazy. She finally hit him on the back of the head with a frying pan and he never hummed again."

We stopped at the outlet mall and I picked up a Kate Spade clutch I found for half price and then I went to the CVS and bought a pregnancy test for Kate. Rosemarie found a corset and matching collar at Frederick's of Hollywood. I hoped that wasn't what she was planning on wearing to dinner with Leroy's parents. She'd tried it on for me and she looked just like Rosie O'Donnell in *Exit to Eden*.

I dropped Rosemarie back at her duplex and made the drive back to Savannah by myself. I stopped at the outskirts of town and took my gun out of my purse and put it in my lap. I didn't want to take any chances.

CHAPTER NINETEEN

I made it to my front door without incident and I remembered to lock the door this time. I needed to change into something more comfortable. I stopped by the bar and picked up the note Phoebe had left. She said she'd found a new studio on the riverfront and she was making arrangements to have her canvasses and other supplies transported. She also said she'd be about ten minutes late for dinner, which was fine by me. Ten minutes was plenty of time for Nick and I to get snockered before we had to sit down at the table.

There was a knock at the door and the handle jiggled. I grabbed my gun and went to look through the peephole. Nick winked at me and I unlocked the door.

"You're early," I said, putting my gun back in my handbag.

"I clocked out just as a double homicide got called out. I wasn't about to stay. I wouldn't make it home until next Tuesday. Hello—" His eyes darkened and the line of his mouth softened. "I really like that sweater."

In heels I was only an inch shorter than he was and he

leaned in to kiss me hello. "I was just about to change into something more comfortable."

"Let me help you with that." And then the sweater was on the floor and my jeans were around my knees. I was up on the dining room table and Nick was looking a little crazed at the sight of my push up bra and matching thong.

"I had no idea you had such a fascination with kitchen tables." He pulled my boots off so my jeans could fall to the floor. "We're going to be late for dinner."

"This will only take a second. Promise." His finger ran just beneath the lace of my thong and it was more than obvious it would only take a second for me as well.

"Time's ticking." I worked at his buckle and had exactly what I wanted in hand when I happened to look up and see the glare from the binoculars. Spock was pressed against the big square window that faced my house and the glass was fogged from where he was breathing.

I squeaked and Nick turned to see what had gotten my attention. That's when Spock got a real eyeful and closed his blinds. I laughed hysterically until I fell back onto the table and tears ran down my face.

"What the hell? You have a peeping Tom next door?"

I could tell Nick was about two seconds away from going next door and beating the shit out of Spock.

"Not really. He's the president of the NAD Squad."

Nick froze and looked at me. His pants were around his knees and his shirt was unbuttoned. He still wore his shoulder holster, and he was still rock hard and raring to go. There wasn't much that got Nick down. This struck me as unusually funny and I burst into laughter again.

"He's the president of the NAD Squad? What in the hell is the NAD Squad?"

"Neighbors Against Delinquency. It's the neighborhood watch."

He sighed and finally gave up and started laughing. "Jesus, it's like you're a magnet. Stuff like this never happens to normal people." He pulled me up off the table and brought me down to the floor so I straddled his hips. "No one can see us down here."

"Not unless they look in the mail slot in the door."

"Comforting thought, but nothing is going to distract me this time."

Then my thong was pulled aside and I was taking him inside of me. A few minutes later both of us were sprawled on the floor and waiting for our breathing to return to normal.

"I don't think my legs work," I said. My eyes weren't focusing and I felt tingling in my toes.

"Maybe we should skip dinner. I think I might have had a small stroke."

"Not even that will save you. But you should probably straighten your clothes. We don't want to scandalize anyone at the dinner table."

"If I remember right we scandalized the hell out of that table. It's going to be difficult to eat remembering what we did there."

My lips twitched and I rolled to my hands and knees. Back when I'd been living at home Nick had paid me a late night visit. It was our first time together and we christened every flat surface, and a few that weren't so flat, in the house.

I managed to make it to my bedroom without falling on my face and looked through my drawers for clean clothes. I needed to do laundry badly and ended up digging out a pair of black cargo pants and another black long-sleeved T-shirt. I tied a windbreaker around my waist and put on my sneakers.

When I came back out Nick was fully dressed and staring at the pregnancy test on the counter. All the color had drained from his face. He looked up at me with and opened his mouth to say something, but then he closed it again and just arched a brow instead.

"It's not mine." I grabbed it and put it back in the sack. "It's for Kate. She's coming over later to take it."

"Oh."

"What?"

"Nothing. I just had a moment. I'm okay now. Why are you dressed like combat Barbie? And more importantly, are you still wearing the red bra? I might like to visit it later."

"I've got to work tonight. Besides, you just visited with the red bra. You'll have to wait until tomorrow to see what else I have in my repertoire."

BY THE TIME we made it back to Whiskey Bayou I was starting to think dinner might be a bad idea. I had a lot on my mind. The Tannenbaum case was bothering me for some reason, not to mention the problem with Johnny Sakko wanting to kill me.

If I was honest with myself the thing that was bothering me the most was the look on Nick's face when he thought the pregnancy test was mine. It wasn't a good look.

"Anything new with Tannenbaum?" I asked.

"Not really. The couple that lives next door was coming in late from a party that night and they think they saw a man standing across the street in the park. But they said they didn't pay much attention because it looked like he was just trying to stay dry under the tree. I went back to talk with my dad about the changing of the will and didn't get anywhere there. He said Tannenbaum called the day before about changing the will and demanded the new one be in place and ready to sign within twenty-four hours. My father isn't a fool, at least not in business, so he had the contracts ready rather than risk the chance of losing him as a client. My father also suggested that you seduced him and he had no choice but to give in because he's only a man."

"What can I say? The red bra is magical over all men, beasts, and assholes. Your mother suggested they could make things hard on me if they wanted."

"That's probably true. This is still the same South it's always been. The same families have all the power and dictate the rules. We liked to think we're an advanced society with freedom to believe what we want and act how we choose, but it's just not true. And when you do fight for those things the consequences might be something you may never recover from."

"So what should I do?"

He pulled up to the curb in front of my mom's house and turned off the car. "I think we should get back together and you should move in with me. Permanently."

"Like marriage?" The thought of marriage freaked me out a little, and all of a sudden I wasn't feeling so good. I'd already been stood up at the altar once. I could do without ever having to go through that hell again.

"Not marriage. Not yet. I can tell you need some time

to get used to the idea. I figure if you move in with me then maybe you'll start to love me like you did before."

I put my head between my knees and took slow deep breaths until the bells stopped clanging in my head.

"I can see you're pleased with the idea and considering it." Nick got out of the truck and came around to my side to open the door.

By the time we made it to the front door I'd gotten my hearing back and I no longer felt like I'd taken a fist to the solar plexus. Vince answered the door and greeted Nick with a beer and me with a large glass of wine.

"Phyllis was starting to wonder if something had come up. Come on back. I've already got the steaks on the grill."

"What happened to the stuffed shells?" I sniffed the house and didn't smell the usual scents of burning.

"Home Depot was having a sale on grills and one caught my eye as we were driving by. I decided to buy it on the spot and talked Phyllis into letting me try it out tonight." He winked and I knew Vince had just saved us all from getting ptomaine. Maybe he was a good fit for my mother after all.

Phoebe arrived twenty minutes later and we all sat down to the table. Mom and Vince at each end, me and Nick on one side, and Phoebe across from me.

"It's been a long time since we all had a dinner together," my mother said. "We should do this more often. And maybe some day I can actually put the leafs in the table."

She looked at Nick as if she was evaluating how strong his swimmers were and Nick took a long drag on his beer and looked at me out of the corner of his eye. "You're going to owe me so big for this." he whispered out of the side of his mouth.

"I'm not doing that anal thing."

Everyone got really still at the table and I realized I'd said that out loud. "Banal," I said. "That banal thing. Nick can be so banal sometimes."

Nick's foot pressed down on top of mine and I gave him a smile with a lot of teeth. My mother cleared her throat and knocked back the sidecar she'd been drinking. "Well, I'm just glad to see the two of you are back together."

"I've been trying to get her to move in with me, but she has cold feet."

My grip tightened on my fork and I resisted the urge to stab Nick in the hand.

"It's understandable," my mother said. "She has terrible luck with men, and she doesn't listen when I tell her not to give up the goods for free without a commitment."

"I'm sitting right here, you know." Phoebe was hiding her laugh behind her wine glass and I kicked her under the table for help.

"I think moving in together is a good step," Nick continued. "She's still a little gun shy about marriage because of the last time."

"Rest in peace," we all said. My former fiancé had bounced off the hood of my car a few months ago and was dead on the spot. Fortunately, I wasn't the cause of death. He'd been poisoned.

"If you move in with Nick I can just take over the lease on your house," Phoebe said.

"Oh, that's a wonderful idea. And I didn't know you were planning to move so close to home. It'll be wonderful to have my girls and grandchildren so close."

"You've got to take a chill pill about the grandkids,"

Phoebe said. "I might get a dog. And I'm thinking about having an affair with one of Addison's neighbors. But there will be no children."

"The guy next door with the binoculars?" Nick asked.

"No. The FBI guy across the street. I don't know his name. Looks like a superhero. Wears cool socks."

"Perfect," Nick said, his smile broadening.

"Wait, I thought you were dating him," my mom said to me. Then she turned to my sister. "I don't think it's good manners to sleep with the same man as your sister."

"She can have him," I said, pushing back from the table. "We were never sleeping together. You can have Nick too if you'd like. I'm going to get dessert and then see if I can join Veronica Wade at her convent." I leaned down and whispered in Nick's ear. "You better kiss the red bra goodbye."

"Meet me back at my place tonight and I bet I could change your mind." He was probably right. I was easily influenced.

"I heard Veronica was trying to become a nun," Phoebe said. "She doesn't seem like the type of woman to be without a man very long."

"I heard she was caught with two priests in the confessional," said Vince. And just like that the subject shifted off me. Vince saves the day again. I went to the kitchen and brought back a homemade chocolate cake Mom had bought at Kroger.

CHAPTER TWENTY

Kate was waiting on me by the time Nick dropped me back at my place. Phoebe had stayed behind and decided to have a girls' night out with one of her friends from high school, so we at least had some privacy.

"Did you get it?" she asked.

"I got a couple of different kinds," I told her. "That way you can be double sure."

"Good idea."

Kate was dressed much like I was—black jeans, sweatshirt, and combat boots. She wasn't wearing her gun on her hip, but I was willing to bet she had one tucked at the small of her back. She had a black baseball cap pulled over her blond hair.

"Here," I said, handing her the sack.

"I can't do this. I'm not ready." She shoved the sack back at me.

"What are you going to do? Wait until you give birth at the office? I wouldn't do that. Lucy looks like the kind of woman who might eat the placenta. Doesn't matter if it's hers or not."

"That's disgusting." Kate grabbed the bag back from me and dumped the boxes out on the counter. "I just figure it won't be real if I don't know the outcome."

"This is ridiculous. Just pee on the damn stick already. How hard can it be?"

"Fine. I'll do one and you'll do one. That way I don't have to do it by myself. And after we're both done peeing we'll put the sticks back in the bag and put them away somewhere for a while and then that'll give me time to get used to the idea before I actually look at it."

"Jesus. Give me that. I can certainly pee on a stick if that's what it takes for you to stop being a pussy. Where do you want me to keep them once we're finished?"

"Just put them in the closet or something?"

"I'm not putting pee sticks in my closet. That's gross."

"Fine. I'll take them with me and put them in my closet. And then maybe five years from now I'll look and see what the result is."

"I'll go first." I went into the bathroom and did my business, tossed the stick into the sack without looking, and then washed my hands. "Your turn. And then we need to get a move on if we're going to catch Carly Mathis doing the nasty."

"Right." Kate took a deep breath and took her box into the bathroom. A couple of minutes later she came out with the sack tied in a knot at the top. She shoved the sack in the side pocket of her shoulder bag and then rolled her shoulders. "No big deal. Now it's done and I don't have to think about it anymore. Lets go catch Carly Mathis in action. I got a call from her husband before I left to come here for the night. She called home and told him she had to work late."

"Why can't people think of a better excuse than

that?" I asked. "That's like admitting you're having an affair. Why don't people say they're going to stop at the grocery store or get their nails done or have a massage?"

"People have no imagination. And most people aren't as good at lying as we are."

"It takes practice," I said, nodding. I looked back and forth between Kate's beige Taurus and Nick's Cabriolet and knew which one we were going to take. I sighed and got in the passenger seat of the Taurus.

"We've got to get a move on. She gets out of her aerobics class in twenty minutes." We parked in the lot of the Anytime Fitness and waited for Carly Mathis to make an appearance. Kate and I studied a recent photograph of her. Late twenties with long blond hair, green eyes, and a cute nose. She looked like the All-American Girl.

"She doesn't look like a cheater," I said.

"They never do."

I checked the clock on the dashboard and rummaged around in my files. Something was bothering me about the Tannenbaum case. I filled in Kate on what I'd gotten from Nick's police report as well as my interviews with the three possible heirs.

"It's weird. My gut instinct says to look at Rose Parker and her great-grandson Jamie a little closer. She admitted that her son wasn't her husband's child, but she didn't want her grandson to be DNA tested. That seems suspicious to me.

"Then we've got Norman Hinkle who is the only remaining heir in the Hinkle line. He's seventy-one years old and spends his days growing and smoking pot in a green house." I told Kate about the enormous crop I'd found at Summer's Eve.

"Holy shit," she said. "You've got to report that."

"But everyone is so old. What if it's medicinal? What if all those old people die because they can't get their weed?" Besides, I was starting to get a feeling about where Johnny Sakko was getting his stash. I wasn't quite ready to pull the plug on SEAL until I could do a little more investigating.

"Then there's the sex god, Eugene Woods. He's likeable in every way. He's handsome and brilliant. But something about him bothers me. He's not that perfect. I feel like we need to dig deeper on him. He's a computer hacker. Maybe he's known all along that his father was Tannenbaum's son. He also wears a size twelve shoe, just like the muddy footprint they found at the murder scene." I chewed on my bottom lip as I thought it through. "I think that's what bothered me about him. It was almost like he was bragging. Letting me know about his hacking abilities and dropping his shoe size."

"I like how you say *we* need to dig deeper on him. I hope what you mean to say is that you're going to turn everything you've found over to Nick so he can be the one doing the digging."

"Right. That's what I meant."

Kate sighed. "Look, there's Carly Mathis." Kate turned on the car but left the headlights off and we watched as Carly got into a canary yellow Jeep Cherokee. Her hair was in a ponytail and her face was scrubbed free of makeup. She'd changed out of her workout clothes into casual jeans and a T-shirt. Not exactly seductive gear.

Carly pulled out of the lot, and Kate waited until a couple of cars were between them before she followed. She flipped on the lights once we turned onto Victory Drive. I got the long range camera out of the bag and slung the strap around my neck. The camera and I had a long and eventful history together. I'd named her Elvira just for the hell of it.

Carly took the exit for the freeway to avoid the city traffic and headed for Bay Street.

"Shit, she's parking street side," Kate said, slowing down as Carly parked the Jeep at a metered spot and got out to put her coins in. "I don't see anything close by. You get out and follow her on foot and I'll get parked and meet you. Keep your phone somewhere you can feel it."

I put my phone inside my bra and got out of the car to follow Carly. She walked along Bay for a bit, looking like she had a destination in mind. She took the River Street access to the lower level down by the waterfront. I gritted my teeth and followed after her.

This was the area that was always teeming with tourists. To get to the riverfront you had to take a road below the city. It was a road of uneven rocks that jarred teeth and ruined tires. Cars were parked in every available space and a big cement truck sat in the middle of the lot blocking the way. They were always trying to patch things down in this area, and when they got done with the cement they used powerful sprayers to move the remaining cement to the bottom of the hill closer to River Street. The lesson to learn is to always watch where you're stepping.

I thought for sure Carly was headed to the Bohemian Hotel, but she kept going and went up another block to a two-story building. She took the stairs up a level and I dashed to the other side of the street.

The area along the docks was made to look like a park, only with brick on the ground instead of grass. There were trees and streetlights and fountains and park benches. I stood on a park bench at first and hoped it would be tall enough for me to see up to the second level of the building across from me. There wasn't a sign I could see on the outside, but there was definitely activity going on on the inside.

I sighted through the camera, but I was only able to see the top railing. I needed to be up higher.

"You're on my bench," a lady said from below me. She swatted at my legs with an old towel.

"Sorry." I jumped down and looked around to see what else I could climb. I didn't have a lot of options. I was going to have to go up the stairs and look in the windows. If anyone asked I could just say I was lost.

I waited until the workers had finished using the high-powered sprayers to send down the next batch of cement and I watched as it gathered in a big gray blob at the bottom of the stairs. I tip-toed across the area, careful to avoid the wet spots or the cement and then I went up the stairs as if I belonged there.

No one screamed at me or told me to leave so I took a chance on looking in the windows. Stacked chairs on top of tables were obstructing my view so I moved down a little ways and put my face to the window again.

"Huh," I said. It looked like a giant kitchen. Like the ones you see on cooking shows on *The Food Network.* Carly was standing behind the counter with a big apron, mixing stuff in a bowl. A woman instructor stood next to her and showed her which steps to do next. Unless they were about to get naked and smear cake batter all over themselves in a lesbian fantasy, I was thinking Hugh was dead wrong about his wife having an affair.

I snapped off a couple of shots to prove it to him and then headed back towards the stairs. I was right at the railing when the door opened and Carly Mathis came storming out. "Hey, you! Why are you following me around? I got a look at you back when I parked my car. It's Hugh, isn't it? He put you up to this."

"Sorry. You're mistaken. I was just thinking about signing up for a cooking class."

"Sure you were," she said, coming closer. She put both her hands on my chest and shoved me back. She didn't look like the All-American Girl anymore. She looked like Linda Blair in the *Exorcist*.

"Hey, stop that."

"You can tell stupid Hugh that if he doesn't start learning to trust me then I'm going to divorce his sorry ass and take all his money. Just because his first two wives cheated doesn't mean I'm going to." She shoved again and my back hit the railing. "I was going to surprise him with a goddamned," *shove,* "birthday cake," *shove.* "And now I'm going to take the cake," *shove,* "and shove it up his ass."

Quite a crowd had gathered below and I could see Kate coming to the rescue out of my periphery, but I knew she wouldn't make it in time. "You need to take some anger management classes. I was just out for a walk."

Her eyes narrowed and I swore I saw them turn red for a second or two. Then she grabbed the camera strap on my neck and jerked it hard enough I was surprised my head didn't pop off.

"You're crazy, lady." I grabbed for the camera to keep it protected and brought my elbow up to block her next shove. Somehow my elbow connected with her nose and she went ballistic. Blood was spraying and her nails raked down my neck. And then I was flying ass over teakettle over the balcony.

The crowd gasped and seemed to hold their breath to

see if I was dead. The air had been knocked out of me and I wasn't sure if my spine was still connected to the rest of my body. Something wet and squishy was under me and I hoped it wasn't my inside leaking out.

"Jeez, Addison," Kate said, kneeling beside me. "Are you okay?"

Carly was standing at the top of the railing and she spit down on me to add insult to injury.

"Do you want to press charges?"

I was finally able to blink my eyes. I wasn't sure if I could actually speak yet. I wiggled my fingers and my toes, and then excruciating pain seemed to catch up with the shock my body had been in until then.

"We need to get you up and hosed off before the cement hardens. Can you stand?"

Kate was asking a lot of questions. Too many for me to answer. But the cement bit got me into motion. I'd already had to get one haircut. IF cement hardened in my hair I'd have to shave myself bald.

Kate got under one arm and one of the cement workers got under the other to bring me to my feet. "Someone called the cops. If you press charges you'll have to stay and answer questions."

"No thanks," I managed to get out. "Just charge Hugh double. It sounds like they deserve each other."

Kate propped me against the wall and the worker took one of the high-powered sprayers and hosed me off from head to toe. There wasn't a crevice that hadn't been violated by the time he turned the hose off.

Kate brought the car down to river level so I wouldn't have to walk so far and I managed to get in under my own steam. I was feeling the aches and pains now from head to toe, and I was going to need a few hundred aspirin.

"Look on the bright side. If we'd brought Nick's car you'd have a lot of explaining to do right now. The Taurus is just the right car for an accident like this."

I hit the recline button on the seat and laid all the way back. It would take fifteen minutes to get to my house. Maybe if I closed my eyes and went to sleep it would all be a dream by the time I woke up.

CHAPTER TWENTY-ONE

Kate helped me to the front door and all of a sudden Savage materialized out of nowhere. "I'll take it from here," he said.

"Call me if you need anything," Kate said.

I waved her off and let Savage prop me up. He took my key from my hand and unlocked the door.

"Do I want to know what happened?" he asked.

"I got violated with a water hose. And I think I have concrete in some very private areas."

"Why don't you get a shower and I'll get you some aspirin and coffee."

"Sounds good." I stumbled into the bathroom and stripped down to nothing. My body was a symphony of colors that would only get worse over the next couple of days. I knew this from experience.

I stood under the hot spray until I felt my muscles start to relax and then I toweled off and realized I had to get from the bathroom to my bedroom with nothing on but a towel. I didn't really care at this point, so I opened the door and went to my bedroom for another change of clothes. I was sore, and was going to be worse in the morning, but for now I was at least functional. I still had work to do, and it couldn't wait another day. It might be too late by then.

I pulled on my last clean pair of jeans and a black Bon Jovi T-shirt. I didn't know if my tennis shoes had survived the cement and hose down, but it wasn't looking too promising. I put on my Chucks instead and did a quick blow dry on my hair.

By the time I made it back to Savage I was feeling halfway human again. He handed me a cup of black coffee and three extra strength pain pills.

"Tell me about your run-in with Anthony Franco?" Savage asked.

"You're working with Nick on getting something on Johnny Sakko, aren't you?"

"We're circling from different directions. Sometimes we have relevant information to pass along to each other."

"It wasn't coincidence that you invited yourself to dinner at his restaurant, was it?"

Savage just smiled. "Tell me what happened at the clinic."

I started at the beginning and told him everything from the moment I found Smash Nose in my apartment to the package I'd had to deliver at the Bayonette Street clinic.

"We've got someone assigned to watching Franco and a few other key men of Sakko's. You should be okay, but you're going to want to stay on your guard. We've got so many drugs coming into the city we can't keep track. We know Sakko is involved somehow but we don't know how. He's making us look like idiots."

"When was the last time you visited Summer's Eve Assisted Living?" I asked. "Heard any rumors?"

Savage shook his head and then I explained about Norman Hinkle and the greenhouse. Savage stood perfectly still, his hands on his hips, and stared at me incredulously.

"You're shitting me," he finally said. "All this time it's been the old folks."

"They're pretty crafty. And they're armed so you might be careful," I said, thinking of Deloris.

"I need to put a team together and get on this. Where's your sister? Isn't she staying with you?"

"She's having a girl's night out with a friend tonight. I think she's staying down in Whiskey Bayou. My sister wants to sleep with you," I said, out of the blue.

"She told me." Savage and I stared at each other for a long while without saying anything. "What do you think about that?" he finally asked.

"Well, I love my sister. And I like you a lot. I think it could work out okay if you didn't kill each other first."

"That was pretty much my thought."

"I'm thinking of moving in with Nick. She's wanting to take over my lease here."

I'd stopped trying to interpret the expressions on Savage's face, but I knew I was feeling a little sad. This was a big step, and the end of something that never really had a chance to get started. I felt a tear slip from the corner of my eye and I wiped at it viciously.

"The NAD Squad won't be the same without you." He smiled a little and opened his arms. I didn't hesitate to walk into his embrace. He held me there for a few minutes, and I might have cried some more. I was a wreck.

"Nick's a good guy. You're good for each other. And it's not like you won't see me around." He kissed me on the top of the head and then let me go.

I stood there in the dark for a few minutes after he left and had a little bit of a pity party. I'd made the adult decision of choosing Nick over Savage. I loved Nick. And I was pretty sure he loved me too. Sometimes that had to be good enough when just starting out in a relationship. I guess we were going to see because I'd just committed myself to moving in with him.

~

A COUPLE of hours later I was in the alley behind the clinic on Bayonette Street. I'd parked the car on the adjacent street and had kept to the shadows behind the buildings. The clinic had closed at ten o'clock and it was well after midnight now. The streetlights were out around the clinic and it seemed Harry and his friends had moved on. The area was completely deserted. It was eerie as hell.

This wasn't a great area of town. I was taking a chance coming here by myself, but I had my gun and I could scream with the best of them. I looked both ways down the alleyway to make sure I was alone. A dumpster and crumpled trash that rolled across the cracked pavement like tumbleweeds were my only company. I'd gotten lucky —the moon was only a sliver in the sky and not enough to make me visible to any passersby. I was still new at this whole breaking and entering thing.

I opened my brand new Kate Spade clutch and pulled out the black cloth packet of lock picking tools I'd bought online. I'd been practicing my B&E skills by watching YouTube videos and using the back door of my house as a test dummy. It had only taken me three tries before I'd managed to click the tumblers into place. Smash Nose should've taken a shot at my back door instead of breaking my window.

It was fortunate the back door of the clinic couldn't afford better locks, but it still took a good fifteen minutes before the tumblers gave. The night air was cool, but I was sweaty as a stripper's G-string due to nerves. I had to rub my hands on my jeans twice before I could turn the knob. I cursed as I thought about fingerprints, so I quickly wiped off every surface I'd touched with the hem of my Bon Jovi T-shirt, pulled a pair of rubber medical gloves out of my purse and snapped them on.

I slipped into the clinic, closed the door at my back and then bit back a yelp when the air conditioning unit came on with a rumble.

"Shit," I breathed out. I relaxed and decided I should've gone to the bathroom before I'd left the house. My bladder couldn't take the stress of illegal activity.

The clinic smelled of Lysol and antiseptic and it was long and rectangular in shape. Patient rooms on both ends, reception and waiting area in the middle, and Dr. Blackbeard's office at the opposite end. After what I'd seen from my previous visit there wasn't enough Lysol in the world to make this place clean.

The door I'd entered was on the opposite side of where I'd been before, and I passed through a long narrow hallway with white floors and wood paneled walls. The lights were off and the only reason I could see at all was because of the red nightlights spaced every twenty feet or so in the ceiling.

I stifled a nervous giggle at the thought that I'd once seen a horror movie that reminded me an awful lot of my current situation. I reached into my purse and pulled out my gun just in case there were zombies. At least I'd worn my Chucks instead of high heels in case I had to make a run for it.

I'd wasted enough time building up my courage so I set forward with determination. I snuck past two bathrooms and a water fountain and wondered if it was against the criminal's code to sneak into the bathroom and relieve myself. But with my luck, that's when the SWAT team would break down the doors and the Enquirer would be standing there to take pictures.

I pulled the strap of my purse over my body and held the gun in a two handed grip. In my mind I was just like Laura Holt from Remington Steele, only curvier and without eighties hair. I made my way to where the hallway met the main area, squatting low and peeping around the corner to make sure I was alone.

The place was silent as a tomb. I squatted low and crossed behind the reception desk so no one could see me through the front windows. There wasn't even a squeak from my sneakers. I was pretty awesome. My stealth abilities had improved by about a hundred and fifty percent since my first day on the job. Which wasn't saying much. It was the same thing as saying a kindergartener could finally use the paste without eating it.

My heart was thudding a hundred miles a minute and the red glow from the lights was creepy as shit. My goal was fairly simple: I needed to get into the locked room I'd noticed on my first visit to the clinic and see if the bag was still locked inside.

I was halfway down the hallway when I heard a horrible moan. My heart stopped and I turned around to run back the way I'd come when I heard it again. And though it *was* horrible, it wasn't a death moan. I'd heard a few of those sounds over the past months. I'd maybe even moaned like that myself over the last couple of days. From the increasing volume I was guessing she was enjoying herself, whoever she was. Either that or she was declawing a cat without anesthesia.

To say my curiosity was piqued was an understatement. I'd never been very good at listening to the part of my mind that told me I shouldn't stick my nose where it didn't belong. I made my way closer to the sounds, hurrying my steps because it sounded like she was winding up for the finale, and I noticed the door was open a crack and light flickered from beneath. It was Doctor Blackbeard's office.

I meant to be quiet. I really did. But the sight that greeted me was enough to draw a gasp from my lips. A pair of familiar blue eyes met mine and widened in surprise. My own eyes narrowed and I felt sick to my stomach as I took in the scene. It was worse than I could've imagined.

The woman reached a climax shrill enough to break glass and the tension ratcheted up the temperature several degrees. A pregnant silence followed her cataclysmic orgasm, and I realized if I didn't breathe a little slower I was likely to end up hyperventilating.

"I should've known you'd show up here," Nick said, closing his eyes and shaking his head in disbelief. "I don't suppose I could talk you into turning around and going back home so I can get this straightened out."

I raised a brow and cut my eyes to the loaded weapon in his hand. "No, I don't think so."

He sighed and put his gun away, reaching over to turn the TV off and the X-rated flick that had been playing.

The smells of old sex and new death assaulted my senses, and I swallowed back the bile that rose at the sight of the body at Nick's feet.

"At least you put on gloves when you came in," he said, nodding at my hands. "I'd hate to think you smudged the prints of whoever broke in."

"Someone broke in?" I asked, guilt sending a rush of heat to my cheeks.

"You didn't see the front door shot to shit and standing open when you came inside?"

"Umm...sure I did. How could I have missed that?" I took a look at the body on the floor and recognized the nurse who'd brought me back to the patient room. She'd been in on whatever they had going on here.

"She was a nurse," I said. "I saw her when I was here." She didn't look so good now. She was naked and sprawled face down on the carpet. Sexual activity was obvious. Her neck was at an odd angle, and I wasn't a medical examiner, but I was guessing that was cause of death. The file cabinet lock had been popped open and all the drawers had been pulled out. The bottom one where the black bag had been was empty.

Nick was on his phone calling in the scene and I stepped around the body to look closer at the file cabinet.

"What?" Nick asked.

"This is where Blackbeard put the bag I traded him for. It's gone now."

"If you don't go now, you're going to have a lot of explaining to do when the other cops get here."

I filled him in briefly on what I'd told Savage about Norman Hinkle and waited for the explosion to come. "Aren't you going to yell at me?"

"I'm too tired to yell. In case you don't remember I

didn't get any sleep last night. It doesn't look like I'm going to get any tonight either."

"My sister stayed in Whiskey Bayou tonight. You're welcome to bunk over if you find yourself at loose ends."

"I'll keep you posted."

I heard the sirens in the distance and slipped back out through the alleyway. My body was starting to feel the aches and pains of the day. I needed an icepack and my bed in a bad way.

CHAPTER TWENTY-TWO

Savage's SUV wasn't in his driveway when I got back home, so I figured he was busy getting things ready to take down the senior citizens at SEAL. I parked Nick's car in the driveway and dug for my house keys before I got out of the car. I should have grabbed my gun too.

A dark shadow appeared just behind me and slapped a hand over my mouth before I could scream. He held a knife to my throat and I felt the nick against my skin. I whimpered once and knew this time was it. I was going to die.

He pushed me forward and somehow my legs started moving. My front door was already unlocked, and he opened it and pushed me inside. My back door was barely on its hinges. And there was a body on the floor. That was new too. The sight of Anthony Franco lying on my floor with his neck gaping open was more than I could bear. I crashed to the ground in a dead faint.

When I woke up I was tied to one of my kitchen chairs. Smash Nose was still dead on the floor, but my attacker was nowhere in sight. My body was in shock and my skin was clammy and ice cold with fear. I scooted the chair toward the kitchen hoping I could make it to a knife, but the noise brought him back again.

I recognized Victor Dawson instantly, though I'd only met him the one time. His black shirt and slacks were wet with blood. Slitting throats was a messy business.

"Has anyone ever told you you're a pain in the ass?" he asked.

I didn't feel like that question deserved an answer, though I'd been told I was a pain in the ass on a fairly frequent basis.

"Why did you kill him?"

"I was doing you a favor." He shrugged and straddled a chair in front of me. "He was here waiting for you to show up. Besides, he and Sakko were getting to be too much trouble. Sakko keeps demanding more volume for less money. We're running a freaking business, not a charity. But Sakko is a greedy bastard. He'll be having an unfortunate accident before too much longer."

"I don't understand any of this." My teeth had started to chatter, and I was trying hard not to let him see how afraid I was. I was failing miserably.

"Don't you? We knew who you were when you came sniffing around the first time. But we let you in to see what you wanted. Deloris was able to find out quite a bit when you were all drinking. You have a loose tongue when you have too much wine."

I would've rolled my eyes if I hadn't been so terrified.

"We've been running a profitable business out of the center for almost a decade now. Norman Hinkle is a horticultural genius, and he grew premium quality plants that could be sold for a premium price. It's not cheap running a home that size you know, and most old people don't have a lot of money. We try to absorb as much of the cost as possible so they're comfortable in their declining years. We want those staying with us to have every luxury at their fingertips."

"They all know what you're doing?"

"Of course they know. Everyone helps with the crops and packaging. Like I told you. We have a business. It costs a million dollars a year to keep the house in good upkeep and employ all the staff."

"But then a couple of years ago Johnny Sakko moves in from somewhere up north and has his own drug trade. He manages to sniff us out and wants to work out a deal, but it's mostly in his favor. Our profits start shrinking. And then you come along and tell us exactly what we needed to hear."

"What was that?" I asked. I'd loosened the ropes around my wrists a bit, and I figured if I could keep him talking another couple of minutes they'd be free.

"Norman has actually known for years that he was the bastard son of Frank Tannenbaum. He didn't particularly care one way or another. His mother told him all about it before she shot herself, but he knew he'd probably never get hold of any of Tannenbaum's money."

"And then Deloris got me drunk and I told her he'd had his will changed."

"Exactly. And that's when we knew we weren't going to need Sakko's business any longer. All we had to do was get rid of Frank Tannenbaum and the money would go to Norman, which means it would go to the whole operation. We would've had enough to keep the house open for the rest of our lives without having to rely on the cannabis crops to see us through. Every year gets riskier."

"So you killed Mr. Tannenbaum?" I caught a flash of

something at my back door, but I couldn't be sure what it was.

"Yep. I knocked right on the door and he let me inside. People are too trusting. I bashed him on the head with the heavy end of his cane and tried to make it look like a robbery. It was pretty easy all in all. I was in and out in just a few minutes and the rain helped keep me hidden. "

I was struggling in earnest now to get the bonds off my wrists, and he just sat there smiling. My time was running out.

"Right now there are Feds swarming all over our home. All of those elderly people are being taken from their beds and questioned like criminals. And their livelihood is being confiscated. All because of you."

Victor had done a pretty good job up until this point of masking his anger. His voice had been calm, almost soothing, as he explained what had happened. But now he was very aware that I was the person who ruined him and everyone else who lived in that house. The hand that held the knife shook as he gripped it tighter and his lips were white with anger.

I pushed back the chair as he slashed the knife in front of me. The only thing that saved me was that I'd tipped the chair over when I'd tried to get away. I'd also landed on my back. Again. I laid there waiting for the next downward stroke of the knife when I heard a war cry from somewhere in the vicinity of my back yard.

Gandalf the Grey broke through what was left of my back door and dozens of Hobbits swarmed inside the room. They all had tiny swords and staffs and were beating the hell out of Victor. He was curled up in the fetal position on the floor.

Sirens sounded in the distance and spotlights shone on the front of the house. And then I looked up and Nick was standing over me. He knelt down and worked at the knots on my hands and feet.

"We've got to stop meeting like this," he said. His hands shook as he tried to get the ropes off. When he finally did, he scooped me into his lap and sat down right on the floor.

"You scared me to death. Dispatch got a call from your neighbor saying you'd been attacked."

I recognized Spock across the room, rallying the other Hobbits as they gave cheers of victory. "Samwise Gamgee is a hero. NAD Squad to the rescue."

"I've got to tell you, this is weird, even for you. I'm not sure what to say about the Hobbits."

"Let's leave them here. I think I'd rather sleep at your house anyway. There's less traffic."

"I also have a bigger bed."

"That too."

CHAPTER TWENTY-THREE

F*riday...three days later*

"WE'VE GOT to pace ourselves better," Nick said. "We get to do this forever. There's no need to try and fit a lifetime's worth of sex into one week."

He rolled off me and onto his back and we watched the ceiling fan spin overhead. My house had been considered a crime scene and was taped up from front to back. Nick had packed a couple of bags for me, scooped me into his truck and driven me home. I hadn't left since then, though Nick had to leave in the mornings for work.

My sister was back at my mother's house and waiting for the cleaning crew to get rid of any leftover blood in my house before she took over the lease. She'd only have to spend another week or so at my Mom's.

I'd fallen behind on the work I was doing for my P.I. license. My body was too sore to do much physical exercise that wasn't on my back, and I'd had to miss one of my classes. I had written exams coming up soon and the physical exam was just before Christmas. Maybe Nick could help me exercise. He seemed to be in excellent shape. I needed to get my ass in gear with no distractions.

The Dragnet theme filled the room and I reached around for it on the nightstand without looking. I was too tired to move, and I realized Nick had started snoring softly beside me at some point.

"What's up?"

"Did I interrupt something?" Kate asked.

"Nah. We're finished. You've got good timing."

"I don't know about that. I've got good news and bad news. Which do you want first?"

"The good news."

"I'm not pregnant. I got my period this morning and my test was negative when I looked in the bag. I think the stress of the job is messing with my hormones."

"That's good news?"

"I think so. I talked it over with Mike and we're going to wait another year or so before starting a family. This was a timely event. We'll be a little more careful with the birth control from now on."

"So what's the bad news?" I asked.

"Your test was positive."

ABOUT THE AUTHOR

Liliana Hart is a *New York Times, USA Today, and Publisher's Weekly* Bestselling Author of more than 40 titles. After starting her first novel her freshman year of college, she immediately became addicted to writing and knew she'd found what she was meant to do with her life. She has no idea why she majored in music. Since self-publishing in June of 2011, Liliana has sold more than 4 million ebooks. She's appeared at #1 on lists all over the world and all three of her series have appeared on the *New York Times* list. Liliana is a sought after speaker and she's given keynote speeches and self-publishing workshops to standing-room-only crowds from California to New York to London.

Liliana can almost always be found at her computer writing or on the road giving workshops for SilverHart International, a company she founded with her husband,

Scott Silverii, where they provide law enforcement, military, and fire resources for writers so they can write it right. When Liliana and her husband aren't spending time with their children, they're living the life of nomads, traveling wherever interests them most.

If you enjoyed reading *Whiskey Sour*, I would appreciate it if you would help others enjoy this book, too.

Lend it. This e-book is lending-enabled, so please, share it with a friend.

Recommend it. Please help other readers find this book by recommending it to friends, readers' groups and discussion boards.

Review it. Please tell other readers why you liked this book by reviewing. If you do write a review, please send me an email at lilianahartauthor@gmail.com so I can thank you with a personal email. Or visit me at http://www.lilianahart.com.

Connect with me online:
www.lilianahart.com
lilianahartauthor@gmail.com

ALSO BY LILIANA HART

The MacKenzies of Montana

Dane: Volume 1

Dane: Volume 2

Thomas: Volume 1

Thomas: Volume 2

Riley: Volume 1

Riley: Volume 2

Cooper: Volume 1

Cooper: Volume 2

A MacKenzie Christmas

MacKenzie Security Series

Cade

Shadows and Silk

Secrets and Satin

Sins and Scarlet Lace

Sizzle

Crave

Trouble Maker

Scorch

Lawmen of Surrender (MacKenzies-1001 Dark Nights)

1001 Dark Nights: Captured in Surrender

1001 Dark Nights: The Promise of Surrender

Sweet Surrender

Dawn of Surrender

The MacKenzie World (read in any order)

Trouble Maker

Bullet Proof

Deep Trouble

Delta Rescue

Desire and Ice

Rush

Spies and Stilettos

Wicked Hot

Hot Witness

Avenged

Never Surrender

JJ Graves Mystery Series

Dirty Little Secrets

A Dirty Shame

Dirty Rotten Scoundrel

Down and Dirty

Dirty Deeds

Dirty Laundry

Dirty Money

Addison Holmes Mystery Series

Whiskey Rebellion

Whiskey Sour

Whiskey For Breakfast

Whiskey, You're The Devil

Whiskey on the Rocks

Whiskey Tango Foxtrot

Whiskey and Gunpowder

The Gravediggers

The Darkest Corner

Gone to Dust

Say No More

Stand Alone Titles

Breath of Fire

Kill Shot

Catch Me If You Can

All About Eve

Paradise Disguised

Island Home

The Witching Hour

Books by Liliana Hart and Scott Silverii

The Harley and Davidson Mystery Series

The Farmer's Slaughter

A Tisket a Casket

I Saw Mommy Killing Santa Claus

Get Your Murder Running

Deceased and Desist

CPSIA information can be obtained
at www.ICGtesting.com
Printed in the USA
LVHW012344111220
673999LV00007B/140